Praise for Mars

"An utterly beautiful tale of familial love that cannot be extinguished through conflict and anger and the rewards of stepping out of one's comfort zone at any stage of life."

—Kyra Davis, *New York Times* bestselling author of *Just One Night*

"If it is possible to write a bildungsroman about a woman in her sixties, Marshall Fine has done it. Fine takes his reserved heroine, Ruth Winters, on a journey through buried resentments, stifled grief, and petty slights until she finally accepts the love and compassion that was within her all along. She blossomed on the page like Austin's Elinor Dashwood right before my eyes. Marshall Fine has created a beautiful and moving character, that if we open our hearts, we will see Ruth Winters everywhere."

—Griffin Dunne, author of *The Friday Afternoon Club*

"A delightfully shrewd and entertaining novel with an aging, quirky heroine who reminds us that some of life's most profound turns can be at the end of the roller coaster. I fell in love with Ruth Winters and think you will too."

—Julia Heaberlin, internationally bestselling author of *Night Will Find You*

"The moving story of a lonely, ordinary woman told with compassion, wit, and an incredible wealth of very human detail. Time, memory, family, and second chances, it deals with it all. I was rooting for Ruth Winters all the way to the end. Highly recommended."

—Paul Giamatti

"As a longtime film critic, Marshall Fine often showed a kinship for the gonzo wallop of Tarantino, Scorsese, and Bloody Sam Peckinpah. So Fine fans may be shocked that his funny, touching, and vital first novel, *The Autumn of Ruth Winters*, features a retired widow in her seventies going it alone in suburban Minnesota. Look deeper and Ruth and her creator, both from Minneapolis, prove a natural fit. Ruth has a gunslinger's mentality when it comes to keeping the world at bay, plus a sharp tongue for those who try her patience, and that includes Marvel movies and a call from her estranged sister. It's a family crisis that gives Ruth a second shot at life and even romance. Don't worry how Fine manages to persuasively enter the head and heart of a woman who's discovering her real self for the first time. Just let this book work its magic. It's an exuberant gift."

—Peter Travers, *ABC News* and *Good Morning America*

"In *The Autumn of Ruth Winters*, Marshall Fine unspools the complex threads of familial relationships and weaves them back into an affecting tapestry of life's biggest and smallest moments."

—Rob Burnett, writer-director, *The Fundamentals of Caring*

"What really hides behind the forced smiles of "Minnesota nice"? Longtime critic Marshall Fine pushes past middle-aged, Midwestern politeness to reveal some surprising drama in *The Autumn of Ruth Winters*. Yet, filled as it is with sibling rivalries, bad marriages, and secret scandals, ultimately this is a novel about forgiveness, uncovering not only disappointments but opportunities—once missed, now reclaimed."

—Stephen Whitty, author of *The Alfred Hitchcock Encyclopedia*

"Only a really great writer can take a story about a somewhat difficult woman and make you care and keep reading till the end. But then, *The Autumn of Ruth Winters* is an absorbing novel for anyone who believes in love, in living life without comparison, and in the idea that, as George Eliot said, 'It's never too late to be what you might have been.'"

—Georgette Gouveia, author of The Games Men Play series

THE AUTUMN OF RUTH WINTERS

THE AUTUMN OF RUTH WINTERS

A Novel

MARSHALL FINE

This is a work of fiction. Names, characters, organizations, places, events, and incidents are either products of the author's imagination or are used fictitiously. Otherwise, any resemblance to actual persons, living or dead, is purely coincidental.

Published by Lake Union Publishing, Seattle

www.apub.com

ISBN-13: 9781662518348 (paperback)
ISBN-13: 9781662518331 (digital)

Cover design by Kathleen Lynch/Black Kat Design
Cover image: © arata / Getty

Printed in the United States of America

To Sandra Solomon

She said, "A good day ain't got no rain."
She said, "A bad day's when I lie in bed
and think of things that might have been."
—Paul Simon, "Slip Slidin' Away"

Comparison is the thief of joy.
—Theodore Roosevelt

CHAPTER 1

Ruth Winters never welcomed change. She tried to avoid it when possible.

Too often, it amounted to change for its own sake, as though *different* were a synonym for *better*. In Ruth's experience, it seldom was.

For Ruth, change upset the balance—if not of the universe in general, then of Ruth's universe in particular, affecting the way Ruth navigated her world. When change also happened to interfere with Ruth's schedule? That was unacceptable on all counts.

Why, for example, did they insist on regularly shifting the location of every food section in her local Cub Foods supermarket? Ruth was running dangerously low on juice boxes, which were like heroin to the children she looked after. But since the last time Ruth had shopped, the beverages had been moved—from aisle three to aisle twelve. *To what possible purpose?* Ruth wondered crossly as she trekked across the sprawling store, after an employee told her where to find them.

She was running late enough that she could not afford a game of hide-and-seek with her staples. Besides juice boxes, she needed a package of Pull-Ups, the not-quite-diapers she kept on hand for when the children had emergencies.

But when she asked, she found that these, also, had been moved—from aisle twelve to aisle three.

How symmetrically inconvenient, Ruth thought.

Between the juice boxes, the diapers, and the little yogurt cups the children devoured, Ruth was convinced that, somewhere, she was responsible for her own private landfill of discarded single-use products.

Ruth hated to feel hurried. It flustered her, and she liked to be calm for the children, who injected their own energy into any moment. But she was running behind schedule.

She had prided herself her entire life on being punctual. "If you're not early, you're late," her father used to say. It wouldn't do to keep the children waiting.

Ruth found her items at last, then tapped her foot as the checkout girl struggled to calculate the change when Ruth gave her $15.21 to pay for an $11.21 bill. Ruth could see the clerk moving the fingers on one hand, though the girl resisted the urge to actually look at them to count. Finally, Ruth said, "The change is four dollars. Please. Thank you." She practically snatched the bills from the clerk's hand.

Out the door she flew. At 10:00 a.m., Samantha, who was four, would be dropped off by her mother. Then, at 11:30 a.m., they would be joined by Jared, who was three. The children would have lunch, then play or nap until their parents collected them at 5:00 p.m. The days when Ruth had as many as three or four of them could be exhausting.

Today would be tiring enough, given her increased stress at running late. Her doctor's appointment wasn't supposed to take as long as it had. It had been, after all, merely an annual dermatology checkup. Even that, however, had required Ruth to accommodate unexpected change.

The dermatologist Ruth had seen for years, a stolid man named Dr. Hickman, had retired in the twelve months between her appointments. Ruth had found herself being examined by his associate who had taken over the practice: Dr. Betsy Everly. *This girl,* Ruth thought, *looks too young to make her own breakfast, let alone wear Dr. Hickman's stethoscope.*

"Has this growth on your back changed in shape or color since the last time you were here?" asked Dr. Everly, who was thirty-five.

"I don't spend my time studying my own naked backside," Ruth said, with an edge that hovered between sarcasm and disdain.

Nonplussed, the young doctor took a beat, then said, "I thought Dr. Hickman might have mentioned that particular spot as something you should keep an eye on."

Ruth looked at her warily, crossing her arms on her chest. This created a gap in the back of her paper examination gown, and she shivered as an air-conditioned draft hit her exposed skin.

"And I imagine you wouldn't have mentioned it if you thought it was nothing."

"Better safe than sorry. You can never be too careful."

"Young lady, I've been careful my entire life, almost seventy years—and yet here I sit," Ruth said.

Undeterred, Dr. Everly said, "I'd like to err on the side of caution and do a biopsy, if that's all right with you, Mrs. Winters. Can I ask you to lie on the table on your stomach and open the back of your gown?"

Twenty unplanned-for minutes later, Ruth had been back in her car, driving to Cub Foods. There was antibiotic ointment and a Band-Aid covering the raw patch where Dr. Everly had used a scalpel to sample her flesh. To Ruth's annoyance, the spot lay directly beneath one of her bra straps, which rubbed against it in an irritating manner.

Ruth looked at the clock in the car when she exited the supermarket: 9:25. She had purposely made the appointment for her dermatology checkup early enough to accommodate her babysitting schedule. But the unexpected outpatient surgery had put her behind.

But, as always, Ruth was on time—it was the rule she lived by. She routinely built extra time into her schedule, which made her perpetually early. This day it meant she got home with ten minutes to spare.

After Samantha arrived, Ruth spent the morning playing tea party and dolls with her until Jared got there, when she made them both lunch. Around two thirty, Ruth left Samantha and Jared digging in the shaded sandbox together, building a castle in the warm July afternoon. She went into the house to sit down in the air-conditioning for a moment and watch them from the kitchen window. Her legs felt heavy, and her hips ached.

She put two ice cubes in a tumbler and poured herself a quarter portion of generic diet lemon-lime soda out of a two-liter bottle, as she did most days at this time. She filled the rest of the glass with seltzer. She found the diet soda too sweet by itself and also felt the beverage was too expensive to be indulged in too freely.

She knew some people might criticize her for "sitting down on the job," particularly as a "childcare professional." She put air quotes around the phrases in her own mind as a form of self-mockery. But these hot, humid late-July afternoons sapped her strength if she didn't get out of the heat once in a while. She was careful with the children and heatstroke, but they never seemed to mind the heat at the point when she needed indoor respite.

Childcare professional? She was merely a retired bookkeeper who now did a little babysitting for mothers on her block.

Ruth had moved to the suburban Minneapolis neighborhood in Saint Louis Park thirty-five years earlier, to a house owned by her late and unlamented husband, Charles. At that point, most of the other people on the block had been their age: couples in their late thirties to midforties, with children who were teens or in college.

Not that she and Charles had ever socialized much in their neighborhood. God forbid Charles should extend himself socially if it didn't help him in business.

Ruth herself was cloaked in a veil of reticence. She lived in perpetual fear of embarrassment and saw danger of it everywhere. If her motto was emblazoned on a needlepoint pillow, it would read **I PROBABLY SHOULDN'T**. She seldom did.

Ruth hated attention, and, from a young age, her height—which topped out at five feet eleven in bare feet—had made her feel overly visible. She tended to slouch, to bring herself level with whatever crowd she found herself in. It was only her imagination, yet she could swear she recalled hearing the words *stork* and *giraffe* whispered behind her back in elevators and at the movies. Heaven forbid she stand up and stand out.

When she went to work as a bookkeeper at Briggs & Oden—her first and only job in her adult life—Ruth created an invisible space around herself. She wasn't unapproachable, but coworkers got the impression that asking for her time would be an imposition to which she would not respond kindly.

The people in her office considered Ruth an odd character, if a highly competent one. When one of the national newsmagazines did a cover story about Asperger's syndrome, Ruth noticed a couple of young secretaries in the break room looking at a copy one day and giggling. But they went quiet and turned the magazine over when they noticed Ruth at the coffee machine. She later glanced through the article on a newsstand and thought, *Well, that's certainly not me.*

People with Asperger's, she read, had difficulty understanding emotional cues in other people. That wasn't Ruth's problem; she understood emotions all too well—and lived in fear of them.

Ruth was convinced of her own worthiness as a person but struggled with the belief that no one else saw her this way and that it was somehow her fault. For her, every conversation was a test she strained to pass, and every social situation was a corner into which she was being painted, in order to be judged and found wanting. So she avoided conversation as much as possible, deploying a sharp tongue as a preemptive defense mechanism.

If Ruth came upon a spill in the grocery store, she would immediately turn and leave the aisle. She did it as much out of embarrassment for the person who had created the mess as for fear of being blamed. She learned which take-out restaurants asked for her name to identify her pickup order and confined her business to the eateries that asked only for her phone number. It never occurred to her to give a phony name. Her stern mien and sometimes-acid remarks were a cover for the near panic she had to suppress during every interpersonal exchange. She found it exhausting.

Yet after marrying Charles and moving to Saint Louis Park from the nearby suburb of Richfield, Ruth made two close friends in her neighborhood, Erica and Tilly, who lived on either side of her. The three would go grocery shopping together on the weekends, followed by coffee.

At those weekly get-togethers, Ruth would listen with guilty pleasure as Erica and Tilly gossiped about their neighbors on the block: who was too cheap to water their lawn, which couples had been having shouting fights in the summer with their windows open, whose kids were in trouble with the local police.

Ruth wished her friends were here now, when she could offer a story of her own, about her recent run-in with one of the mothers whose children she had taken care of. Past tense.

A few weeks earlier, Ruth had caught little Roy McMillan, four, going through the jewelry box on her dresser. He'd climbed the drawers like they were the steps of a ladder so he could reach the top. When Ruth came upon him, Roy sat on the dresser, legs dangling over the side, casually stuffing what little costume jewelry Ruth owned into his bulging pockets.

Ruth set him on the floor and forced him to empty the treasure from his pants. She gave him a stern lecture on the crime of theft, and, from that day forward, she subjected the doughy little boy to a quick search before he left each afternoon, which he accepted passively. More often than not, she found something, despite her vigilance when Roy was in her house.

Roy's mother, Merry, was habitually late to retrieve him. So on a day when she did happen to show up on time, she was surprised to see Ruth walk over to where Roy was putting on his jacket.

"OK, Roy, assume the position," Ruth said, dropping to one knee in front of him. Roy automatically turned and faced her, extending his arms like airplane wings. She frisked him with brisk efficiency.

"Excuse me!" Merry McMillan said, stepping out from behind a taller parent. "What do you think you're doing?"

Merry was a short, round woman who, Ruth thought, looked like a sentient beach ball with glasses. Ruth, who was kneeling next to Roy, stood up and, at almost six feet in sneakers, towered over Merry.

"I'm searching his pockets because, on several occasions, I've caught Roy trying to take things that don't belong to him."

"What?" Merry glared at Roy. Roy, arms still extended, stared at his shoes, offering neither denial nor confession.

"We've talked more than once about why stealing is wrong," Ruth added.

Merry turned on Ruth: "My son is not a thief, and I'll thank you to stop implying that he is."

"I'm not implying anything—I'm saying it outright," Ruth replied, speaking slowly, as though addressing a dim-witted employee. "I've caught Roy stealing, and it's happened more than once."

Merry puffed up even further and said, "And I'll thank you to stop touching him in his, um, pocket area."

"Mrs. McMillan," Ruth said, speaking even more slowly, "the other day I caught Roy with a bottle of my blood pressure medication from the medicine cabinet. I don't even want to know how he got up there. That could have been dangerous for him."

"This is outrageous," Merry exclaimed.

"And just now I caught him with this," Ruth had said, holding up a plastic dental appliance she used because she ground her teeth in her sleep, which she had retrieved from Roy's pocket.

Recalling the moment, Ruth smiled at how funny Tilly and Erica would think it was that she was babysitting. Quiet, solitary Ruth, playing with small children—they wouldn't believe it.

She missed her time with her long-departed neighbors. They'd provided a weekend buffer for her when Charles would come in from selling on the road, usually in a bad mood. Charles didn't care how Ruth spent her weeks while he was gone or his weekends while he was home. His weekends were reserved for watching televised sports—year round, whatever happened to be on, around the clock if possible.

Ruth's friends offered a source of support when Charles died, twenty years ago. Then, a few years later, Tilly and her husband sold their house and moved to Omaha, where their son and grandchildren lived. Tilly sent Ruth a Christmas card for a few years after that, before stopping.

After Erica's husband died, she sold her house and moved into an apartment in Saint Paul to be closer to her older daughter's family. But Ruth harbored the kind of disdain for Saint Paul common among Minneapolitans of a certain age.

During Ruth's formative years, Saint Paul was regarded as the lesser of the Twin Cities, the farm team striving to belong in the big leagues like its sibling metropolis. Minneapolis boasted the Guthrie Theater, the Minnesota Orchestra, the Minnesota Twins and Vikings, and the University of Minnesota, while Saint Paul had . . . the Minnesota state capitol. And stockyards. Hardly identical twins. While Saint Paul had evened the cultural playing field in intervening decades, the prejudices of longtime Minneapolitans died hard. As far as Ruth was concerned, Erica might as well have moved to the moon.

After her friends left, the neighborhood began to change. Ruth's generation of neighbors retired and moved on, and there was an influx of newcomers with young children. Ruth's block turned over quickly, its benign little post-WWII houses attractive and affordable to newly minted families.

Ruth would see the young mothers walk by, pushing strollers. They waved at Ruth as she dug in her flower bed, and she would wave back. But she was too reticent to do more than wave, and the new neighbors were too busy, it seemed, to reach out to her. She couldn't imagine what she would have to say to these young mothers, who seemed so caught up in their own lives.

Then one day, to Ruth's surprise, one of those young mothers parked her stroller in Ruth's driveway and walked across the lawn to where Ruth was kneeling in the dirt, trying to discipline a leggy azalea.

"Hi—excuse me?" the younger woman said.

She was waving at Ruth, even though Ruth was looking directly at her.

"Yes? What is it?"

"Hi, I'm Jane Mallory from Number Forty-Five? Next door?"

"Yes, I know where Number Forty-Five is," Ruth said.

"You're Ruth, right?"

"Um, yes." She realized she was still kneeling and stood. When Jane extended her hand, Ruth started to extend hers, then noticed she was still wearing a dirty garden glove and stopped to take it off. "Ruth Winters."

Jane shook her hand eagerly and a little longer than Ruth would have liked.

"Anyway," Jane said as she paused to summon courage. "I know this is out of the blue, and normally, I wouldn't think to ask, but I'm desperate."

Ruth looked at her. "Yes? And?"

"Oh, uh, well, I was wondering if you ever did any babysitting. I'm about to start a part-time job and could use someone dependable."

Ruth cocked her head, not sure she'd heard correctly.

"And you thought I'd be interested?"

"Oh, I'd pay you, of course. It would be about three days a week and not all day. Erica—we bought her house—told us how good you were with her kids."

"That was ages ago."

"Hey, it's like riding a bike—you never forget, right? Would you consider it? Please? You'd be saving my life. I wouldn't need you to start until next week. Come over and meet Sam. Maybe that will persuade you."

Samantha turned out to be a sweet, well-behaved little girl with a sparkle that softened Ruth. She surprised herself by saying, "Yes, all right, I guess I could."

Babysitting took Ruth out of her unemployment funk, and before she knew it, she was doing it almost full time. Jane was wired in to the neighborhood, and the word spread quickly among the mothers on the block. Ruth shortly had a roster of children she looked after on different days and a handprinted schedule on her kitchen bulletin board to keep track of who would be there on which day.

Gradually, she began to open up to Jane. They would talk a little at pickup time, or when they would see each other in the yard, as amiable, distant next-door neighbors will. She was the closest thing Ruth had to a friend, though Ruth never let her guard down completely, with anyone.

When she began babysitting, Ruth realized she would need equipment and supplies for the job. She bought a sandbox with an umbrella for her fenced backyard and some sturdy plastic jungle gym pieces, sized for small fry who tended to be easily toppled. She filled her den with blocks, crayons, coloring books, simple puzzles, and such elementary games as Candy Land and Old Maid, for Minnesota winter days indoors.

Ruth had long ago come to terms with a childless life, so it came as a revelation that children were fun to be around. When she was with the children, Ruth discovered that she had an unexpected capacity for play and an ability to relate to the kids on their own level without talking down to them. For a few hours each day, her face lost its resting scowl. She could forget everything else in her life and be as focused on the children as they were on their own sense of play.

When Ruth had first found herself unemployed, part of a "reduction in force" after almost forty years at the same company, she had tried various things to occupy herself. She enjoyed movies, but there weren't that many films she wanted to see. She visited the art museums in Minneapolis but knew both of their collections by heart—and they mounted new exhibits only slightly more often than quarterly.

She didn't like going to the museums on weekends, when parents seemed to think it was appropriate for their children to treat the museum as their playground. On weekdays, which Ruth preferred, the museums were less crowded. But, whether it was the large stark galleries of the Walker Art Center or the slightly warmer ones at the Minneapolis Institute of Art, Ruth felt uncomfortably conspicuous as she wandered from room to room, hearing her own footsteps, even when she wore sneakers.

Staying home, she tired of spending her days filling the pages of sudoku puzzle books. If it wasn't sudoku, it was crosswords, or watching old movies and soap operas (really, only the one, *General Hospital*; it was all that was left of the daytime shows she'd watched in the years when she was nursing her father).

When she was laid off, her severance pay amounted to a half year's salary. But she worried, because no further revenue would be incoming. When Jane Mallory approached her about babysitting, it seemed like a supplement that could augment her Social Security check after her unemployment ran out, while she put the severance away for a rainy day.

During her life, Ruth had experienced a couple of serious financial setbacks. They had left her perpetually agitated by fiscal concerns that were as much a product of her imagination as the fears that fueled her anxiety about being embarrassed.

Sipping her watered-down diet soda as she watched the children through the window, Ruth had stirrings of a familiar feeling: the sense of dissatisfaction that could overtake her and turn her days sour, for a week at a time.

Ruth's unhappiness with her own life was long standing. She tried to wall off those feelings, but, inevitably, they escaped the mental storage locker into which she forced them, the lock to the compartment forced open by one memory or another.

When she was in the workforce, she could distract herself with her job at Briggs & Oden. That sufficed for long stretches of her marriage.

She had little opportunity to fret about life during her twenties, which she spent acting as caregiver for her incapacitated father. She had few moments to consider what a bad hand life had dealt her because she was too busy dealing with life itself, on the most basic level.

Until her husband died, their life had run smoothly enough that she hadn't noticed how little satisfaction it gave her. It was only after Charles's death that she realized what a demand he made on her supply of mental energy when he was home. She always felt depleted by the time he left for the road each Monday.

The dark cloud that babysitting kept at bay had been at its worst for the first month Ruth was unemployed. She would plan chores and make lists—as mundane as "1. Go grocery shopping. 2. Weed the side garden"—and then complete those chores. But when the tasks came to an end, she felt untethered once again. With nothing she was required to do, Ruth was forced to confront the eternal question: *What now?*

Babysitting proved a welcome respite from herself. With her time occupied by the concerns of small children, Ruth only occasionally found herself susceptible to that particular cloud, though it hovered at the edge of her consciousness on this day.

Her age cutoff for the children was three. At that age, they were mostly toilet trained (hence, the emergency supply of Pull-Ups). They understood the word *no* and still complied with commands on a "Because I said so" basis.

They could communicate in full sentences and possessed imaginations that were amusingly unbridled. While they were able to express themselves verbally and get involved in cooperative play, these were still preschoolers: old enough to engage in conversation but too young to be left alone for long, especially in a group.

As if on cue, Samantha ran in, startling Ruth, who'd been staring into her glass for a moment.

"Mzwnnrs! Mzwnnrs!" she yelled in her squeaky voice, pulling at the hem of Ruth's jumper as she hopped from one foot to the other. She had a tendency to run Ruth's name together when she was excited and to call her *Miss* Winters when she wasn't, despite being reminded by her mother that her caretaker was a *Mrs.*

"Samantha, dear, do you remember what I told you about your indoor voice?" Ruth said, a little more sharply than she intended.

Samantha thought, then said quietly, "Yes, ma'am."

"Very good," Ruth said.

Samantha, now almost whispering, enunciated more clearly as she said, "Scuse me, Miss Winters? Jared is pooping in the sandbox."

Ruth leaped to her feet and hurried out the back door, pulling Samantha by the hand behind her.

Sure enough, there was Jared, triumphantly rising from a crouch after executing a successful bowel movement from a two-point stance in the middle of the sandbox. He then bent over and started shoveling sand backward between his legs at the little pile, using his hands as scoops, like a football center hiking the ball. His pants were still around his ankles, and his shorts quickly filled with sand from his frenzied digging. Only an act of God prevented him from stepping in his own droppings.

When he saw Ruth, Jared grinned and pointed proudly to his little pile of sand-crusted scat, which already had begun to attract flies on the warm afternoon.

"This is how our cat does it," he said, standing up for a second.

Before he could explain further, Ruth hoisted him by one arm out of the sandbox and away from the scene of his crime.

Ruth set him on his feet on the grass, then dropped to one knee and steadied him as he stepped out of his sand-filled shorts. She shook the sand out of his pants, then took Jared's hand and walked him, bare bottomed, across the backyard to the house as Samantha gawked.

Ruth turned back to Samantha and said, "Stay out of the sandbox until I get it cleaned out. Why don't you come in and color while I take care of Jared?"

As Samantha trailed behind them, Ruth focused on the task at hand: getting Jared indoors to clean him up and put his clothes back on.

"Why did you do that, Jared? You're not a cat," Ruth said with genuine curiosity as they walked.

Jared said, "Well, I really had to go potty, and I didn't want to make in my pants. And that's where my cat goes—in the sand."

"I don't really like cats, which is why I take care of young gentlemen and ladies instead. Now, we've never talked about this before, so I'm not angry with you. But people don't do that in their backyard, even if cats do. That's what the bathroom is for. So next time, run for the bathroom as fast as you can."

"Yes, Mrs.," he said, nodding earnestly.

She was walking him in the back door toward the bathroom when her landline rang. Still holding his balled-up shorts and underpants in one hand, Ruth pointed Samantha to the coloring books in the den, then aimed the little boy down the hall and said, "Go to the bathroom, and wait for me to come clean you up, please, Jared. Stand still, and try not to touch anything while I'm on the phone."

She set Jared's sandy clothes in the kitchen sink, then grabbed the wall phone on the third ring: "Hello?"

"Ruth, it's Ronnie. How are you?"

"Veronica," Ruth said. "This is a surprise."

Ruth did a quick mental calculation. It was almost the end of July, so it had been roughly a year since she and her sister had talked. It was a little longer since they'd been in the same room.

A silence hung between them, and Ruth thought, *The first to speak loses.* She easily outwaited her sister.

Finally, Veronica said, "Am I calling at a bad time, Ruthie?"

"As good a time as any," Ruth said. "What can I do for you?"

Ruth knew she shouldn't be surprised to hear from her sister. She'd received a phone call from her niece—Veronica's daughter, Chloe—the day before. And as night follows day . . .

"Chloe told me she asked you to be godmother to her baby," Veronica said, as though reading Ruth's mind.

"Yes, she did. I'm so flattered she asked me. I'm very excited for her."

"So you're going to do it?"

The note of disapproval in Veronica's voice was audible. Ruth couldn't resist baiting her.

"Of course I'm much too old for something like that," Ruth said.

Veronica took the bait. "That's what I told Chloe—"

"On the other hand," Ruth said, "Chloe seemed to have her heart set on having me do it. I think I'm going to have to say yes."

The phone went so quiet that Ruth thought she might have been disconnected. Then she heard Veronica sigh before she grumbled, "She told you she was pregnant before she told me."

"Don't worry," Ruth said. "The last I heard, *granny* still outranks *godmother*."

That drew a chuckle from Veronica.

"Oh my God, don't call me that! Can you imagine? Me? A grandmother?" Veronica said, sounding human to Ruth for the first time in a long while. "And don't ever call me *Granny*. It makes me sound like a kind of apple."

Ruth smiled at that. But, again, the phone line went silent.

This time, Ruth spoke first, when she remembered that Jared was shedding sand on the floor of her bathroom. "Was that all you wanted? To register your disapproval of me as godmother? That seems petty even for you, Veronica."

"Please—don't," Veronica said, and her pained tone surprised Ruth. It sounded less like a defensive feint than an actual plea for mercy.

"I'm sorry," Ruth said. "Was there something else you needed to talk about?"

Again, the pause and the sound of Veronica exhaling, then: "I need a favor."

"From me?" Ruth was unable to keep the shock out of her voice. "What sort of favor?"

Another pause; then Veronica said, "A ride. Are you free a week from Monday?"

"A ride," Ruth repeated, her anger rising. "And so, after not speaking to me for a year—and after the way you treated me at Chloe's wedding—you decide to call me. To ask for a ride."

"Ruth—"

"Honestly, Veronica. You call me out of the blue just to be snotty about this godmother business. And then you ask me to drop everything to be your chauffeur? Even for you, that's approaching a new peak in gall."

"If you'd just listen—"

"Yes, well, I've listened to you my entire life, haven't I? Because the only thing you have ever been concerned about is Veronica."

"Ruth—I have cancer."

"What?"

"I need a ride to chemotherapy."

Ruth felt as though the wind was knocked out of her.

"You have cancer? When did you find out?"

"About four months ago."

"Four months? And you're just telling me now?"

"It wasn't about you. No one knew except Irwin. And my doctors."

Emotions clashed tumultuously within Ruth. Her sister—the last living member of her nuclear family—had cancer. She might be dying. The thought shook Ruth for a moment.

But that shock was overwhelmed by a lifetime of resentment, which sparked her sense of betrayal now at being such an afterthought for her sister—except when Veronica needed a functionary. *The story of my life,* Ruth thought. *She waited four months to tell me—and she's only telling me now because she wants a favor from me.*

Before she knew it, she said, "I'm sorry. I'm not sure I can do it that day. I'll have to get back to you."

And with that, Ruth hung up the phone. Then she thought, *I've never hung up on anyone before in my life.*

CHAPTER 2

For most of their adult lives, Ruth's relationship with her younger sister, Veronica, had run the gamut from antagonistic to poisonous. The sisters had gone years at a time without speaking.

Their truces tended to be short lived, far briefer than the battles that the cease-fires separated. Inevitably it was Ruth, the dutiful one, who would be conciliatory and negotiate a halt in hostilities.

"You only have one sister," her mother had hammered home when they were girls. But once they were past childhood, the siblings had ridden a pendulum that swung less often toward *peace* than toward *conflict*.

That dynamic was already on Ruth's mind, in fact, during her conversation with her niece the day before.

"Auntie Ruth? It's Chloe. Did you get my email?"

Ruth realized she hadn't taken her iPhone out of the kitchen drawer in a couple of weeks. It was the only device she owned that received email. Because she never used email, Ruth seldom thought to take it out and turn it on.

"I'm sorry, dear. I don't think I saw it," Ruth replied, finding a seat in the kitchen from which she could watch the children outside. "You know how I am with technology. How are you? Is anything wrong?"

"No, it was just a note saying that you should give me a call because I had some news. When I didn't hear from you, I thought I'd call you myself."

"Well, I already know it's not something that would make me feel bad, or I'd have heard about it from your mother."

"No, Mom doesn't know yet." She paused, then added, "I'm sorry for the way she treated you at our wedding."

"Oh, honey, that's water under the bridge. It certainly wasn't your fault. I had a nice time anyway."

Chloe had married a software designer named David the previous year in San Francisco, at a point when Veronica had frozen Ruth out for several months, in a snit over . . . what? Ruth couldn't even remember. Veronica had unsuccessfully tried to talk Chloe into disinviting Ruth, a fact that Veronica had "let slip" to Ruth before the wedding.

For the entire weekend of wedding events in San Francisco, Veronica made a point of not speaking to Ruth, keeping her distance from her to emphasize the slight. When Ruth came through the receiving line after the ceremony, Veronica refused to acknowledge her or introduce her to Chloe's new father-in-law, Clark.

Mortified, but fortified with a couple of glasses of champagne, Ruth strode up to Clark, shook his hand, and said, "Congratulations. Your son is a lovely young man, and he's very lucky to have my niece. I'm Chloe's aunt, Ruth Winters. So nice to meet you."

She saw Veronica's jaw drop. Then Ruth strode away, even as she heard Clark say, "Do you know that woman?"

A little farther down the reception line, Ruth performed the same bit of theater with Chloe's new mother-in-law, Marlene, who was standing next to Veronica's latest husband, Irwin (whom Ruth had also never met). She put on a big smile, offered a hearty handshake and self-introduction to both, and then made a quick exit, but not before she heard Irwin say, "I think that's Veronica's sister."

Ruth spent the rest of the wedding dinner talking with one of the groom's elderly aunts, who was unhappy about the location of the table to which she'd been assigned.

"I don't know anyone at this table!" she complained to Ruth, who was seated next to her.

"Well, now you know me," Ruth said with champagne-fueled vivacity. She spent the dinner regaling the older woman with tales of the sisters' lifelong antipathy, which Ruth blamed on Veronica's innate selfishness.

A few days after the wedding, when Ruth answered her phone, Veronica didn't even bother to say hello, opening instead with "What did you tell David's aunt Delores?" Apparently, Ruth had been seated next to the biggest gossip in the groom's family.

"Well, I talked to a lot of new people that night," Ruth said. "I don't remember exactly what I said to whom."

"She said you described me as a spoiled, small-town socialite!"

"I'm sorry, Veronica," Ruth said. "You'll have to narrow it down further than that. As I said, I spoke to so many people."

"Small town? Really?"

"What's wrong with that?"

"*You* live in that same small town."

"But I don't pretend otherwise, the way you do."

Veronica hung up. It was the last time the two sisters had spoken.

"So anyway, about my news," Chloe said.

"Yes, of course, dear, tell me everything."

"I'm pregnant!"

"Oh, honey, that's wonderful."

"David and I want you to be the baby's godmother."

"Really? Oh, it's lovely of you to ask, but what kind of godmother would I be if I never saw your baby in order to spoil her? I hardly get to see *you*, as it is."

"Don't you ever think about escaping from Minnesota?" Chloe asked. "People do it all the time. Look at me. I can't tell you how happy I am in the Bay Area."

"What's wrong with Minneapolis?"

"How many more of those winters do you want to go through? You're not getting any younger, Auntie Ruth. I worry about you slipping on ice, or getting caught in one of those polar vortexes I've read about. There are alternatives, you know."

"Well, that's a discussion for another day," Ruth said, wanting to change the subject. "Oh, sweetie, a baby—that's such happy news. Are you excited? How do you feel?"

"So far, so good—a little morning sickness, but nothing extreme. We're both going a little crazy in anticipation. Now—tell me you'll agree to be my baby's godmother so I can stop worrying about that."

"I don't think your mother would approve."

"It's my baby, not hers. What do you say?"

"Let me think about it, honey. You can't imagine how pleased I am to be asked. But don't you also need a godfather?"

"David is asking Eric, his brother, who was his best man."

"I remember him. A rather hirsute young man, if I recall."

"Yeah, that beard, right? But Eric is still single, and you're my favorite aunt."

"I'm your only aunt."

"Yes, true. But you seemed like the logical choice, someone solid and sensible to balance out Eric. So please say yes—and think about moving somewhere warmer. Like out here to California."

Ruth hadn't had a genuine laugh in a while, but the notion of her living in California nudged a chortle loose from deep down.

"What's so funny?"

"Nothing, honey. I tickled myself, is all. I did enjoy San Francisco when I was there for your wedding. But it's precisely because I *am* solid and sensible that I would never consider moving to California. And also, I'm allergic to sunscreen."

That made Chloe laugh. Then Ruth heard a two-part beep on the line, and Chloe said, "I'm sorry, Auntie Ruth. That's David calling. I had my ultrasound today, and he wants to know how it went."

"How *did* it go?"

"The baby seems to have all its fingers and toes, so that's good."

"When are you due, dear?"

"In January, a little less than six months."

"Well, congratulations, honey. You must be chuffed, as the British say."

"I am. We are. Love you, Auntie. And think about what I asked, OK?"

CHAPTER 3

Ruth was still steaming from Veronica's phone call when the mothers arrived for the 5:00 p.m. pickup. She let her anger obscure the larger issue—Veronica's illness—as years of memories bubbled to the surface, and she wished she could be alone with her indignation.

The first to arrive was Jared's mother, Judith, a fussy, birdlike woman. Jared, who had spent the rest of the afternoon wearing his underwear without pants, now struggled to put his shorts on over his sneakers. His mother hovered ineffectually, seemingly incapable of assisting him.

Clucking impatiently with Judith's dithering, Ruth finally stepped in. Despite her anger, she handled Jared with playful brusqueness, instructing him to stand still even as she tickled his knee.

"Miss-*us*," he squealed, his giggle extending the two syllables merrily.

A few minutes later, Jane Mallory arrived. As they waited for Samantha to finish a protracted potty break, Ruth realized she was tapping her foot with impatience. Jane noticed as well.

"Is anything the matter, Ruth?"

"I'm sorry, I'm upset about something that happened this afternoon."

"Was it something Samantha did?" Jane asked.

"Oh, no, of course not. Samantha is a lovely girl," Ruth said. "No, nothing like that. It was something with my family."

"I hope it's nothing serious."

"Oh, it's my hateful younger sister," Ruth said, then made a face. "I shouldn't say that."

"What makes your sister hateful?"

"Really, we're hateful to each other in equal measure and have been for as long as I can remember. Now she's got cancer, and she waited four months to tell me."

"Oh my God, I'm so sorry," Jane said. Ruth realized Jane seemed more upset than Ruth, who sounded less concerned than vexed.

"And the thing is, I have such mixed feelings about it," Ruth admitted.

Jane looked at her, then said, "Why don't I get Samantha set up coloring in the other room and then we can talk?"

Just then, Samantha came in, the hem of her skirt tucked into the back of her underwear.

"I put my clothes back on by myself," she announced.

"C'mon, sweetie," Jane said to her, adjusting her clothing and taking her back into the den to find a coloring book. As they left, Ruth heard Samantha say, "Mommy, Jared pooped in the sandbox today, like a cat."

When Jane returned, Ruth was sitting at the kitchen table, staring blankly into space. She snapped to attention when Jane entered. "Would you like something to drink?"

Jane sat down opposite her. "No, I'm not going to stay. But you seem upset. Like you're angry at your sister for being sick."

"No, it's that she deliberately kept this from me. She only told me because she needs a ride to chemotherapy next week," Ruth said with surprising heat. "Apparently, none of her snooty Lake Minnetonka friends want to risk having her throw up in their Teslas. But *my* car is just fine for that."

After a pause, Jane said, "Well, she obviously needs your help," with a note of sympathy that stopped Ruth.

She looked at Jane: young, earnest, open. Jane looked at her with a sense of expectation, then said, "You're going to do it, aren't you? I mean, she's your sister."

Ruth was about to blurt out "No, of course not" but saw the look on Jane's face: hope triumphing over possible disappointment. Ruth directed her gaze out the window, saying nothing.

"Do you know how bad it is?" Jane prodded carefully.

"Honestly, I have no idea. She was very vague on the phone."

"Is she your only sister?"

That also brought Ruth up short. She heard echoes of her mother: "You only have one sister, and you have to look out for her."

Before Ruth could answer, Jane added, "Don't you think she'd do it for you if you needed her help?"

"I wouldn't be too sure of that," Ruth said. But even as she tried to summon negative thoughts about her sister, she found her head flooded again with thoughts of her mother's admonition: "You have to look out for her."

At that moment, Samantha stuck her head in the kitchen and said, "Mommy, I'm hungry."

Jane glanced at her watch and said, "Look at the time. OK, sweetie, let's go home and make dinner."

She stood up, then turned back to Ruth and gently put a hand on her shoulder. Ruth, whose formal bearing usually precluded that kind of contact, accepted the intimacy gratefully.

"I had an aunt who used to say, 'The right thing is always the hardest thing to do,'" Jane said, just before she and Samantha left. "You'll figure it out, Ruth."

CHAPTER 4

Ruth had a restless night, filled with dreams in which she was rushing endlessly to catch a bus that always seemed to be a half block away, no matter how fast she walked. She would gain on it a little and think, *Almost there*, then realize that it was farther than she thought. When she did reach the bus at last, she found a long line waiting to board, because it was already full. Then she woke up.

"The right thing is always the hardest thing to do," Jane had said. Ruth could feel the sentiment scratching at her conscience as she contemplated the day ahead.

Veronica had cancer. She could be dying. She needed Ruth's help. She had never asked Ruth for help before.

On the other hand, there had been at least one point in the past when Ruth had desperately needed Veronica's aid—and Veronica had turned her down.

Then Ruth thought again of her mother and of being children with Veronica. The subsequent years, stuffed with bitter memories or simply silence from her sister: How could she weigh them against this plea for help?

It was, after all, just one ride. They didn't have to talk.

Veronica is probably used to being driven while she looks at her phone, Ruth thought. *She won't even know I'm there—just like the rest of our life.*

And so, though she resented doing it, she decided to call her.

Ruth pulled out her overstuffed address book, filled with paper-clipped notes and loose Post-its; slipped off the rubber band that held it all in; and flipped to where Veronica had commandeered two yellowing pages with crossed-out addresses and phone numbers. She dialed the only un-crossed-out phone number and heard it ring twice before Veronica answered.

"Ruth?" she said, sounding surprised.

Ruth, herself surprised, said, "How did you know it was me?"

"I have caller ID. Don't you?"

"I have no idea."

There was a moment of awkward silence, and then Veronica said, "How are you?"

"I've decided," Ruth said, plunging straight in, "to drive you, as you asked."

"Oh, Ruth," Veronica said, the relief in her voice warm in Ruth's ear. "Thank you."

"Yes, well, that doesn't mean I'm not angry."

"I'm the one who's sick. What are you angry about?"

"That you waited so long to tell me this—that you waited until you needed a favor. And then you ask me to be your servant."

"I never said that."

"Whatever else there is between us, we're still sisters. You are the only family I have."

"Yes, well . . ." Veronica's voice trailed off.

After a moment, Ruth said, "What kind of cancer is it?"

"Liver. I never ate liver—why would mine do this to me?"

Ruth smiled at the weak attempt at humor, then said, "Does Chloe know you're sick?"

"No."

"But the surgery, the chemo—you have to tell her. She needs to know. She'll want to come home."

"Oh, Chloe has her job—and now this baby. She can't be flying back and forth across the country from California."

"You're her mother. She will want to be with you."

"Don't be melodramatic. It's not like I'm going to die next week. Next month? Maybe. But not next week."

"How can you be so flip about this?"

"Oh, I've already cried, a lot. I make jokes to keep it at arm's length. I have to make a lot of jokes."

"Why can't your husband take you to your treatment?"

"Irwin has to go to New York. So I need a couple of rides to and from chemotherapy, because I'm not supposed to drive myself. Now he's threatening to cancel his trip if I don't confirm someone to drive me before he leaves. And he won't let me Uber or take a taxi."

"What's so important about this trip of his?"

"He's selling his business to a European multinational. It's a great opportunity for him to finally retire, but he was going to pass it up if I didn't get this transportation business taken care of."

Ruth was quiet a moment, then said, not without a certain satisfaction, "You *must* be desperate if you called me."

"Calling you was Irwin's idea. In fact, he insisted on it."

Why would he do that? Ruth wondered. *I've barely met the man.* But Veronica broke that train of thought.

"And friends? None that I would let see me in that condition. Ever."

But with me, it's OK, because I've already seen you at your worst, Ruth thought.

"I feel so honored," Ruth said. Then, recognizing her sarcastic tone, she said, "Sorry. I didn't mean that. Yes, I'll give you a ride."

"Thank you."

There was a moment of silence before Ruth said, "How are you feeling, Ronnie? Physically?"

"I feel like shit. About the same as I look." Veronica was quiet for a moment, then said, "I'm scared, Ruthie." She sounded like the little girl Ruth used to know.

"I'm sorry this is happening to you" was all Ruth could manage. "When do you need me?"

"The chemo is a week from Monday at eleven a.m. Are you free?"

"I'll rearrange my schedule with the mothers. It won't be a problem."

"Mothers?"

"I've been doing some babysitting since I was laid off at Briggs & Oden last year."

"You? Babysitting? I'm having trouble picturing that."

"It's a stopgap, until I find something else."

"Ruth, you're almost seventy. Why don't you just retire?"

Ruth's response wasn't meant to draw blood, but reflexes died hard: "Retirement isn't an option for me right now. We don't all have businesses we can sell to multinationals."

There was a chill on the line. But instead of responding in kind, Veronica held her tongue, and so did Ruth.

After a moment, Veronica said, "I'll tell Irwin we're all set so he'll finally go ahead and make his travel arrangements. I appreciate you doing this, Ruth. Why don't you pick me up around ten fifteen? That will give us a buffer in case there's traffic or it takes time to find parking."

"I know you live in Minnetonka now, but I'll need a specific address."

"It's the one on Incognito Lane."

Ruth checked her book. "The last address I have is on Beavertail Circle."

"Oh, that was a husband and a half ago. I'll email you the info."

"OK," Ruth said. She paused, then added, "Veronica, my whole life I've thought you were the most willful person I ever knew. How does cancer stand a chance if you make up your mind to beat it?"

She thought she heard a catch in Veronica's voice as she rang off with "Thanks, Ruth. See you a week from Monday."

Ruth tried to sort through her feelings after the call, all colored by her lifelong resentment of her sister. Yet that longtime connection now tore at her heart in unaccustomed places after her sister's news. That, and something Ruth had heard in Veronica's voice. *She sounds scared,* Ruth thought. And that scared her—because she thought nothing scared her sister.

CHAPTER 5

Ever methodical, Ruth decided she needed to learn as much as she could about liver cancer. The place to do that, she decided, was the local library. While the children napped that afternoon, she phoned the library, and, after working her way through a cumbersome phone tree, she learned the library would be open until 9:00 p.m.

When the last child had been picked up, Ruth retrieved that day's mail from the front door before she left for the library. She found the usual assortment: catalogs, direct-mail advertising, a couple of bills—and what appeared to be a handwritten letter.

The envelope was neatly addressed to her—to her maiden name, Ruth Abraham—in distinctive cursive handwriting, as though the writer had designed his own font. She looked at the return address: Denver, but no name for who had sent it. She had never visited Denver (one of a long list of places she'd never been), and Ruth could not think of a soul she might know there.

She found a letter opener and slit the envelope. The letter inside was neatly folded, typed single-spaced. She began to read without looking at the signature:

> Dear Ruth,
>
> I've been working with the committee for our Richfield High class's fiftieth reunion and took advantage of that lofty perch to obtain your snail-mail address, since

> they don't seem to have an email address for you. I hope you still remember me—

Ruth scanned down to the bottom of the page for the signature: *Martin Daly.*

Though it had been fifty years, she could picture him: tall and scarecrow thin, lank brown hair covering his ears and touching his collar, mischievous eyes, and a wardrobe comprised, at least in her memory, of corduroy pants and interchangeable plaid flannel shirts.

She remembered him being in trouble—not the kind of trouble that got him sent to juvie, but she recalled that Martin had spent time in detention after school on a regular basis. The charge usually was *insolence*, because he tended to talk back to teachers in class in what was described as a *smart* way.

Otherwise, his infractions ranged from chewing gum in class to parking his car in one of the spots reserved for teachers. He was accused of vandalism after someone sneaked into the building one weekend and papered the school with orange peel-off stickers. Each was printed with the question, "Whose stupid idea was this?" (including one plastered across the face of the principal's portrait hanging in the school's foyer). But it could never be proved that he did it. (He later admitted to Ruth that, in fact, he had.)

Then she remembered laughing in German class at his jokes about their teacher, Frau Morrison.

They both took German through high school, starting sophomore year. The only German teacher at their school, Frau Morrison, was a barrel-shaped woman of comically formal bearing and a fruity voice that tended to crack in unexpected places.

Frau Morrison had created a seating chart that randomly assigned students to desks for the year. She seated Ruth in the back of the room, just in front of Martin Daly, a stranger who'd attended a different elementary school and junior high in the Richfield school system.

As the teacher spoke to the class the first day, she would say something in English, then repeat it in German, before saying, "*Jah*?"—as though to say, "Do you understand?"

When Martin muttered a hilariously accurate imitation under his breath ("Oh, yaaaaah," he yawned), Ruth giggled more loudly than she'd meant to.

"*Jah*, fräulein?" Frau Morrison said to Ruth, turning from the chalkboard, where she was conjugating the present tense of *to walk*.

"*Nichts*, Frau Morrison," Ruth replied, nearly exhausting her supply of German words. Frau Morrison had announced when class began that as much classroom conversation as possible should be in German. But Ruth knew next to no vocabulary yet, so all she could say was, "I coughed."

"*Ich hustete*," Frau Morrison corrected her. "*Bitte—wiederholden.*"

Ruth stared at her blankly, embarrassed not to understand, though it was only the first day of class.

"Repeat, please—*bitte, wiederholden*," Frau Morrison said. "*Ich hustete.*"

"Oh," Ruth said. "*Ich hustete.*"

"*Sehr gut*," Frau Morrison said and turned back to the chalkboard.

When Martin Daly said, "Bitter, wiener holder," in a high-pitched whisper, Ruth managed to smother her next giggle with an actual cough so as not to draw further attention from their teacher.

Standing in her living room with Martin's letter in her hand, Ruth thought, *Martin Daly took me out on a date once.* It hit her like a bolt.

It was a half century ago, yet she suddenly remembered that she had ordered soup and that he had kissed her on her doorstep.

She went back to the top of the letter and continued reading:

> I hope you still remember me because I remember you quite clearly. The Ruth Abraham I remember (is it still Abraham?) wouldn't be caught dead at a high school reunion.

Well, he had that right. Ruth wasn't sure how the "Richfield 69/50" reunion committee, as they referred to themselves, had tracked down her home address. After Charles's death, Ruth had continued to use Winters as her last name and left her telephone listed under Charles Winters. Yet, for the past six months, the committee had used the US Postal Service to bombard her with flyers, fundraising letters, and save-the-date cards. She did not respond to any of them. She assumed that their pursuit would be even more relentless if they had her email address.

Which was why she had never given anyone her email.

She went back to the letter:

> I know, because I've gone to the reunions every ten years since we graduated, hoping I'd run into you, though I never did. I'm planning to come in from Denver for this one as well and I hoped that I'd see you—and then realized that, if you didn't come to any of the others, you probably won't come to this one either.
>
> So here I am, being pro-active, writing you an actual letter, to see if we might be able to get together when I'm in town, totally outside the scope of the reunion. I'm not proposing anything elaborate—coffee or perhaps lunch? I'm including my email address below so, hopefully, we can connect a little more efficiently than in the days of the Pony Express.

Though she didn't own a computer, Ruth had her iPhone, thanks to Chloe. Chloe had talked Ruth into the purchase when she'd left for college so they could stay in touch via email.

But Chloe was the only person to whom Ruth had given her email address or cell phone number. Veronica had obtained the email address by wheedling it from Chloe.

Ruth's sister tended to use email only to lob bombs at Ruth. Sometimes it was as childish as forwarding ads for dating services or designer sample sales (Brighten your wardrobe—and save!), which Ruth understood were meant as insults.

When Ruth and Veronica argued, Veronica would always try to get the last word via email. She inevitably did so after a couple of glasses of wine, sending off invective-filled accusations flecked with all-caps exclamations. One subject line read: That YOU could be so GODDAM SELF-RIGHTEOUS! And thin-skinned at the same time!!!

Ruth would give Veronica's emails a cursory glance, long enough to determine that a closer look would only be upsetting. Then she would delete them. She rarely read them all the way through and never, ever responded.

She looked at Martin's letter again. When did he say he would be in town? Not that she had any interest in *getting together* with a man who was, for all intents and purposes, a stranger. *He would only be disappointed in me,* she thought, remembering the kiss again and what had come after. When Ruth saw that the reunion was at the beginning of September, a little over seven weeks hence, she decided a quick and flat *no* would probably be best.

She dug her iPhone out of the kitchen drawer where it lived, searched for a charging cord, and, once connected, powered up the phone.

Ruth copied Martin's email address from his letter. Not sure what to put in the subject line, she wrote, Nice to hear from you. That seemed appropriately anodyne.

> Dear Martin,
>
> Things are unsettled right now. The time doesn't seem opportune to meet, I'm afraid. Thanks for thinking of me.

All the best,

Ruth (Abraham) Winters

P.S.: Please do not share my email address with any third parties—particularly not the reunion committee.

She tapped the "Send" button on the phone's screen, then set the phone on the counter. She picked up a windbreaker and went to the front door to head for the library. But when she stepped outside, she decided it was too warm for a coat and went back in to set it down. As she glanced at her iPhone, she saw the screen flash as a little flag appeared, alerting her to the presence of a new email.

On those infrequent occasions when Ruth did retrieve her iPhone from the drawer for a few minutes of use, those little flags let her know she'd missed an email from Chloe, anywhere from a week to a month earlier. That was how seldom Ruth looked at the device—much to the consternation of Chloe, who worried about her aging aunt and still tended to reach her via landline. Chloe had learned from experience that Ruth's lack of response to an email didn't mean something tragic had befallen her.

This flag's sudden appearance put Ruth off balance. Who could be bothering her now?

Martin Daly, as it turned out.

Dear Ruth,

When I sent my letter to you last week, I assumed I wouldn't hear back from you, or at least not this quickly.

So imagine my surprise—my pleasant surprise, I should add—to receive your email. I'm sorry we won't be able to get together. Still, I will check back when my trip gets a little closer, in a few weeks, in case you have a change of heart.

I remember you as sharp, funny, no-nonsense and determined. Where did all that determination take you, I wonder? You are someone I wished I'd stayed in touch with. So I'm still hopeful that you might find a little time to see me when I'm in town.

I should warn you: I'm not easily discouraged. I spent my career in advertising, and I was known for my persistence in landing a client. Fondly, Martin

CHAPTER 6

After a career as a bookkeeper, Ruth viewed her life as a spreadsheet, on which she plotted the various data points of her existence. It helped to put things in a logical order, even if the data revealed a long-running deficit.

The spreadsheet showed that Ruth hadn't had five consecutive years since the accident when her life had felt like her own, or even five years cumulatively.

Instead, in the forty-plus years since her parents' car accident, most of her life felt like a job from which she was not allowed to resign. One of many reasons she rarely examined that particular spreadsheet.

Ruth's parents suffered the accident, she thought, but Ruth's life was the victim.

Ruth spent years walling off the memories of what she vaguely thought of as *before the accident*: Childhood. High school. College. All before her parents' encounter with a drunk driver. All of it seemed so far in the distant past.

Martin's letter brought that time back. The memory of their date shook loose other memories. Each new one nudged free the next one and the next. It created an avalanche of nostalgia, which buried Ruth where she stood in her kitchen, distracted from her research trip to the library.

She hadn't erected the barriers against those memories because the memories were painful. Just the opposite: the pain arose from the fact that those years through adolescence had been happy and carefree, relatively speaking, though she hadn't known it then. So she made a point of not thinking about that time.

It made her sad to think about her mother, who had vanished from Ruth's life in the instant of the phone call about the accident. Her mother had worked with her father, managing the shoe stores he owned.

When Ruth and Veronica were girls, they would pester their mother to tell them stories about her life before she got married and had children. She would tell them, "I never imagined myself selling shoes for a living when I was in college at the U."

Ruth's mother grew up in Mankato, in southern Minnesota, and went to the University of Minnesota to fulfill her dream of becoming an elementary school teacher in Minneapolis. After graduation, she found a job teaching third grade in suburban Richfield, where she met Ruth's father.

Ruth's father grew up in North Minneapolis. He earned a bachelor's degree with a business major at the U, and, fresh out of college, he and a friend pooled their funds to buy a shoe store in southeast Minneapolis. In short order, the friend decided he wanted to move into ladies' ready-to-wear, so Ruth's father bought him out.

Her father made a success of the shoe store by focusing on the family market. That meant selling to families with kids, who grew out of their shoes almost annually, if not more often. There was, after all, a baby boom in progress. Shortly afterward, he met Ruth's mother, married her, and settled in Richfield.

A few years later, when he had a chance to buy a second store, he took it.

As the second outlet found its footing, the wholesale price of shoes began to rise. To maintain a profit margin on which they could live, he asked his wife to take charge of the second store so he wouldn't have to pay a manager. The difference between paying a manager's salary and losing her teaching salary made unfortunate economic sense.

Having Ruth's mother at the second store meant her father didn't have to worry that it was being run correctly. But it meant her mother had to give up teaching.

Her father eventually added two more stores, and the business consumed her parents' lives. They owned four stores in different Minneapolis suburbs, and, between the two of them, they were running the four stores themselves when they had their car accident.

But Ruth and Veronica knew that their mother lived another existence before she was their mother, a life shaping young minds. "When I was teaching" was Ruth and Veronica's favorite opening line for one of their mother's tales. The girls found her stories hilarious, because they focused on the bad behavior of students in her past life.

The misbehaving students in the stories were always little boys. In Ruth's memory, none of her mother's stories involved little girls, who, the young Ruth presumed, were all little angels. But the boys tended to be, um, spirited.

There was one boy named Samuel who, her mother said, was always climbing up on the school's flat roof, which was obviously off limits to the elementary school students. Another boy, Edward, would wet his pants in class and then deny that he had done so, despite the wet spot on his pants and the puddle under his desk.

"He would always say, 'I spilled!'—even though there wasn't anything on his desk for him to spill," her mother said. It always sent the girls into a gale of giggles.

A third boy, a particular favorite of Ruth's, was caught with an arsenal of small homemade darts, constructed of straight pins and scraps of cloth for a feather, both stuck through small cubes of rubber eraser. He would throw them at classmates when they weren't looking, limiting his prank to children wearing thick sweaters. The small dart would dangle from the sweater all day, or until it got jostled loose at recess or someone noticed it. The boy, whose name was Stevie, got caught when he threw one of the darts so hard it pierced another boy's shoulder, drawing blood.

"The darts were actually kind of ingenious," her mother recalled. "Surprisingly aerodynamic."

Their mother was much more available to Ruth and Veronica than their father was. As the demands of the shoe stores increased, however, the time she had for Ruth and Veronica shrank.

Ruth felt she could talk to her mother and that her mother loved her and understood her. But too many of their conversations came while her mother was putting dinner on the table or cleaning up afterward.

Ruth stopped trying to recount her school day to her mother when she was cooking, because her mother inevitably got distracted—"Wait, a tablespoon or a teaspoon?"—and Ruth would have to start her story over or repeat salient details more than once. Her mother rarely had the kind of time for Ruth that Ruth needed.

Her mother did take Ruth aside one day when she was twelve to explain what she might feel and what she should do at the point in the near future when she would start menstruating. But it was the school nurse who instructed Ruth in the use of a sanitary napkin when her first period happened one day at school.

When Ruth told her mother that night before dinner, her mother stopped mashing potatoes long enough to give her a hug and say, "Are you OK?" But that was the end of it, because Ronnie came in and announced that she was failing arithmetic. In many ways, Ruth took care of herself from that time onward.

Once Ronnie made school friends of her own, the two sisters rarely shared interests. The three years between them was already a significant gap, and the differences in their personalities made it feel wider.

Ronnie and her friends played dolls together, until they discovered pop idols like the Monkees and TV stars like David Cassidy and the stars of *The Mod Squad*. It was a short step from there to developing an interest in actual boys.

Ruth, on the other hand, discovered a passion for art at a young age. From elementary school through high school, her drawings were featured regularly on the schools' communal bulletin boards. She may not have had many friends, but everyone knew how well she could draw. She took pride in the reputation, even as she was forced to endure the attention it brought with it.

Through high school, she took all the art classes her school offered. By the end of her sophomore year, she realized that while her talent at sketching—and, later, painting—was real, it wasn't any better than above average. The last thing the world needed, Ruth thought, was another self-deluding, mediocre artist. There were already too many of those for her taste.

Yet she was passionate to know about artists and why they did what they did: how they were able to look at the world and express what they saw in an abstract way that other people felt and understood. So she decided she would major in art history in college and become a museum curator.

Ruth began to haunt the Richfield library—and then the main branch of the Minneapolis Public Library downtown. Every week, she checked out at least three large art books, which featured either color plates of the work by a particular artist or examples of a specific artistic movement or period. She would devote one index card to each artist or movement, carefully printing salient facts she gleaned from each book on a card, then filing it in a file box that originally had been for recipes. By the time she graduated from high school, her box contained more than one hundred annotated cards, most of which she knew by heart because she spent so much time flipping through them.

She saw all the exhibits at the Walker and the Institute of Art. She scoured the *Minneapolis Tribune*'s Sunday arts section each week for announcements of free public lectures at the university and the museums and attended as many as her studies allowed. She interned at the institute two summers during high school and again between her junior and senior years of college.

Even as she read biographies of Vermeer, Michelangelo, and da Vinci, she read the newspaper and the magazines her parents subscribed to—*Time*, *Life*, *Look*—to see the latest about modernist provocateurs like Picasso and Dalí and successors like Andy Warhol, Jasper Johns, and Roy Lichtenstein.

At the time of her parents' accident, Ruth was wrestling with that dichotomy: her love and appreciation for the work of the old masters bumping up against her intellectual curiosity about the audacity, humor, and challenge of modernism and its many branches.

She had heard a comedian say, "All art was modern art at some point." As she looked at nineteenth- and twentieth-century modernism on the continuum of art history, it was apparent that each leap forward felt like an effort to distance itself from what had come before, if not to erase it outright. Yet, in the end, the past contained the seeds of the present and future. Ruth loved finding the threads that tied ideas together across decades and even centuries.

She wrote a senior paper at Northwestern that connected the Renaissance, Dadaism, and pop art. But even as her academic adviser complimented Ruth on the intellectual reach of the paper, the older woman counseled Ruth to figure out whether she wanted to devote her graduate studies to the classics or to modernism.

"You can't focus on two things at once," the adviser said, as though it should have been obvious to someone at Ruth's level of education.

"But isn't it *all* art?" Ruth asked, to which her adviser replied, "Yes. But all art is not of equal importance. You need to spend your time focusing on what's important."

Ruth looked at catalogs for several graduate schools with prestigious art-history programs in the college library. Still, she knew Northwestern's department was well regarded. The more she considered other schools, the more she realized that the idea of uprooting and starting over—at Harvard? UCLA? Even Michigan?—made her anxious.

After almost four years at Northwestern, Ruth had developed a level of comfort in Evanston. She was familiar with the faculty at the university, and the professors in the art-history department all knew and liked her. She even enjoyed forays on the train into Chicago to visit its museums.

Finally, she applied for early acceptance to Northwestern's program. At the end of fall semester of her senior year, just before she went home for Christmas break, Ruth learned she had been accepted to Northwestern's graduate school for the following autumn.

She spent the winter and early spring of her final semester tracking down everything she could find to read about Andy Warhol and the scene he was creating in New York. At the beginning of May, as she finished her last senior-year finals, Ruth's parents had their accident, and Ruth left Northwestern, never to return.

What was important to Ruth after that had little to do with art or art history. A career as a museum curator became a distant, bitter memory.

A head-on collision killed her mother and left her father with brain damage and other lingering injuries. He was wheelchair bound and, after a couple of years, bedridden.

The drunk driver, who emerged from the collision with only a broken wrist, went to prison. He was an assembly-line worker at the Ford plant in Saint Paul who had lost his job because of his drinking. Not surprisingly, the driver's car insurance had lapsed a few months before the accident. He had no money for Ruth and Veronica to claim as compensation for the wrongful death of their mother or to pay for the care that their father's condition demanded. What compensation there was for the accident proved wildly insufficient for the needs Ruth's father faced.

With her mother gone, Ruth took on the full-time job of caregiver for her father. From the accident until her father died almost eight years later, Ruth focused on getting through each day with as little incident as possible. One foot in front of the other, one step at a time, for the rest of her twenties. Once she'd settled into that way of thinking, life seemed more manageable.

At the start, Ruth received two months of a home health-care worker's help, during days, while she closed her father's stores. Then Medicare stopped paying for that, and Ruth's father's Social Security wouldn't provide for it. The benefit from her mother's life insurance kept them afloat because Ruth took over as her father's sole caregiver.

Ruth assisted the nurse during those two months when she could so she could learn the keys to her father's routine. She became steeped in the minutiae of his daily care and feeding, including the disposal of by-products.

For the first couple of years after the accident, Ruth accepted holiday invitations from her mother's sisters, who lived in the far-flung Saint Paul suburb of White Bear Lake. Those gatherings left Ruth feeling tired and defeated. Eventually, she declined the invitations, because traveling with her father, even the short distances in and out of cars and houses, became increasingly difficult.

After that, neither of her aunts called to ask about her or her father. Ruth believed her aunts held her father responsible for her mother's death, though he was in no way at fault. While her aunts were sympathetic to Ruth during the holiday visits, she remembered only the disapproval in their eyes for her father, which she could not help feeling was meant for her as well.

Her father's head injury left him confused and irritable, particularly at the end of the day (which, she later discovered, was a phenomenon known as *sundowning*). But she learned what set him off, as well as what soothed him.

At first, when he still had some use of his legs and could be helped to the toilet, his care felt manageable to her. Then a stroke left him semiparalyzed, and Ruth found herself in uncharted waters. She needed to develop expertise in nutrition and its impact on bowel motility. She learned to time the trips when she assisted him to the toilet to move his bowels, to minimize his need for diapers, until moving him from the bed to the toilet became too challenging physically.

Before long, everything was systematized. Ruth had clipboards, charts, and calendars, meticulously recording her father's medications, his caloric intake, his weight, his output of urine and stool.

She began to see her father as a science project. She was able to relegate his physical being to a set of numbers that charted a downhill arc so she would not have to think about the diminished man she loved who clung to life.

She nearly surrendered to her sense of hopelessness when he was hospitalized in howling pain with a bowel obstruction. He came home with both a colostomy bag and a catheter leading to a urine collector.

This time, Medicaid provided for the aid of a nurse, but only for a month after his return from the hospital. The nurse gave her a tutorial in dealing with the bodily-waste products she would now be required to handle, more than once a day. Ruth was surprised how quickly she became inured to the tasks.

The nurse, an older Black woman whose name was Hazelle ("That's huh-*zelle*," she corrected Ruth), offered a pair of commonsense tips. The first: "You never get used to the smell. When it gets bad, rub a little Mentholatum or Vicks VapoRub under your nose. It covers it up real good."

Hazelle's other nugget of wisdom had to do with always wearing rubber gloves when changing the colostomy bag or the catheter, to protect against the chance of infection from spills: "Gotta do it—that shit is nasty, full of germs," she said.

"But remember: If you get some on you, it all washes off with soap and hot water. Good as new. Same thing I tell new parents about changing diapers. Circle of life, honey."

Eventually, her father needed a feeding tube inserted in his stomach, which required Ruth to squeeze the bags of nutritional paste through the tube into her father, a little at a time. She finally started sedating him before feedings so she could put his hands in restraints, because he would thrash and try to bat the tube out of Ruth's hands.

Ruth tried not to be repulsed by her father as she changed, cleaned, and bathed him and otherwise attended to all but one of his most intimate needs. She played a mental game of disassociation, trying to memorize and recite the calories, sugar, fat, and sodium content of each item on her father's menu, to distract herself while she performed the necessary tasks. If she could perfectly recite the breakdown of nutritional elements, she didn't have to be present for the scrubbing, sanitizing, and rediapering of which her day largely consisted.

By the time her father died, she barely noticed the smells, smears, and spills involved in his personal care. She was now well versed in vigilance for and care of the bedsores that plagued immobile patients like her father.

Even before he became comatose, she administered a daily pair of physical therapy sessions, in which she put his limbs through sets of repetitive movements and massaged his muscles to prevent atrophy. That was in addition to the rest of his complicated and time-consuming care schedule.

After the accident, Ruth also immediately had to take the reins of her father's four shoe stores. By that point, however, the stores were beginning to fall victim to the growth of suburban malls. Each new mall came with its own chain discount shoe store, always in a location that impinged on the territory of one of her father's stores.

Ruth promoted the most-experienced employee at each store to be manager, as a holding action. But she spent the first two months after the accident looking for a buyer and then hacking her way through the details of actually selling the stores so she could focus on her father's care.

As she watched her father fade into a coma that lasted for almost six months, she longed to be back working at his original store, though she'd hated working there during her high school years. When her father finally died, she wept when remembering the Saturday afternoons spent with him alone at the store after closing, straightening the stockroom together as she chattered to him about art history and what she referred to as *the calling* of being an art curator.

She spent most of her father's final year alone in the house with her silent patient. At one point, she realized that the only people she'd spoken to in a month were the men who delivered groceries and the paperboy, who'd collected for delivering the morning paper. She hadn't been outside in even longer. She barely knew the people in her old neighborhood. But she rarely left the house, so this wasn't an issue.

To pass the time, she would carry on conversations with her mute father, voicing both sides of the dialogue. At the point where he could still communicate by grunting and pointing, the conversations were limited to discovering what he needed. Eventually, he was reduced to communicating with eyeblinks, *yes* or *no*, when the rest of his limited ability to communicate deserted him.

Eventually Ruth began to take on both sides of the conversation as she gave him a bath or brushed his teeth or changed his pajamas. It was a way to distract herself (and him) from the task at hand or where it was all eventually going to lead.

Sometimes, it was as simple as recognizing that she'd jostled him unnecessarily, in dressing or moving him. She'd assume a gruff voice for her father and say, "Not so rough, Ruthie."

To which she'd reply in her own voice, "Sorry, Daddy. I'll try to be more careful."

More often, she would carry on conversations about current events, to try to keep both of them interested in the world outside the confines of their little house in Richfield.

"Oh my God, Daddy, that ridiculous Evel Knievel is going to do another one of his big stunts. It's all over the news. You can't get away from it."

"Really, Ruthie? What's he going to do?"

"He's going to try to jump over a tank full of sharks in Chicago."

"Well, Ruthie, that is his job. He's a professional daredevil."

"Yes, Daddy, but what kind of profession is that? A daredevil? How can anyone expect to live long enough to have a career doing that?"

"It takes all kinds, honey. He's done all right for himself so far."

At times, she let her dark humor seep into the dialogue:

"Daddy, did you see? Teddy Kennedy is going to run against Jimmy Carter for the Democratic nomination."

"Now, Ruthie—how would I see that? Did you forget? I'm in a coma. I can't get up to turn on the TV or read a paper."

"Stop making excuses—you could keep up with the news if you really tried. You are ignoring the entire world, and it's extremely selfish."

"Oh, Ruthie, you're such a kidder."

Assuming both roles in the conversation gave Ruth comfort after her father went into a coma. It took her mind off the fact that she was now left to bathe, exercise, feed, and otherwise tend to this human husk. Her father had spoken his last actual word more than a year earlier, but his most basic care would be Ruth's responsibility as long as he was drawing breath. She pretended to talk with him to avoid confronting that fact.

Shortly after he died, she caught herself carrying on another of her imaginary conversations and gave herself a good talking-to.

"Do you want to become the neighborhood crazy person, having conversations with people who aren't there?" she said to herself. "Stop talking to yourself—now!" And she did.

Ruth was surprised at the loneliness she felt after her father's death. Even though he hadn't been able to hold up his end of a conversation for some time, at least he had been there, a presence in the house, the proof that her life had purpose, if not meaning.

Without him, the emptiness of the house pressed on her. As anxious as she was about social interaction, she craved contact with someone—anyone—though she preferred to do it on her own terms.

But she believed no one would ever let her do that. She learned to focus on the pleasures—the simple lack of social pressure of any sort—of solitude. It sustained her until Charles Winters came along.

~

When Ruth was in high school, her mother taught her to help do the bookkeeping for the shoe stores and paid her for her labors. Ruth enjoyed the precision of doing the books, how everything needed to add up just so. Though she didn't know it at the time, it also offered insight into the stores' finances, which Ruth would use to value and sell the business, when that moment arrived.

She also saved enough in high school, between working in the store for her father and doing books for her mother, to buy a car, a used Volkswagen Bug, which she used to visit museums and attend lectures.

An inveterate autodidact with hours of time on her hands as she cared for her father and the house, Ruth studied bookkeeping from textbooks she checked out of the library.

By the time her father died, Ruth was thirty and in no mood to plunge into postgraduate studies in art history. Applying to graduate school at her age felt shameful and self-indulgent.

Ruth knew she would have to earn a living. Bookkeeping was the logical place to start. The newspaper classifieds were full of help wanted ads for bookkeepers of even limited experience. It had been several years since she'd kept the books for the shoe stores, but numbers were numbers, and accounting formulas remained unchanged.

When Ruth began to apply for bookkeeping jobs, however, no one would consider her without some proof of training, despite her experience. She found a local secretarial school and sailed through a six-week bookkeeping course that included a certificate of completion at the end. She then landed the first job she applied for after receiving her certification, at the insurance company Briggs & Oden, and spent thirty-seven years in the same job.

When the company announced it was trimming its staff, it came as a surprise to Ruth, though not to the other employees who were let go at the same time. The rumors about the merger of the agency's Minneapolis and Saint Paul offices had been floating around since the arrival of a new CEO, after the company had been sold to a larger Twin Cities firm. It was a cost cutting measure at a moment when business was off because of competition from the internet.

In the twenty years since her husband's death, Ruth had become increasingly isolated at work—although, in truth, she'd never had *work friends*. The secretaries and sales staff turned over regularly, seemingly always replenished by increasingly younger workers. She had once overheard one of the newer ones refer to her as *the strict old lady in accounting*. Because of her own inertia, by the end of her tenure there, she was the senior bookkeeper for the company by a factor of decades.

Ruth only ever had one friend at work, and that was shortly after she'd started at Briggs & Oden. On her first day, Ruth had been taken under the wing of Doris Taggart, the head bookkeeper, a bit of a mother hen, who took a liking to the quiet younger woman.

Doris befriended Ruth, showed her the job, explained the office politics and how to avoid them, and regularly ate lunch with Ruth in the small break room. Doris became the one person Ruth could talk to at work, though Doris did most of the talking.

She enjoyed hearing Doris's stories about her husband, Ralph ("God, that man is lazy"), and their grown son, Eddie, who was studying computer repair. Ruth never had any stories of her own to share but still found she was able to talk to Doris, even if it was only about the office and the news headlines.

Doris retired the year after Ruth's arrival, drastically shrinking Ruth's work world. She never joined watercooler chatter or break room discussions and began eating lunch at her desk. By the time rumors about the company's future swirled, the younger employees assumed Ruth's age and tenure meant she was part of the permanent management structure.

Ruth had met Jillian Blair, the company's new human resources executive, in passing a year or so earlier, when Bob Thompson, the longtime HR person, had retired. After that, Ruth and Jillian nodded hello when they saw each other in the hall. But they had not spoken until the day Jillian poked her head into Ruth's small office and said, "Ruth, could you come with me, please?"

Ruth followed her to the conference room, where Jillian pointed to one of the chairs at the large table. Jillian sat down opposite her and began to rummage through the pile of personnel folders scattered on the table.

Ruth decided the fortyish Jillian had a hard look. Her bubble-shaped hairdo appeared brittle, more a construction than a coiffure. Ruth also decided that her elaborate eye makeup, a style known as a *smoky eye*, made her look cheap.

Jillian finally unearthed the paperwork she sought. Ruth could see her own name typed on a label on the outside of the folder.

"Ruth, as you know," Jillian began, "we are merging the staffs of the Minneapolis and Saint Paul offices in order to create a more dynamic corporate structure."

"I didn't realize that was happening this quickly," Ruth said.

"You didn't?" Jillian said, and Ruth heard the surprise in her voice. Jillian's eyes seemed to do a little dance, like a computer taking a moment to reboot. She took two slow breaths in and out while looking down at her hands.

Then she looked up, smiled, and once more assumed a tone of corporate sympathy, saying, "Yes, I'm afraid so. As you can imagine, blending the two offices creates a number of staff redundancies, including in accounting. So I'm afraid your services are no longer required and that this is your last day at Briggs & Oden."

"What?"

"I'm afraid I have to ask you to clean out your office."

Ruth saw stars for a moment, as though she'd bumped her head hard. Then her vision cleared, and she said, "But I've been here since 1981."

"And we thank you for your years of service. But those services are no longer required, I'm afraid."

"You've said that four times. What exactly are you afraid *of*? That I might think badly of you? Because I already do."

"Well, I—"

"What am I supposed to do now?" Ruth snapped.

Though Ruth hadn't raised her voice, the question sounded like a demand, one that caused Jillian to sit back in her chair. She looked at Ruth—who stared intently at her—then down at her papers again. She took another calming breath before straightening her skirt and looking up again.

"We will be giving you a severance package and can provide career guidance—or retirement planning, as may be the case."

She smiled hopefully, as though she were a food server who had offered Ruth an unexpected amuse-bouche.

"But I'm not retiring," Ruth said. "I'm being fired."

"You're not being fired," Jillian pointed out. "Your position has been made redundant by a reduction in force. You're being downsized."

"How is that any different, in terms of how it affects me?" Ruth demanded.

Ruth watched Jillian go through the same brief routine: the look down at her hands, the slow breath in and out, the return of an empathetic but professional smile. *Do they teach this technique in business school?* Ruth wondered.

"I naturally assumed that, at your age, you have grandchildren who will keep you busy."

Ruth glared at her. "I do not, not that it's your business." Ruth thought a moment, then said, "How am I supposed to get the belongings in my office to my house?"

"The janitors have put boxes in your office while we've been talking here," Jillian said. "Let me know if you need more or if you require help to carry things to your car. Thank you, Ruth."

As it turned out, she required only one box. Not wanting to call attention to herself, Ruth had never decorated her office with personal photos or whimsical knickknacks. Her box contained one box of tissues, one small bottle of hand lotion and one of hand sanitizer, one half-full bottle of Tylenol, and a coffee mug with the Briggs & Oden logo on the side.

Looking at the box's contents as she prepared to leave, Ruth paused, then removed the coffee mug from the box and dropped it in the wastebasket before closing the door behind her.

CHAPTER 7

Ruth's quest to learn more about liver cancer started at the library and, to her surprise, resulted in her buying an iPad.

And so Ruth Winters ended her long, stubborn holdout—analog and unwired—against the invasion of the personal computer that had conquered the rest of the world in the late 1990s.

During her tenure at Briggs & Oden, Ruth had easily surfed the office evolution of the 1980s: the transition from mechanical adding machines to electronic calculators to desktop computers with digital bookkeeping programs. She had kept up with the shifts in technology as the accounting and bookkeeping software had grown more sophisticated.

But, until she developed a need to learn about liver cancer and its possible treatments, Ruth had never previously seen a reason to own a home computer.

In her entire career, there had never been a moment when she'd thought, *I should bring home an adding machine this weekend, in case I need to do a little extra work.* She felt the same about having a computer in her house. It was a work tool, an implement of labor—period. When the internet had appeared on the scene, she'd decided it was frivolous and distracting and had no interest in accessing it from home—or work, for that matter.

To Ruth, doing research meant one thing: a trip to the library. So she visited the one near her house in Saint Louis Park, in hopes of amassing a pile of articles and other materials in which to submerge herself.

It had been decades since Ruth had visited a library, the last time being while she was caring for her father. Walking into her local branch to find information about cancer, she discovered that much had changed. Of most concern was the fact that the endless shelves of reference books she remembered were gone, replaced by rows of computer terminals at small desks.

When Ruth went to the reference desk to ask about the books she sought, she was told they now existed at this branch only on microfilm and microfiche, a term Ruth heard as *micro-fish*. She wanted no part of that.

"But really," the young librarian said, "most of what you're looking for is available on the internet; it's kind of made us obsolete, in terms of reference books. Have you looked at WebMD or one of the other medical websites? Some of them are quite good. You could use one of our computers, if you have a library card."

Ruth had a card, though she hadn't used it in a while. Then she noticed how close together the computer desks were. The people who used them looked like sailors peering through portholes. They appeared to be seated shoulder to shoulder, able to easily glance left or right at the contents of their neighbors' screens. *No, thank you,* Ruth thought.

Which was why, after the children went home the next day, Ruth found herself at a counter in a Best Buy store in suburban Hopkins.

She initially thought about getting a desktop computer. But, after asking her a few questions about how she planned to use it, the young man behind the counter, whose name tag said **Mitch B.**, convinced her that an iPad was all she needed.

"Do you have access to Wi-Fi?" he asked.

"I'm not sure I know what that is," she said. His explanation included words like *router*, *coverage*, *cell service*—until Ruth finally understood what he was asking.

"My late husband used to have a laptop computer to access the internet. So we must have something that works."

"Well, if you have any problems, just call whoever handles your phone service or cable service, and they'll fix you right up."

Another expense, she thought as the clerk disappeared into the storeroom to retrieve Ruth's purchase. Ruth looked around the store, which was mostly empty on a summer weekday afternoon. Even without people, it felt like an electronic hellscape to Ruth. Under the silvery glare of fluorescent lights, guitar-heavy rock music blared from the public-address system.

To Ruth, much of the other merchandise looked mysterious and unfamiliar. She could identify headphones (which now resembled cupcakes that were worn over the ears), but what was a mesh extender? A halo light?

Ruth's eye was drawn to a wall of flat-screen TVs. The flat-screens, large and small, all showed the same movie simultaneously, which appeared to consist solely of exploding fireballs. The sound of the explosions rumbled across the store, providing a throbbing accent to the loud music.

Some of those televisions are bigger than the windshield of my car, Ruth thought.

When she got home, Ruth was intercepted on her way into the house by her neighbor Jane.

"Ruth, I got your message about not being available next Monday. Is everything OK with your sister?"

"Yes, but I will be driving her that day," Ruth explained.

Before she could go further, Jane said, "Oooh—is that the new iPad? I've seen the ads. Mine's so old."

On impulse, Ruth said, "Maybe you can come in and help me figure out how to use it."

The idea excited Jane, who followed Ruth into the house and helped her unbox the device. Jane expertly powered it up, then searched for a Wi-Fi signal. Finding none, she asked Ruth about it but drew only a blank look. So Jane located the signal from her own house next door and latched on to it.

"You can hook on to ours, rather than signing up for Wi-Fi of your own," Jane said, typing in her Wi-Fi password. "I don't think I have to worry about you stealing our identities."

"Even if I knew why someone would do that, I would never know how."

Before long, Jane had Ruth cruising internet medical sites on her new tablet. Ruth approached the device with the trepidation of a child learning to ride a two-wheeler. But shortly, she had the hang of the touch screen and was toggling between tabs expertly.

"What made you decide to buy an iPad?" Jane asked.

"I went to the library last night to do some research and found that they'd replaced their entire reference collection with computer terminals. I decided that if I was going to use a computer to find out about liver cancer, I'd rather do it in the privacy of my own home, thanks very much."

"Well, let's just see here," Jane said and beckoned for the iPad. Ruth handed it to her, and Jane began methodically searching for and bookmarking articles. Ruth watched for a few minutes and then stood up.

"Where are my manners? Would you like something to drink? I can make coffee, or . . ."

"Or what?"

"Well, perhaps a glass of wine?"

"Now you're talking."

It was the first time in ages that Ruth had entertained someone other than preschoolers. Even if it was only her next-door neighbor with a glass of chardonnay at the end of a long day, it was, Ruth had to admit, quite pleasant to chat as they took turns fiddling with the iPad.

Finally, Jane said, "Was there ever a time when you and your sister *were* friends?"

Unsure how to answer Jane's question, she finally said, "The list of things she's done since we were teenagers is too long for that to make a difference." But she was still stewing about it after Jane left.

Ruth summoned a memory of playing Barbies with her sister. How old would she have been? Ruth could remember when the first Barbies came out. She must have been—what? Nine? Ten? Which meant that Ronnie would have been six or seven.

Ruth had seen the Barbie commercials on Saturday-morning cartoons and asked for the doll for her birthday. Then she started saving her allowance and doing chores around the house to earn money to buy Barbie clothes.

Not that there was much that was childlike in Ruth's relationship with Barbie. A serious child, she was less interested in fantasy play about ponies, proms, and boyfriends than she was in organizing and reorganizing Barbie's wardrobe. Initially, she did it chronologically, in the order she bought the outfits. Then, for a while, she organized them by color. She was painfully precise, agonizing for an hour once over an aquamarine swimsuit: *Does this go with blue? Or green?*

When Ronnie would play Barbies with Ruth, she earned her place by reorganizing the clothes once the girls finished trying them all on their dolls. At the age of six, Veronica could spot the difference between cornflower blue and robin's-egg blue without looking at a color chart.

Ruth took credit for the fact that Ronnie was an early reader. She made Ronnie arrange the Barbie clothes in alphabetical order, using a small scrapbook Ruth kept, in which each page contained a photo of one outfit and its official name and date of purchase. She taught her little sister how to use it for reference, helping her sound out the name of the outfit on each page.

Yes, we did get along when we were girls, Ruth thought. *We played dolls and did other little-girl things together.* Ruth felt a quiver of warmth at the memory.

So what happened? When did things change?

Ruth thought about school. In junior high and high school, Ruth's mother had cajoled and encouraged her into participating in extracurricular activities. But the ones she pointed Ruth toward always focused more on service than enjoyment, such as working at the refreshment stand at school sporting events or on the stage crew for school plays. Her mother believed activities like these would open the introverted teen's world a little and keep her from being so solitary. She pushed Ruth to stick with the groups with each new school year, even though Ruth complained about the time it took away from her studies. "You're a good enough student to do both," her mother replied. "It will look good on your résumé for college."

Ruth understood that socialization was her mother's goal, just as it was when she had Ruth's father put Ruth to work at the shoe store on weekends. Her parents believed waiting on customers could only help break down the barrier of shyness and anxiety behind which Ruth lived.

But Ruth was so terse with the customers that her mother said, "You should try to meet people halfway." It was something she still struggled with.

Working at the shoe store and the concession counter at basketball games did hone Ruth's skill in the use of masks, faces she could put on to buffer her from social discourse. Most of the time, she wore a furrowed-brow look that bordered on a frown, as though she were considering serious things that displeased her. People often mistook this for aloofness or even rudeness. Her father once scolded her, "Be a little nicer to the customers, Ruthie, can you?"

Her mother did everything she could think of to help Ruth get out of her own head. Yet Ruth didn't walk through life; she sidled through it, ever wary of any moment that would draw unwanted public attention—and ridicule—to her. In her mind, embarrassment hovered over her like a cargo net, waiting to fall and entrap her.

When Ruth was ten, she confided her fear to her mother. Boiled down, it amounted to this: "What if something happens and people laugh at me?"

To which her mother replied, "Oh, honey, please don't take this the wrong way, because I love you. But the rest of the world doesn't care. And if people laugh at you? Guess what? You'll live."

Still, Ruth stayed home from school for a week out of embarrassment after she vomited in the hallway at school in eighth grade. Though she kept up with her schoolwork easily, a week was the longest her mother would let her stay home from school without actually being sick.

When she returned the next week, Ruth slunk from class to class, afraid to look anyone in the face for fear of finding disgust or revulsion, though she never did. In her last class of the day, though, a boy named Kenny Keith made an exaggerated vomiting sound as she walked to her desk, to snorts of laughter from other boys. She stopped, angry, then turned to Kenny and said calmly, "Everyone knows you're getting a D in this class." The retching sound stopped.

Whereas Ruth grew anxious in social situations, Ronnie thrived in them. She had an ease with people and facility with small talk that Ruth could only envy—and, as they got older, Ruth's envy grew. From an early age, she saw Ronnie's life as a rebuke to her own: a constant churn of playdates, sleepovers, and birthday parties and a crew of pretty, chirpy friends with whom Ronnie was joined at the charm bracelet from elementary school all the way through high school graduation. Most of them were bridesmaids at Veronica's first wedding—some at more than one.

In junior high and high school, Ruth always placed at or near the top of the honor roll. As a senior, she received an invitation to join the National Honor Society (which she accepted after she confirmed she wouldn't have to attend any meetings). At graduation, she ranked among the top ten students academically, in a class of over six hundred. She ended up in fourth place, which was fine with her. Any higher and she would have been in danger of being asked to speak at the cap and gown ceremony. There was no way she could ever imagine doing that.

Just walking across the stage to accept her diploma when they called her name was difficult enough.

Her parents were proud of her academic achievements. But, by the time she got to high school, it was a given: Ruth would get As. Ho hum, what else was new?

Veronica, on the other hand, was a mediocre student at best. Her school performance became a source of perpetual stress in the family, because she struggled with every level of math, starting with long division. Fractions, decimals, algebra, geometry—Ruth's parents had to be hands on, eventually hiring a tutor to ensure that Veronica's academic progress kept pace with her classmates', even as they left Ruth on autopilot to bring home stellar report cards.

When Ronnie found herself in danger of failing math and repeating grade 6, their father spent what little free time he had working on homework with her. He was expanding his chain with another store that particular year, and so his time for Ruth and Ronnie was limited. But what there was went to coaching Ronnie on her math studies.

A memory suddenly resurfaced: Ruth was fourteen and already interested in art history, particularly the Impressionists. A traveling exhibit of Monet's water lily paintings was showing at the Minneapolis Institute of Art, and Ruth wanted to go. And she wanted her father to take her.

While there is a behavioral pattern of daughters being close to their fathers and at odds with their mothers, Ruth's father was an exception. Reared in a family with three brothers, he was unnerved when he found himself the father to two girls. He loved Ruth and Veronica; Ruth knew that. But her father never was able to act like Ruth's daddy, instead of her parent or guardian. And that was something Ruth didn't know how to ask for. Ruth was an undemonstrative child, and her father rarely let his feelings show. It made an unfortunate combination.

She remembered her unhappiness after she begged him unsuccessfully to take her to the Monet show. Her father had encouraged her fascination with art, though his own interest was minimal. Now he sighed and said, "Oh, Ruthie—an art museum? You know how busy I am with the new store."

"The exhibit is only here for another month!" she implored.

"Can't you go with one of your friends?"

"I don't have any friends who are interested in art," she said, thinking, *Or any friends at all.* "I wanted to go with you."

"I'm sorry, sweetie. I just don't have the time."

Still too young to drive, Ruth figured out how to get to the museum from her house using Minneapolis city buses. She called the bus company to find out the schedule, the closest bus stop to her house, which bus she would need to take, and what a student fare cost. Then she rode the bus to the museum one afternoon when there was no school and both of her parents were working, without telling them.

Not a month later, her sister saw a TV commercial for the annual Minneapolis engagement by the Zuhrah Shrine Circus and begged to be taken. When Veronica received a C on a math test she was expected to fail, their father celebrated by taking the whole family to the circus—closing the stores early on a school night, no less.

Though Ruth said she had no interest in attending, her parents decided it was important that this be an activity for the whole family and wouldn't let Ruth stay home alone. She went along under protest.

When they got to the Minneapolis Auditorium, Ruth was intimidated by the size of the crowd (*What if we get separated?*), unhappy about the odors (*Do I smell elephant poop?*), and, of course, incensed by the ridiculous unfairness of it all: the fact that Ronnie got what she wanted from their father and Ruth did not.

She began to keep a tally of what she considered acts of unfairness involving her parents and her sister. That only made her unhappier.

Not long after that, Ruth realized that not only could Ronnie hurt her feelings, but she could do it casually and heedlessly.

Ruth was a high school sophomore, working on the stage crew for a school production of *Inherit the Wind.* One day, at the end of her work shift, she shed the coveralls she wore while she painted scenery and went back to the stage. She needed to talk to the stage manager about her duties regarding props once the show opened. But the stage manager was talking to someone else, so Ruth took a seat at the side of the stage to wait her turn.

When she stood up, she discovered her chair had been freshly painted for the set. Ruth's turquoise jumper had large brown stains on the seat and back. As she turned slowly to try to survey the damage, the stage crew's mouthiest wiseass, a kid known as Bobber, saw her dress and laughed loudly.

"Hey, Ruth, did you take too much Ex-Lax today?" he said, and the entire crew turned and then laughed. It was Ruth's worst nightmare come to life, worse even than the day she had thrown up. No one had laughed at her that day.

A week later, Ronnie had a friend over after school to watch TV and play Barbies. Ruth was in the kitchen, finishing homework before that night's technical rehearsal, when she overheard Ronnie and her friend, Vicky, talking in the other room.

"My sister is in the play at the high school," Vicky said. "We're going to see it this weekend."

"Who does she play?"

"I think she's Mrs. Blair."

"Who's that?"

"Like, a townsperson."

"We're going too. My sister is on the stage crew."

"I know," Vicky said, and Ruth's ears perked up. "My sister said your sister sat in wet paint on the stage, and, when she stood up, it looked like she'd pooped in her pants."

Veronica's melodic peal of laughter sounded as mean as a cackle to Ruth.

"My sister says your sister's backstage nickname is Poopdeck."

Ronnie, who had finally stopped gasping from laughter, said, "Poopdeck?" and off she went again. Her unrestrained giggles stabbed

Ruth like a spear, casually tearing through her rib cage as it searched unerringly for her heart.

Face burning, unbeknownst to Ronnie, Ruth quietly got up from the kitchen table and walked into their bedroom. She closed the door and let angry, silent tears come. Then she went over to Ronnie's little display case, full of trophies for the various sports teams in which Ronnie was honored as a *participant*. Ronnie was never a gifted athlete, but she was coordinated enough, and team settings fed her bottomless social appetite.

Ruth saw the one trophy she knew Veronica was proud of: second place in an archery competition at summer camp. Ruth picked up the small statuette and looked at the little gold-colored plastic figure atop it: an archer with an arrow drawn in his bow. Then she deliberately broke off the little bow and arrow and one of the archer's arms with it. She set the statue and its now-detached fragment on the floor, to make it look like it was accidentally knocked over.

So it had gone for the rest of their lives: each jealous of what the other had, expressing those feelings through passive-aggressive acts. Some slights, of course, were intentional: the noninvitation to Veronica's first wedding (and any of her subsequent weddings); the events of Chloe's wedding; and a laundry list of small unkind acts that left a mark, if not a scar.

Other times, however, simple mistakes—phone calls that were missed rather than ignored—were mistaken for deliberate provocation. The sense of outrage expressed on either side inevitably was made worse by the size of the chip each sister carried on her shoulder.

Ruth spent the rest of that evening on her new iPad. She read the articles Jane had bookmarked for her about different liver-cancer treatments and used the Google search engine to seek information about the survival rates of each.

As she drifted off to another night of restless sleep, Ruth thought, *If we weren't sisters, Veronica is not someone I ever would have been friends with. As it is, I can barely tolerate her.*

CHAPTER 8

The first time one of Ruth's children—a three-year-old named Evan—wet his pants at her house, he burst into tears, out of embarrassment and simple discomfort.

Ruth thought of how many mornings she'd had to change her father's wet bedding as she calmed Evan, saying, "Now, Evan, these things happen, even to people as old as me."

"Really?" he said, snuffling.

"Sometimes older people wet the bed," she said. "It's just an accident, dear. Nothing to be done but get you into some dry clothes. I know you'll try harder next time."

Until she began babysitting, Ruth had little interaction with small children in her life. She was thirty-five when she married Charles Winters, and they were never able to have children. Neither of them had living parents, so there was no pressure to produce grandchildren. After a few years, when no pregnancy occurred, the absence of children had little impact on a marriage that was already in the doldrums and destined to remain there.

When Ruth began babysitting, she found her anxiety disappeared with the children, because they all looked at her as a cross between their grandmother and a superhero. Her superpowers included tush wiping, boo-boo kissing, and tear drying, along with hugs and snacks.

The children were at a perfect age: happy little people, blissfully unaware that they weren't the center of the universe. Cheerful honesty was their default setting; they all said exactly what they thought or observed. They did it without malice and often with a sense of wonder, because they had not yet learned to be mean or sarcastic. They just wanted to have fun. She enjoyed their company, as exhausting as it could be to keep up with them physically.

Ruth found that young children responded to someone taking them seriously and expecting them to take themselves seriously in the bargain. The occasional parent who happened to see Ruth in action may have found her manner terse, but Ruth knew what worked. Children liked to have boundaries set.

And children liked feeling grown up. They seemed to brighten whenever Ruth addressed one of them as *young lady* or *young man* or reminded them to act *like ladies and gentlemen*.

She also refused to use nicknames. To one mother, Ruth said, "If you want to call him Xander at home, that's up to you. In this house, his name is Alexander." She imparted the same message—perhaps even more firmly—to the mother of a boy named Phillip, who insisted on calling him "Buzzy." To Ruth, Sam was always Samantha, and Jane stopped using the diminutive at Ruth's house.

Ruth always spoke to her young charges as though they were adults, as she had with Chloe when she was a girl—and Chloe had always risen to the challenge. Ruth's affection for the children reminded her of how little time she'd gotten to spend with Chloe when she was little.

Ruth's access to her niece had always hinged on the state of play between Ruth and Veronica. When Chloe was young, Ruth and Veronica could go months without speaking, which also meant months of Ruth not seeing Chloe.

Chloe was now almost thirty-five, and Ruth saw her only when she came to Minneapolis from California to visit Veronica. At least Veronica was no longer the gatekeeper—and hadn't been for a long time.

Still, Ruth retained bitterness about how little significant time she had been allowed with Chloe when she was a little girl.

For that she blamed Veronica. It was always Veronica.

Ruth believed Veronica was to blame for the lifelong friction and fractiousness between the sisters—because Veronica had abandoned her to the tidal wave of personal and financial worries Ruth had been forced to swim against from the time she was twenty-two. That was the first of many reasons why Ruth believed she could never forgive Veronica. But it always came back to the fact that Veronica had ducked her responsibility and Ruth hadn't.

Ruth skipped her college graduation ceremony to come home to care for her father and never left. Ronnie left and never came back.

When the accident occurred, Ronnie was finishing her freshman year at Saint Cloud State College. She came home for her mother's funeral, then went back to school for finals. She returned for the summer, but her help during her school break was both grudging and infrequent. She and her friends had jobs for the summer at a local Dairy Queen, and Ronnie was also leading an active social life, with several would-be boyfriends jostling for her attention.

Ruth spent the summer hounding Ronnie to handle her share of their father's care. Ronnie couldn't wait to escape back to school for her sophomore year.

Once she escaped, Ronnie didn't come home for Thanksgiving or Christmas, because she was invited to spend the holidays with a steady new beau and his well-off family. Nor did she drive down for weekend visits. Ruth didn't see her sister for almost five months.

By Christmas of Ronnie's sophomore year, she was engaged to marry her boyfriend, whose name was Tad Mills ("Of the General Mills," Veronica joked). They set a Labor Day wedding date the following autumn. Veronica phoned Ruth, telling her the news mostly so Ruth would be sure not to miss the engagement announcement in that Sunday's *Minneapolis Tribune*. She wanted Ruth to cut it out and send it to her so Veronica could have extra copies.

Tad, a graduating senior, slid into a vice presidency at his father's investment firm in Minneapolis. At the end of her sophomore year, Veronica moved into an apartment in Minneapolis with girlfriends

(Tad paid her portion of the rent), rather than live at home. She spent the summer doing wedding planning and decorating the house on Lake Harriet that she and Tad would move into after the wedding. On one of the few occasions she came by to see her father and Ruth, she announced her decision to quit college to be a wife, homemaker, and, with luck, a mother.

To Ruth, that was the moment Veronica forever absconded into a world of suburban luxury, a life marred only by a series of divorces, which came at regular intervals. Ruth knew none of the details.

Ruth couldn't imagine her sister doing anything that would make her angrier than the way she'd walked away with nary a backward glance, leaving their father's care in Ruth's hands. Then Veronica phoned Ruth about her wedding—her first wedding, that is—and proved her wrong.

Friends of Tad's parents had invited the happy couple to hold their wedding in the rose garden of the friends' Long Island estate. She was calling, Veronica said, to say she understood how hard it would be for their father to travel to New York for the wedding, given his condition. She also knew that Ruth probably couldn't afford the cost of a nurse to look after him, if Ruth decided to attend.

"So I won't even send you an invitation, OK?" Veronica said, as though performing an act of noblesse oblige. "That way, you don't have to RSVP *no*, and you won't have to feel bad. Isn't that simpler?"

The memory of that moment could darken Ruth's mood instantly. Yet Veronica managed to top even that a few years later, after their father died. By then she was on her second husband, Peter, Chloe's father. The day after the reading of the will, Peter and Veronica sued Ruth to force her to sell their parents' house and split the proceeds.

The sisters didn't speak for several years after that. When Chloe was born, Ruth was willing to bury the hatchet with her sister, in order to spend time with her only niece. But she and Veronica were unable to avoid squabbling when they were together.

Things would always begin cordially, but inevitably Veronica would say something Ruth found insulting, and Ruth would respond in kind. And that would be that.

The two sisters happened to be on good enough terms the year Chloe turned ten that Veronica allowed her to have an overnight at Ruth's house, as a birthday treat. From that point on, Chloe insisted on making her "Auntie Ruth sleepover" an annual tradition, even in the years when Ruth and Veronica were not speaking. It was the birthday tradition Chloe stuck to, no matter how her mother tried to distract her from it.

Veronica even scheduled a family trip for the week surrounding Chloe's thirteenth birthday, which coincided with a school break: Six Flags! Universal Studios Florida! Disney World! Chloe returned from the vacation and, the following weekend, demanded her sleepover at Ruth's house.

Chloe proved to be a strong-willed teen who understood how to push Veronica's buttons. She did so with enough skill to keep her mother at bay when it came to securing her time with Ruth.

For their special night, Ruth would pick Chloe up after school on Friday and take her to Ruth's house. They would order pizza or Chinese food—Chloe liked plain cheese pizza and pupu platters. Then they'd watch one of Chloe's Friday-night shows—*Sabrina the Teenage Witch* or *Boy Meets World*—and one of the videocassettes Chloe would bring with her, most of which were animated.

On Saturday, the two of them would put on dresses—not dress-up, exactly, but more an unspoken lesson Ruth offered in the correct way to present yourself to the world at large. Then they would get in Ruth's car and drive to one of the local malls that contained both a multiplex and a food court.

Chloe got to choose both the movie and the eatery. Her taste in restaurants seldom varied. For years, McDonald's chicken nuggets had pride of place on her food court tray, though, as she got older, she began directing them to the mall's TGI Fridays.

Chloe's taste in movies began with Disney, but, as she got older, she dragged Ruth to an increasing variety of films. Ruth loved the music of *The Lion King* and marveled at the computer animation in *Toy Story*. But she found herself unimpressed by a film as frantic and unfunny as the live remake of *101 Dalmatians* (while Chloe loved it). She was charmed, however, by the talking animals in *Babe* (which Chloe loved as well).

Then, one afternoon, about a year after Charles died, Ruth's office phone rang.

"Accounting. Ruth Winters speaking."

"Auntie Ruth?"

"Chloe? Is something wrong, dear?"

Chloe began crying and said, "I bought a ticket to see Bon Jovi with my friends at the Target Center on Saturday, and now Mom won't take me. She says I can't go alone because I'm only fourteen, even though I'd be with my friends."

"Slow down, honey. Tell me again—who's at the Target Center?"

"Bon Jovi—my favorite band."

"I'm sure your mother had a good reason—" Ruth began, not wanting to insert herself into a parental squabble.

"But Mom promised. She even bought a ticket so she could chaperone us. Then it turned out she and Errol have some other event that night. So she can't go. And now she says I can't go either."

Errol, Ruth thought. *Is that Veronica's third husband or her fourth?* She said, "I'm not sure what I can do, dear. Your mother certainly wouldn't listen to me. Can't one of your friends' parents do it?"

"They all said no." She paused, then said, "All my friends bought tickets because Mom promised to take us. Now it's going to be my fault when none of us can go."

"I'm not sure—"

"Auntie Ruth, what if you chaperoned instead?"

"Oh, honey, I don't know."

"Are you free on Saturday?"

"Well, yes, but—"

"Please, Auntie Ruth. I would owe you—like, forever!"

"I'm not sure your mother would approve of this plan."

"Her exact words were 'If you can find an appropriate adult to chaperone, they can have my ticket.' That's what she said."

The thought of irritating Veronica, while getting to spend unscheduled time with her adolescent niece, proved irresistible. Ruth wound up driving Chloe and three of her friends to the Target Center, an arena in downtown Minneapolis she'd never visited before, where she played sheepdog to her small herd of teenage girls at the rock concert.

She found tissues in her purse and created impromptu earplugs to block out the high-decibel rock 'n' roll. Then she could enjoy the enthusiasm of Chloe, her friends, and the girls around them.

Almost as soon as the lights went down, the screaming started. It was a high-pitched squeal that built in intensity, bleeding through Ruth's Kleenex-packed ears. The screaming crested when the stage lights blazed to life, revealing the strutting, colorfully dressed rock stars, who commanded the stage.

Though she had been the right age, Ruth was not the type to succumb to Beatlemania when she was a young teen. But she remembered seeing the crowds of her screaming peers in news film on TV and hearing the shrieks when the Beatles performed on *The Ed Sullivan Show*. The screams of Chloe and her friends reminded Ruth of that time, though Bon Jovi and their music left little impression on her.

On the drive home, Ruth's car was abuzz with teenage chatter.

"Did you like the way Jon had his hair?" Chloe's friend Beth asked.

"It's too short—and I didn't like that headband," countered a serious-looking girl named Darlene.

"Did you know that Richie is married to that actress Heather Locklear?" said Diane, the group's fourth member.

"Wasn't she married to the drummer from Mötley Crüe?" Chloe said.

"Never mind that," Darlene put in. "Did you see how tight Richie's pants were, if you know what I mean?"

"Darlene!" Chloe remonstrated, and all four girls giggled. Ruth smiled and kept driving.

"I wish they'd done 'Shot Through the Heart,'" Diane said.

"They can't do every song," Beth said. "At least they did 'Runaway.'"

"I love that one," Chloe agreed.

Chloe still bubbled with excitement as she and Ruth pulled into the driveway at Veronica's house. As they arrived, the porch light clicked on.

The front door opened, and Veronica stepped out, dramatically illuminated by the porch light as though onstage. She stood there, arms crossed, performing her tableau of silent disapproval from a distance.

"Uh-oh, the warden looks angry," Chloe said.

Struggling to mask her amusement at the smart-aleck remark, Ruth asked, "Did you have a curfew? You should have told me."

"No, no, I'm fine—but look at her. She didn't want to go. And now she's mad at me for having fun without her."

"Oh, honey," Ruth said with a chuckle. "I'm sure it's more the fact that you had fun with me. She's never happy about that."

"I know," Chloe said. "Why is that?"

"I'll tell you someday. When you're older."

Through the rest of Chloe's high school and college years, she and Ruth shared a closer relationship than Veronica knew. By the time Veronica got around to discussing a problem with Chloe, Chloe usually had resolved the issue by talking to Ruth.

Every week or so, Chloe would call Ruth to talk about boys and friends and college and all the other things she was trying to figure out in her life.

Ruth could talk to Chloe in a way that was affectionately parental, without being judgmental. She treated her with maternal affection, and whether she could verbalize it or not, she saw her as a surrogate daughter.

It was their unspoken secret.

CHAPTER 9

One day, while reading to Samantha from one of her picture books, Ruth noticed that Samantha was reading aloud along with her—and that she recognized words when Ruth pointed to them. The day Samantha announced, "I know my two-pluses," Ruth realized she was ready for arithmetic, as were the other children.

Ruth bought some simple word-and-number workbooks, which also served as coloring books. The children raced through the first batch so quickly—and then the second and then each subsequent batch—that Ruth was forced to make regular trips to the remaining Barnes & Noble store in her area. The children's eagerness surprised her: not only with their spongelike avidity to learn but with the unexpected tingle it gave her to encourage that quest.

Ruth remembered her mother talking about those moments when she saw something click behind the eyes of one of her students: a synapse being formed, a conceptual connection being made, something that would last their whole life. For Ruth, it was as though Samantha and the other children emitted tiny sparks when that happened—and it was occurring with greater and greater frequency.

As she began her latest search through the Barnes & Noble children's section, a few days before she was supposed to drive Veronica, she heard a voice behind her.

"Ruth? Ruth Abraham?"

She turned to see a balding, overweight man with glasses.

"Ruth?" he said again.

"Yes?"

"I just knew it was you. Boy, you haven't changed at all. Except, you know, the gray hair."

Ruth squinted at him, then said, "I'm sorry, you have me at a disadvantage."

"It's Teddy." She still stared blankly. "Teddy Arnold? I sat next to you in Advanced Sophomore English at Richfield High. Mrs. Ungaro's class?"

Ruth adjusted her glasses and stared at him. She certainly remembered Mrs. Ungaro, a pixieish teacher with a sharp mind and a needling sense of humor. But, though she searched her memory, Ruth could not extract an image of the boy this man once was. Perhaps she was being thrown by the comb-over and the double chin.

"Teddy, of course, how are you?" she said, unhappy to have to pretend familiarity.

"Pretty good. Remember Cindy Pearson?" *Cindy who?* "Well, I married her after college. We've got three kids and four grandkids. I retired from 3M a couple years ago. And you?"

He paused.

"Are you married? Retired? Kids? Grandkids?" he prodded her, unleashing a torrent of senior citizen signifiers intended to elicit a Pavlovian response.

Ruth felt the pressure build to reciprocate with a quick recitation of her own history. Teddy's attention bore down on her like a thumb pressing into her forehead. She wanted the conversation with this pushy little man to be over.

"You'll have to excuse me, Ed—"

"Teddy."

"Yes, of course. I'm sorry, Teddy. But I have a doctor's appointment that I'm going to be late for. It was nice to see you."

She worried that he could tell she was lying, though he appeared to believe her. She turned to leave, but wasn't quick enough.

"Listen, Ruth, before you go . . ."

"Yes?" she said, reluctantly turning back.

"I'm glad I ran into you. Did you know the class of '69 is having its fiftieth reunion in September? I'm working on the committee."

"Yes, I believe I did hear about that."

"Lucky I ran into you. You're one of our unicorns."

"Excuse me?"

"A unicorn—something that's impossible to find. You are one of the few people from the class that we haven't heard from, who are still alive. But since I ran into you, can I give the committee your RSVP? They need a head count for the caterer. I hope you're planning to come."

"I'm afraid I won't be attending," Ruth said. "I have another commitment that weekend. Out of town. A family gathering in . . ." Why couldn't she think of a plausible destination? *Because,* she thought, *I am a terrible liar.* She wound up saying the first name that came to mind. "Sioux City."

"Oh, I have family there too," Teddy enthused. *Of course he does,* Ruth thought. "We get down there every so often. They have a pretty good art museum, considering that it's, you know, Iowa. I remember you used to be into art, right? If you give me your email address, I can send you a list of my favorite restaurants down there."

"I'm sorry, I don't share my email," Ruth said, amazed that this stranger remembered her youthful passion for art. "But thank you for the offer."

"It was good seeing you, Ruth. And if your plans should change, I hope you'll consider coming to the reunion."

"Thank you. Goodbye."

She walked briskly to her car, then immediately drove away, afraid he might follow her and keep talking. At the stoplight, she realized she'd fled the bookstore before she'd had a chance to buy any workbooks. So Ruth drove to another bookstore, where she bought what she wanted without having any further unexpected reunions.

CHAPTER 10

On the drive home from the bookstore, the oldies radio station she favored played "Revolution," by the Beatles. The song, with its screaming lead guitar, dislodged a stray memory about Martin Daly.

She could remember debating the song's meaning with Martin when it had first come out in 1968. But what was the disagreement? She couldn't quite remember.

As a teen, she had owned a handful of Beatles' records, including the 45 rpm single that had "Revolution" on one side and "Hey Jude" on the other. For her, music was pleasant background noise while she did her homework or drove her car. She rarely understood the lyrics when she listened to most rock songs.

Martin, on the other hand, frequently came into German class with words of a song by some new rock band handprinted in a spiral notebook. He would listen to the record over and over on headphones, painstakingly lifting and dropping the needle in the same spot, copying down the lyrics until he had them all.

Instead of schoolwork, Martin worked at being a rock-critic manqué. He wrote album reviews for the high school paper and even submitted some pieces to a local alternative weekly, which promptly sent them back.

When she got home, Ruth dug the iPhone out of the drawer again. She found Martin's email address and typed him a note.

Dear Martin,

Do you remember the Beatles' song, "Revolution"? I seem to recall us having a debate about it, but, for the life of me, I can't remember what the issue was. Do you?
Best, Ruth

The return email arrived later that day.

Dear Ruth,

Wow! I hadn't thought of that discussion in a loooong time. But here's what I remember.

Our debate was about whether the song was pro- or anti-revolution. From this distance, it's obvious what it's saying: Be careful what you ask for—and how you ask for it.

Which you figured out and I didn't, at least back then. I thought the song was anti-revolution, and I couldn't square that with John Lennon's obviously antiwar political ideas.

But you knew, Ruth. I even remember you pointing to one specific lyric to make your point, the one about carrying pictures of Chairman Mao. You understood: How can you change the world if your methods alienate the people you're trying to help and wind up turning them against you?

Very profound for a seventeen-year-old. I was thinking about high school after I wrote you and remembering

> how cool I thought you were. I wish I'd told you that back then.

Me? Cool? Ruth's head spun a little. She continued reading.

> Do you remember that, just before my family moved to Colorado at the end of senior year, you and I went on a date? We saw the movie *Midnight Cowboy* and went to Embers after. Somehow, I worked up the nerve to kiss you goodnight. I always wondered what might have happened if my family hadn't moved away from Minneapolis.
>
> Sorry, don't mean to get nostalgic here. Just my way of saying that I'm glad we're back in touch. Your email gave me hope that you might change your mind and find time to see me when I'm in town. I do hope we can connect when I'm there. All my best, Martin

Ruth realized she'd been holding her breath as she read and exhaled. She set the iPhone down, then picked it up and reread the email.

She did remember her date with Martin. She remembered how nervous she had been because she'd developed a secret crush on Martin in German class. But she'd heard (or overheard) that, aside from being in trouble for his casual approach to school rules, Martin had a reputation for being *fast* with girls. She'd even heard that he had a nickname—the Martinizer—though she had no idea what it meant.

She was also unsure what it meant to be *fast*. Would he expect her to drink beer or smoke cigarettes? Would he want to take her to Lake Harriet to *park*? *Parking* was a term she only vaguely understood, though she assumed it involved some sort of sexual activity, in a car. If she was honest, Ruth was dying to be asked to do any of those things, though she also knew there was no way she would say *yes* if asked.

The memory of their date loosened a bubble of longing that was trapped somewhere among the recesses of Ruth's repressed feelings. She remembered feeling something for Martin Daly, long before he had surprised her by asking her out just before the end of their senior year.

Every day in German class, Martin went out of his way to try to make her laugh at least once. Ruth was too rule bound to do more than give in to muffled giggles, which she learned to hide from Frau Morrison. She and Martin shared a lunch period immediately following German class sophomore year, and he would use it to lampoon Frau Morrison while Ruth ate the cafeteria lunch and laughed quietly.

Martin always came to class with an imitation of one of the school's authority figures—usually Mr. Walker, the vice principal, who took particular interest in catching Martin in the act of misbehaving. Or he had a joke he'd heard on *Rowan & Martin's Laugh-In*. Or an impression of an actor he'd seen on *The Tonight Show*. He tried to engage her every day; even when she didn't laugh, he would make a joke.

"Oh, it's the stern Ruth today," he'd say, mimicking Ruth's composure when one of his German-class gibes met a deadpan response.

Ruth wished with all her being that she could join in with Martin's daily improv performance in the back row of the German classroom, before Frau Morrison called them to order (and, more than occasionally, after). Ruth could think of funny responses to some of his wisecracks, but she could never give them voice.

Eventually, Ruth decided that Martin might be too daring for her risk-averse approach to life. Martin was smart and funny, which fueled Ruth's crush. But he was perpetually in some kind of trouble in school—and that made her nervous. It felt dangerous to have feelings for him.

In retrospect, Martin scared her as much as he thrilled her, yet she was surprised at the level of unspoken feeling she retained for him. She still remembered her shock when, late in May of their senior year, Martin asked her out to a movie.

It was only the third date she'd ever had. The first two, sophomore year, had been arranged by her mother, with sons of her mother's friends. The dates were textbook examples of mismatchmaking.

As her evening with Martin approached, the teenage Ruth ran through the usual cluster of worries. But, on the appointed evening, Martin was sweet and polite, opening the door on the passenger side of his rusty (but clean) Camaro when he came to pick her up.

He took her to see the film *Midnight Cowboy* downtown at the Gopher Theater, where Ruth had seen films with her parents and Veronica when they were children. She and Martin needed to show IDs to confirm they were old enough to be allowed into the X-rated feature.

Afterward, he took her for a bite to eat at an Embers, one of a chain of family restaurants that was open around the clock. It was across the street from Dudley Riggs's Brave New Workshop, a comedy theater that put on mildly scandalous satirical revues on the weekend: "I love that place," Martin said, pointing to it as they walked into the restaurant.

"I've never been," Ruth replied.

"Oh, you'd like it," he said. "Maybe I can take you sometime."

The thought made Ruth feel as though she were floating for a moment.

Not knowing what to eat in a restaurant at that time of night, Ruth settled on a cup of navy bean soup. Martin, on the other hand, ordered a Jumbo Emberger Royal Deluxe, a massive cheeseburger with bacon, lettuce, and tomato that came with enough french fries to feed a family of four.

Ruth began the evening racked with tension, something to which Martin appeared oblivious. Even as she fretted about every moment they were together before the movie began—*Is this silence too long? Does my hair look crazy? How does my breath smell?*—she settled down as she and Martin chatted in the restaurant.

She wasn't particularly talkative, but he was happy to carry the conversational load. Before long, Ruth felt the same ease with Martin that she felt when they were in class.

They talked about the movie, and Martin, who regularly read the entertainment section of the *New York Times* in the school library, quoted his favorite critics. He commented on the film's message about loneliness and its love story between two men in the heart of unfeeling New York City. For someone with a reputation for skating by academically, Martin seemed very perceptive to Ruth.

When Martin mentioned the film's treatment of sexuality, Ruth spoke up: "Why does that subject have to be so forbidden? I mean, I understand that they put the homosexual material in to be controversial, but I wish there was a way to talk about that without being so sensational. Those people never hurt anyone. Why pick on them?"

"I don't know how I feel about how Ratso and Joe ended up—except, of course, that Ratso was dead, so that was sad," Martin said. "But, I mean, they weren't homosexuals—they were just close friends who learned to look out for each other. Maybe a little too late, but still . . ."

"Do you have any friends like that?" Ruth asked.

"You mean who walk with a limp? Or who want to act as my pimp? Neither, so far," he said, with a straight face. "But I'm still young."

Ruth laughed and said, "I have no idea what was going on in that one party scene. That was weird."

"Really?" Martin said. "I thought it was fascinating—I read that they filmed that at Andy Warhol's Factory in New York."

"I *thought* some of those people looked familiar, when the camera held still long enough to see what was going on. I've read a lot about Warhol, as an artist."

"I've read about those parties at the Factory," Martin said. "I don't think they could show what really goes on there in a movie, except maybe in some of those films that Warhol makes. Have you seen any of his films?"

"I went to see *Chelsea Girls* when it played at the Cedar," said Ruth, who had told her parents only that she was going to see "a movie" when she had gone out, not Andy Warhol's underground film. "I couldn't sit through it all. They seemed to say and do whatever would be the most shocking. But it wasn't particularly interesting as a film."

Ruth sipped her water and considered that evening's movie.

"I thought that friendship was so sad because Joe was so dumb and Ratso was obviously doomed," Ruth said. "He reminded me of Smike in *Nicholas Nickleby*. The kind of character who, the first time he shows up, you know is doomed to die tragically."

"Deep reference," Martin said with a nod. Then, pulling a face, he grabbed a french fry and savored it in a comically exaggerated way that made Ruth laugh. His compliment gave her a small thrill. She couldn't quite believe it: *I'm on a date with Martin Daly,* she thought, uncertain whether to be pleased or concerned, but mostly feeling excited.

As Ruth thought back, she remembered how the evening had ended: with a kiss—a moment from fifty years ago that now felt unbearably poignant.

Ruth started to get out of the car after Martin pulled into her driveway. But he said, "Wait—let me," then hopped out and ran around to open her door for her before walking her to the front steps.

"I had a good time, Ruth," he said.

"Yes, so did I," she said. "Thanks for taking me. And for the bite to eat."

"Sure. Well, I mean, I was just glad you were willing to go out with me."

With a look of determination, Martin squared up opposite her. Then, putting a hand gently but firmly on each of her arms, he leaned in and kissed her.

Having spent the drive home worried that he might instead drive them to a lakeside parking spot, Ruth was unprepared for the chasteness of the moment. His lips felt warm, dry, and soft, and she could feel the fuzz of his upper lip, which did not yet rise to the level of an actual mustache.

Despite her surprise at being kissed, Ruth responded, putting her arms around his waist and kissing him back, though it was mostly an ardent pressing together of their lips. As she did so, Ruth tried to catalog her feelings and sensations so she could sort them out later.

Before she could, the front-porch light clicked on.

Ruth and Martin jumped apart, as if shocked by an electric current. They both laughed; then Martin smiled and said "Thanks" and hurried off to his car.

Ruth took out her key and opened the door. Her mother, dressed in a bathrobe over her nightgown, was halfway from the front door to the kitchen when Ruth came in.

"Oh, honey—you're home," she said.

"Isn't that why you turned on the porch light?"

"Oh, no—I thought you would be later than this and didn't want you to come home to a dark house." She looked at Ruth a moment, then said with a slight smile, "I didn't interrupt anything, I hope."

Ruth, blushing, pushed past her, saying, "No. Good night."

That was the Friday before Memorial Day. Not having dated frequently, Ruth had no expectations of a follow-up phone call from Martin and, so, wasn't surprised not to hear from him. She knew Martin had an active social life. She also knew it was a busy season of teen parties, because Veronica was invited to so many of them. Ruth assumed that Martin was caught up in the same social whirlwind. He must have had better things to do than call her. Perhaps he'd kissed her only out of politeness.

When Ruth returned to school for the last week before final exams, Martin wasn't in German class the first day, or the second, or any other day as June loomed. Finally, at the end of class on Friday, Ruth asked Frau Morrison if she knew anything about Martin's whereabouts.

"I believe his family moved out of the school district" came the reply—in German, of course.

A couple of weeks later, not long after graduation, Ruth received a letter from Martin. It was typed, with a number of cross-outs and strikeovers. The return address was a town whose name was unfamiliar to Ruth, though it struck her as poetic: Golden, Colorado.

Dear Ruth,

I'm sorry to write you like this, but I didn't really have much choice. My father's job transferred him to Colorado in May, so we were busy moving or I would have called you. Kind of a last-minute deal that was complete bulls**t (pardon my French—hey, now I'm trilingual!), not that anyone asked what I think! Anyway, I had a good time with you at the movies and in German class. Maybe we'll meet up again in college! Like I'd even go there. Good luck with the rest of your life—ha ha!

Your "freund," Martin Daly

Ruth considered writing back to him but couldn't convince herself that her reply would be welcome. That was the last time she'd heard from him, until his letter had arrived the previous week, fifty years later. Now here she was in an epistolary relationship with him after all these years, if an electronic one.

Ruth looked at Martin's email again and realized that she'd missed a postscript. She scrolled up.

PS: Can I get you to give me a quick thumbnail history of what you've been up to for, oh, the last half-century? Here's mine, in less than two hundred words (because who would want to read more?):

After barely graduating high school, I backpacked through Europe, where I decided to skip college and become a writer. After a year of struggle, I realized that going to college was much easier than writing. So I enrolled at the University of Colorado to major in advertising and that's where I met my wife Betty. We got married after graduation and I got a job at an advertising agency in Denver. After about five years, I started my own agency here in Golden, and, about five years ago, I sold the agency and retired. I lost Betty about two years ago to leukemia. We have a boy and two girls who are grown and married, and now I have a brood of grandchildren who delight me on a regular basis. I've lived in the Denver area since my family moved away from Minneapolis in May 1969.

OK—your turn. /M

CHAPTER 11

Dear Martin,

I apologize for not responding sooner. I assumed that the older that you got, the simpler that life would become. But the opposite seems to be the case.

How to summarize a half-century: The numbers tell a story, but not a particularly interesting one.

I spent almost eight years after college taking care of my ailing father (until his death) after closing down his business.

After that, I was married for fifteen years. My husband died and I have been a widow for the twenty years since then.

I worked as a bookkeeper at the same company for almost forty years until they laid me off a year or so ago. Since then, I've been babysitting for neighborhood children, which, I was surprised to find, I enjoy. They lift my spirits every day. Not having children of my own, I had not realized what I was missing, so finding it at this age feels like a gift.

Still, at the moment, I can't decide if life is telling me to stay in my rut or trying to force me out of it.

I'm sorry if this is a little incoherent. I've had some bad news about my sister's health. It's thrown me a little, because we've never gotten along. I spent so many years with negative feelings about her that my reaction to her news has confused me. I resented her for so long; I still harbor resentments, if I'm honest. Yet now I'm filled with sadness and concern. Normal feelings for most people, I know. Yet I've wished her ill on so many occasions—how can I be having these feelings now?

My apologies for rambling. I disapprove of self-pity, particularly in myself. Does this seem like someone you want to have lunch with when you're in town? I have my doubts, but have decided that, if you're still interested, I would be willing to meet.

Sincerely,

Ruth

~

Dear Ruth,

I'm so sorry to hear about your sister's health. Here's hoping things have improved; if not, you have my sympathy. Let me know if there's anything I can do.

I'm elated that you decided to meet when I'm in Minneapolis. I've thought about seeing you more often over the years than I should admit.

As the date for my trip gets closer—can't believe it's only five weeks—I will be back in touch to firm up plans. And, again, if you need anything, please don't hesitate to reach out. All my best, Martin

~

Dear Martin,

When I think back (something I don't often let myself do), my memories of you are fond, and that fondness comforts me. Honestly, it is nice to have someone express an interest. It has been a long time.

I'm afraid my sister has liver cancer. I'm unsettled by how this makes me feel. If I were being melodramatic, I would describe her as my lifelong nemesis. I have essentially spent my adult years at odds with her over one thing or another.

I will admit that, along with that sadness, I have also not been able to shake a certain feeling of gratitude that I'm not the one who's sick. I can scare myself silly, imagining myself in the same situation. Which is why I try not to think about it.

You mentioned that your wife was also a cancer patient. I can only imagine how hard that must have been for her—and for you, who had to care for her.

Your concern is greatly appreciated. I can't help but think of how I have always envied my sister's beauty, her confidence and, if I'm honest, her wealth. Yet none of those things can help her now. If even my sister is powerless against this, what hope do I have? It's an unnerving thought, so I try not to think about that too much, either.

Hearing from you has made me recall so many things I haven't thought of in ages, at a moment of flux in my life. It is a challenge for me to adjust to unexpected changes to my routine. Yet my life continues to be upended by them. It gets trickier, with age, to maintain my equilibrium. I look forward to seeing you soon. Best wishes, Ruth

CHAPTER 12

What if Veronica dies?

Ruth had the thought while preparing dinner one evening as she brooded over the favor she'd agreed to for her sister.

She suddenly considered the possibility that her sister not only might die, but might expire in her car on the way to chemotherapy.

What now?

Mostly it was her sister's impending mortality that registered with her (though she put a mental pin in the dies-in-the-car scenario for later anxious consideration). The idea that Veronica would die aroused unexpected sadness, but Ruth still found herself entertaining the thought, *Why should I care at this point?*

Yet she did care, and she resented the fact. *Why do I always have such mixed feelings when the significant people in my life die? Why can't I simply feel grief? Or relief?* She hated how the combination made her feel.

Ruth had been awash in conflicting emotions at the funeral of her husband, Charles. But then, Ruth had never been more than mixed positive on Charles, even early on. Yet, somehow, she had wound up married to him.

Charles Winters joined the sales team at Briggs & Oden a few years after Ruth was hired as a bookkeeper. Charles was five years older than Ruth and divorced for a decade. He'd been lured away from another Minneapolis firm with a promise of executive advancement.

Charles had a salesman's smile: quick, ingratiating, genuine seeming. He was confident, outgoing, ready with a good word for everyone. To the cumulative surprise of the Briggs & Oden office staff, he set his romantic sights on the tall, standoffish bookkeeper, whose office was next to the executive offices at B&O.

Ruth had never been courted successfully in her life. Few tried, and the ones who did weren't able to penetrate the hard shell of personal rigor and fear of embarrassment behind which she hid, shielding herself with cutting remarks meant to fend off attention.

With the exception of Martin Daly, the boys she attracted in high school all belonged to roughly the same geeky demographic: the chess club, the A/V club, the math club, or, worst of all, the debate club. The males in this substratum tended to be undersocialized adolescents, awash in the kind of self-deluding hormonal cockiness that believes that a superior intellect compensates for a deficit of looks, charm, manners, maturity, and, often, hygiene.

Ruth was painfully blunt in assessing the shortcomings of those young men who did seek a date with her. When one young swain suggested that Ruth might like to come watch him compete in a chess tournament, a laugh burst from her like a sneeze, and she said, "Why would I ever want to do that?"

A different suitor, an A/V nerd, invited her to a movie, *2001: A Space Odyssey*.

"They've got the new Cinerama projector at the Cooper Theater," he told her, as though this would seal the deal. When she turned him down, the boy made the mistake of asking her why.

"Maybe if you brushed your teeth more often," she said. Ruth, who was interested in the movie, eventually saw it with her mother.

Ruth's experience with courtship and romance was as limited as her interest in it, even as a teen. She found hormonal urges unseemly and undisciplined, even when they couldn't be avoided.

If she lacked a physical interest in sex, Ruth did have intellectual curiosity. In high school, she'd once read a reference to the *Kama Sutra* in a racy novel, then looked it up in an encyclopedia, which was maddeningly oblique about what this mysterious ancient volume contained.

Though she was not by nature a rule flouter, Ruth used a part-time job at the Minneapolis Public Library downtown to sneak back in the stacks to a section for restricted books. There, she tracked down an illustrated copy of the *Kama Sutra.* She scrutinized the pen-and-ink drawings by Japanese artists of what looked like geishas and samurais joined in a variety of sexual positions. The drawings made the genitals of both genders look unappetizingly bewhiskered.

Most of the positions in the drawings struck her as so much showing off. Were those gymnastics necessary? Her feelings didn't change after she'd been initiated into the actual physical act; she had no particular interest in frills.

Despite her lack of carnal interest (and confidence), Ruth fell into an unlikely romance in the fall semester of her freshman year at Northwestern. It was her first and only such relationship until she met her husband.

Corey Walters was a sophomore art-history major from Buffalo who lived in her dorm, which was one of the first on the Northwestern campus to go coed. Ruth was finishing lunch and reading an art-history textbook in the dorm cafeteria a week into the semester when Corey sat down across the table from her with his tray and, instead of eating, began talking to her. Afraid of making a bad impression on a stranger her first week on campus, Ruth listened.

He began by pontificating about how overrated Marcel Duchamp was. Mistaking Ruth's silence for interest, he worked his way through a well-curated list of jejune opinions, slagging off Picasso, Warhol, Pollock, and Man Ray, while Ruth finished her fish sticks, macaroni and cheese, and coleslaw. Corey took encouragement from the fact that she didn't walk away.

"I'm sorry, I have a class to get to," Ruth finally said when she got up to leave, as though it was she who had asked for his attention.

Corey staked out the cafeteria at dinner that evening, and, when Ruth walked in, he made a production of seeing her, waving to her, and then sitting by her. He badgered her into seeing him again, this time for a movie on campus that weekend.

No one had ever done this to Ruth before. While she did say no at first, Corey persisted, pursuing her with puppyish exuberance. After they'd gone out a few times, he begged her for a kiss, and when she complied, he pronounced them boyfriend and girlfriend. Ruth was too surprised to correct him.

When Corey found out that Ruth was a freshman, he assumed the role of the experienced older man, though he was barely two months Ruth's senior. He wooed her with poetry (his own and that of others), and they learned to smoke marijuana together. Ruth wasn't fond of the sensation it produced and demurred after the first couple of times.

Ruth was still a virgin at the point that she began sleeping with Corey, and so, unsurprisingly, was Corey. He was honest with Ruth, this reticent freshman, telling her that he was eager to shed his pesky virtue before the end of the semester, when he turned nineteen. But, he claimed, he'd waited until he found a true soulmate, another description that surprised Ruth. He made a solemn candlelight-and-incense ritual out of surrendering their chastity to each other in his dorm room one weekend night before Halloween, while his roommate was out of town.

During their first week of discovery, Corey insisted they have sex as often as Ruth's demanding midterm study schedule permitted, factoring in the walking distance from campus to their dorm and their ability to secure a dorm room for themselves. As was typical of his age and experience, Corey was a vigorous but inexpert lover who assumed the quantity of their couplings was an acceptable substitute for their inconsistent quality.

Ruth couldn't swear she ever achieved an actual orgasm, as defined by Masters and Johnson, at least during the short peek Ruth had sneaked of their bestselling book in the student union bookstore. But Corey was the first boy who had ever persisted in this sort of attraction to Ruth and the first who wasn't intimidated by her standoffish personality. She had no experience against which to judge Corey as either boyfriend or lover. But she enjoyed having someone devote this kind of attention to her.

He called her at her parents' house on Christmas and again on New Year's and sent her a Christmas card with a box of candy, a small Fannie Farmer sampler. Ruth explained to her inquisitive mother that the gift was "from a study partner—so I guess I have to get her something too," uncomfortable in the white lie.

It turned out to be for the best that she'd kept the news of a boyfriend a secret. When she returned for classes at the beginning of January, Corey announced that he had slept with another girl in their dorm but told Ruth he'd be willing to see both of them (preferably together in one bed), an offer Ruth disgustedly declined. Ruth was glad she'd never mentioned Corey to her parents; she would not have wanted to explain that breakup.

She threw herself into academics and wound up at the top of the dean's list for the spring semester. She remained there for the rest of her undergraduate years, her perfect grades contrasting with her empty social calendar.

At the point when she met Charles Winters, Ruth was in her thirties, and whatever curiosity she may have had about men physically had been extinguished by the last few years of caring for her father. The male anatomy was no longer a mystery, in any sense.

But Ruth had little experience in the give-and-take of romantic attraction when Charles began to stop at her office door to chat with her, even if it was just a quick "Hi, Ruth" as he passed. When he offered to bring her something on his way back from the break room ("No, thanks," she quickly said), Ruth failed to recognize it for the aggressive act of flirtation that it was.

Then he asked her out and nearly scared her to death.

He found her in the break room one day and said, "Hey, Ruth, I have to go to a dinner next week where I'm getting a sales award, and I'd rather not go alone. Would you like to go with me?"

Ruth was so shocked that she blurted out, "Certainly not."

Then she hurried out, forgetting her plastic tub of mushroom-barley soup heating in the microwave oven. A veteran salesman who was used to the rejection that went with that job, Charles looked surprised, nevertheless.

He knocked at her office door the next day and said, "Hi, Ruth—do you have a minute?"

Ruth, flustered, started to say, "I don't—" but Charles cut her off.

"I only need a minute—please?" he said, sounding reasonable enough that she acquiesced with an unsure "Well, all right."

When he reached to close the door, she said, "If you don't mind, I prefer you leave that open."

"Oh," Charles said, then smiled and said, "OK if I sit down?" Ruth nodded, and he took the chair in front of her desk, then leaned forward, elbows on his knees, and looked at her seriously.

"I only have one question," he said. "Did I do something to offend you?"

"What?" Ruth said. "No, of course not. I hardly know you."

"Really? The way you turned down my dinner invitation, you'd think I ran over your dog."

"Don't be ridiculous. I don't own a dog."

"Figure of speech. My point is: You said *no* so quickly that I thought I must have done something to upset you that I didn't realize. But for the life of me, I can't imagine what."

"No, that's not it," Ruth said, trying to collect herself and finding it difficult. "You surprised me, that's all. I said *no* in case I was already going to be busy that night."

"I didn't tell you when it was."

"Oh. When is it?"

"Next Saturday." He paused, and when she said nothing, he continued, "The offer is still open, if you'd like to join me."

She reached for her perpetually empty calendar and scanned it briefly. "As it turns out, I'm free that night."

"Good. I'd love you to be my guest, and this time I won't take *no* for an answer."

"Is that how you close the deal with your insurance customers?"

Charles laughed, then offered Ruth a look that gave her an unfamiliar shiver. If a man had ever looked at Ruth with real desire before, she hadn't noticed or recognized it for what it was. But this look from Charles Winters was direct enough for her to feel physically.

At the industry dinner, for which Ruth felt compelled to buy a new dress (and then fretted about the price), Charles was a charming escort, treating her with a deference and solicitousness she'd never experienced. He was a lively raconteur, regaling their table with surprisingly entertaining stories from the trenches of the insurance industry. And he was a gentleman when she refused his request to come in for a nightcap.

Married and divorced in his early twenties, Charles told Ruth that he was ready to make that commitment again with her, to truly settle down. This came after eight weeks of dating, during which she refused to sleep with him. Ruth was too flattered to say no to his proposal. Ruth was thirty-five when she married Charles, and he was forty.

What did Charles see in her? Ruth wished she knew. She thought she understood what kind of women men wanted to look at and be with. Every TV show and movie she'd ever seen was created from what was labeled the *male gaze*. That gaze never focused on women who looked like her, and Ruth appreciated being left alone.

But during their courtship, Charles showered her with attention, and when her social discomfort translated to brusqueness, he took it in stride by kidding about it. It was as though he assumed Ruth was joking and simply moved forward. It was the same in the early years of their marriage.

"I snagged a couple of tickets to the after-party for the Vulcan Victory Torchlight Parade at the Saint Paul Winter Carnival," Charles would say. "I'm friends with this year's King Boreas."

"Oh, I don't want to go to that," Ruth would reply quickly, with a sour look.

Charles would laugh and say, "Of course you don't. You never do."

And they would end up going.

Eventually, Ruth learned to understand the transactional nature of Charles's personality. It was the perfect trait for a salesman but something he also applied to her without acknowledging it. She was there to play the role of wife, which came with a certain lifestyle attached and wasn't all that difficult, though not terribly engaging. Once he'd cast the role, Charles appeared to lose interest in the actress.

What did Ruth find in Charles? At first, it was the simple relief from loneliness. Her solitude was so self-contained that she was puzzled at emotions Charles elicited. She began to feel a pleasant sense of anticipation before their dates. After their small wedding (to which she sent Veronica an invitation, after the fact—two could play that game), she started to look forward to sitting down for dinner at home with Charles each evening to hear about his day, tell him about hers, and chat about their mutual acquaintances at the office.

What did she want from Charles? She didn't know. She had not asked for anything for herself since she was fourteen.

She knew what her parents' marriage had looked like to her as a girl. She remembered it being at odds with the way married life appeared on TV programs like *Father Knows Best*, *The Donna Reed Show*, and other family sitcoms in the early 1960s. None of the families in those shows appeared to suffer the stress and tension caused by the pressures of owning one's own business.

It wasn't as though the changes to her life were profound after she and Charles were married. She sold her father's house in Richfield (and, according to Veronica's husband Peter, didn't get nearly enough for it) to move into the house Charles owned in Saint Louis Park. She still went to work every morning, but on many mornings, she now rode with Charles.

Given her day-to-day schedule when her father was alive, marriage to Charles felt like a vacation, with someone who knew how to take care of himself. Charles staked out his areas of household responsibility:

yard work, home maintenance, keeping the cars in working order, and family finances. He made it clear that the cooking, shopping, laundry, and housework were her bailiwick alone, but Ruth was doing that for herself already, so it wasn't a strain to do it for two.

Ruth was surprised at how she responded to those moments early on, when Charles came up behind her and slipped an arm around her waist, giving her a kiss on the cheek and smelling her neck and hair. That kind of affection felt unexpectedly welcome after a life without it.

Charles would take her out to dinner and movies. He would go to sporting events with male clients and indulge her by taking her to the Guthrie Theater and to the occasional touring Broadway show, which Ruth enjoyed.

In his first few years, Charles was the top salesman at B&O, so he and Ruth frequently dined out with clients. Though it made Ruth uncomfortable, she forced herself to be part of the conversation with the clients' wives.

As time went on, however, there was a perfunctory quality to those moments when Charles would come up behind Ruth to massage her shoulders as she did the dishes, as though it was a task on a mental checklist he could now tick off. She enjoyed those moments of physical closeness when they came, for the fleeting touch they brought, until she realized that these encounters were a substitute for feelings he no longer could summon.

Around the end of year three, Ruth noticed that Charles stopped expressing interest in hearing about her day when they talked at dinner. She also noticed that he spent more of their dinner conversation talking at her than with her, most often to complain about something at the office. Nor did he listen to what she said, marking time until it was his turn to talk again.

Then Reynolds Oden, Briggs & Oden's CEO, died before making good on his promise to move Charles to the executive suite. Oden also neglected to leave any record of that agreement with Charles. When the position that Charles had been promised became open, it went to someone younger.

Even worse, the new CEO decided that, based on Charles's track record, he was the perfect person to expand the agency by pursuing new clients in Minneapolis's most far-flung exurbs, which meant the municipalities in a one-hundred-mile radius. Rather than trying to harpoon the whales that glided through Minneapolis's financial waters, Charles was forced to troll for perch on Minnesota's rural Rotary and Kiwanis circuit.

It also meant Charles had to go out on the road. He was gone Monday morning through Thursday night, then in the office on Fridays and home on weekends.

Just like that, Ruth was living alone for most of each week. For Ruth, Charles's absence came as a surprising relief. Ruth enjoyed having the house to herself and began to look forward to Monday mornings, when Charles would drive off. She scolded herself at her resentment when he came home for the weekend and worried that he could see how she felt. But if her true feelings showed, Charles wasn't paying enough attention to notice.

This man, who had appeared to be on a perpetual winning streak when she'd married him, now appeared to be defeated by his own life. He resented the fact that she still worked at a company that had so obviously wronged him, while he was forced to drive a repetitive circuit of Minnesota farm towns. He hunted for another position, but the other agencies weren't looking outside their own shops for executives, certainly not of his age. Charles said he would not trade being a salesman at B&O for being one somewhere else, because he'd have to start at the bottom again.

Charles began to drink beer to the point of sodden silence, with a regularity that Ruth found upsetting. On weekends, he would plant himself in front of the TV in the den with a succession of beers, flicking the TV channel restlessly from sporting event to sporting event.

Charles died at the age of fifty-five on a Friday at the office during lunch hour. He was leaning against a counter in the break room, when, by all accounts, he put a hand to his head, said, "Jesus Christ, that hurts"—then collapsed to the floor and stopped breathing.

Someone performed CPR and mouth-to-mouth while they waited for an ambulance to respond to their 911 call, but there was nothing to be done. A massive blood clot had lodged in an artery in Charles's neck, bringing his circulatory system—and then the rest of him—to a screeching halt.

Ruth was gone from the office for a dentist appointment over lunch hour. When she returned, an ambulance was parked in front of the Briggs & Oden building, with lights flashing. Ruth parked in her spot in the office lot as the paramedics closed the back of the ambulance. The siren whooped, and the vehicle sped off.

Ruth wondered vaguely who was being taken away. Though she had spent more than fifteen years at that office, there were still employees she had never met or spoken to. She knew their names from doing the payroll and taxes but couldn't necessarily match those names to faces.

Bob Thompson, the head of human resources, was waiting for Ruth at the building entrance. He rehearsed in his mind how to deliver the bad news. What he'd come up with was: "Ruth, I'm afraid Charles collapsed in the break room and died of a stroke before the ambulance arrived." In fact, those were almost the exact words he used.

But, as he waited for Ruth to return from her dental appointment, he had no idea how the deeply reserved woman would take the news.

Ruth was already a veteran at B&O when Thompson had been hired to run the HR department. In the subsequent decade, his interactions with her had been minimal. She had once pointed out a math error in the calculations for a new employee benefit, saving the company money. That may have been their most complex personal interaction ever, other than a passing nod in the hallway.

Charles Winters, on the other hand, had been a frequent visitor to HR.

Half of Thompson's encounters with Charles had to do with Charles's complaints about his lack of upward mobility in the company. The other half were complaints *about* Charles, which Thompson received from Charles's coworkers and supervisors. On those days when he was in the office, Charles had a habit of "joking" to his fellow employees about colleagues and bosses in a manner they found insulting.

In truth, Charles Winters was on thin ice at Briggs & Oden when he died. Aside from his increasingly unpleasant manner in the office, his sales numbers had declined, and there were questions about his expense account that were headed toward further scrutiny when Charles dropped dead.

Did Ruth know any of this? Thompson wondered. She lived with the man, so she must have been aware of how mordant he could be. But the falloff in his job performance? The ethical questions that threatened his continued employment at B&O? How much of that was Ruth aware of?

Thompson was a firm believer in the truism that no one knew what went on in a marriage except the two people directly involved. He hesitated to make assumptions about Ruth's.

Now he stood in the front vestibule, watching the ambulance pull away as Ruth came up the front sidewalk.

"What's going on, Bob?" Ruth asked, looking back at the ambulance.

"Ruth, I'm afraid I have some bad news," Thompson said, walking her in. "Why don't we go to my office?"

In his encounters with Ruth over the years, Thompson had never seen her display even the slightest emotion. It made him wonder about the formality that Ruth brought to any exchange. Though she was quiet, there was nothing timid about Ruth that Thompson ever saw, in terms of straightforward business interactions. Yet he always sensed an underlying tension beneath the otherwise unflappable surface.

When he told her that Charles was dead, Ruth gasped and seemed to collapse in on herself physically. Her eyes fixed on some point in the middle distance, and her breathing grew shallow. He saw her eyes glisten, and she cried quietly for a minute. Thompson sat there in uncomfortable silence, finally pushing a box of tissues across his desk in her direction.

Ruth took one, dabbed at her eyes, and blew her nose. Then she took a deep breath, sat upright, wiped her eyes once more, and said, "What happened?"

For a moment, Thompson thought he'd seen real sadness and loss in Ruth. Then she clicked into gear as pragmatic facilitator, gathering information about the tasks that faced her: identifying and retrieving Charles's body and getting the death certificate signed and a funeral home alerted. Thompson never did get his answer about how knowledgeable Ruth was about Charles's work life. (As it turned out, she knew very little.)

~

Charles's wake and funeral were out-of-body experiences for Ruth, a blur of handshakes and hugs from people she hardly knew, rarely saw, and would probably never see again. She wondered who most of them were and how they knew her husband. For most of that day, she had two words repeating in her head: *What now?*

The official funeral planning, including the wake, was done by Charles's younger sister, Arlene, whom Ruth barely knew. Charles was ten years older than Arlene, and he had never been close to her. His sister's efforts to deepen the relationship had been either ignored or rebuffed by Charles.

A few times, Arlene, who lived in Iowa, even tried to enlist Ruth on her behalf: "Would you mind just asking?" she'd say, invariably catching Ruth with a phone call in the evening during the week, while Charles was out of town.

Uncomfortable with the idea, Ruth nonetheless would mention to Charles that Arlene would be coming to the Twin Cities, and would Charles have time to see her? The answer invariably was no.

Charles never gave Ruth a reason for his lack of interest in his younger sibling, and she never asked. In the decade and a half that Ruth and Charles were married, Ruth saw or spoke to her sister-in-law on fewer than a dozen occasions.

Ruth notified Arlene, who lived in Des Moines with her husband and grown son, of Charles's death on a phone call the evening he died. Ruth was surprised when Arlene turned up unannounced at the funeral home in Minneapolis the next morning. There, she informed Ruth that, as a devout Catholic, Charles would have a wake, at which his casket would be open, as it would be at the funeral.

The prospect startled Ruth. For one thing, her memory of her minimal upbringing in Judaism did include the fact that Jewish funerals never involved any viewing of the deceased. For another, in all the years she had known Charles Winters, Ruth had never once seen him go to Mass.

"Charles wasn't an observant Catholic," Ruth said, in mild protest to Arlene at the mortuary.

"My brother was baptized in the same church I was," Arlene replied firmly. "As far as the church is concerned, he will always be a Catholic. He was my only brother; I am his only surviving blood relation. So I'd say my preferences take precedence here."

From the time she'd been told of Charles's death to this encounter with Arlene, Ruth had suffered guilt at not feeling worse that her husband had expired. Acquiescing to Arlene's interference helped extinguish that guilt.

Still, Ruth was ashamed at the sense of relief his passing gave her. Charles had been less like a husband than a sullen weekend boarder for at least a decade. The sense of reprieve she felt after his death seemed at odds with the genuine sadness she had about the fact that he was dead.

Ruth selected a suit, shirt, and tie so the funeral home could dress Charles for the viewing. Then she had to figure out how she was going to get through the wake and funeral mass while staring at her husband's remains in an open casket.

It wasn't the first time Ruth had seen a cadaver. She'd identified her mother's remains after the car accident that killed her. Then she had watched her father die slowly, literally holding his hand as he went, before helping prepare him for his funeral.

But the idea of putting a lifelike corpse on public display struck Ruth as . . . unseemly. She didn't want to use words like *primitive* or *barbaric*, because they sounded intolerant. Still, the Vikings of old supposedly put their dead into boats, which were set adrift and afire. To Ruth, that somehow felt less embarrassing than this show.

The wake and funeral were overseen by the bossy Arlene. Ruth's job was to perch on an uncomfortable pew in the church and then a bad folding chair at graveside, performing the role of widow while Arlene acted as funeral social director and chief mourner.

Ruth hadn't had feelings for Charles that could be described as *romantic* or even *warm* since shortly after they were married. But, sitting graveside with Arlene and her family, Ruth felt choked with emotion, if only for the memories the funeral evoked of burying her parents.

At that point, she had become an orphan. Now she could add *widow* to her résumé of life traumas.

Alone in her house after a day of company following the funeral, Ruth went upstairs to the attic, to Charles's office, a room whose door he always kept closed. Charles had never locked the door, but Ruth had taken the fact that it was closed as a personal warning to her: keep out. He'd never invited her in, and she'd never asked for admission. Nor had she had the courage to explore on her own, even when she had known he was out on the road, driving to one of those bleak little towns that dotted the southern Minnesota prairie.

But now she did open the door—and immediately smelled the cigars. She spotted an ashtray with a half-smoked butt. The ashtray sat on a small table, next to an easy chair with an ottoman, which was next to a half-open window in an alcove.

Ruth and Charles had never argued; it was not in her nature to be confrontational or show her anger. But she had drawn a line after he'd lit a cigar at the table after dinner one evening, giving him the silent treatment for three days until he had agreed not to indulge indoors. Now Ruth realized Charles had sneaked cigars by keeping the window open and the door closed. The room was scented with the dark tang of old tobacco, but the closed door had kept Charles from discovery.

The top of his desk was a daunting shambles: a nonfunctioning laptop computer, buried under a haystack of papers that looked as though she'd need a pitchfork to sort through. Ruth decided instead to focus her initial cleanup work on something more manageable, like an individual drawer. She would sort through the paper maelstrom of the desktop another time.

Ruth didn't get further than the first drawer in Charles's desk when she uncovered a sheaf of "Past Due" notices from the water department, the electric and phone companies, the bank that owned their mortgage—and both the state and federal tax departments. The further she dug, the more she found—each notice older than the last. Ever methodical, she began to phone the various entities that had sent the dunning notices, only to confirm that things were as dire as they appeared.

Ruth discovered that her husband, Charles Winters, had gone to his grave carrying the secret of a gambling addiction she had known nothing about. Charles didn't owe money to bookies; he'd always paid off the lavishly wrongheaded bets he'd placed on college football, professional basketball, and anything else on which he could lay some action. He'd had to, if he wanted to keep betting.

He had paid his bookies by ignoring most of his and Ruth's bills. When he got in a squeeze, he would buckle down at work and churn sales for a couple of weeks, earning enough in commissions to keep the gambling gods appeased. But he had a spotty record with mortgage and insurance payments, though not enough that it ever jeopardized anything—until now. He'd figured out a way to sprinkle payments around, when he occasionally won a little money, so that everyone got paid something once in a while, even as Charles's total debt continued to mount.

Ruth kicked herself when she figured it out: *I am a professional bookkeeper, and yet I let this man do our books for all those years because I assumed . . .*

What had she assumed?

Her whole marriage had been an assumption, she realized, and a mostly incorrect assumption, at that.

But she didn't have time for a relationship autopsy at this late date. She knew there was little to dissect and even less to be gained from the dissection. Charles had left her in financial jeopardy, with thousands in unpaid state and federal taxes and nothing in savings, an IRA, a pension fund, or life insurance. What else did she need to know about their relationship at this point?

Really, Charles? Ruth thought. *You sold the damn stuff, but you never thought to leave me any?*

Ruth hired an attorney, who was able to help her make a deal with the IRS and her various creditors to save her house and car, but not a lot else. Her back-tax repayment schedule was severe, requiring every extra penny she could squeeze from the income of a single-earner household and her dead husband's Social Security for the better part of a decade.

When the extent of the financial damage Charles had created became clear, any grief Ruth felt gave way to fury and frustration. Her anger at Charles reached a depth of emotion that her late husband had never inspired in life. She felt betrayal, not only at the economic hole in which he'd left her but that he'd hidden it from her.

Because he knew how angry this would make me.

There was a moment when, desperate at the prospect of possibly losing her house, Ruth swallowed hard and called Veronica, who'd recently split from the third of what would be four husbands.

When she called her sister and told her she needed ten thousand dollars or she would lose her house, Ruth could sense the iciness through the phone line. Veronica launched into a tale of woe about what a terrible time this was for her, how overextended she was—between household expenses and Errol losing a pile of money in the recession and falling behind on his support payments. As Veronica put it, she was having *liquidity problems*. She deployed this phrase as though it were a "Get Out of Jail Free" card that allowed her to ignore Ruth's request with impunity.

"I can't put my hands on that kind of money right now," Veronica said.

Ruth swallowed hard, then asked, with an edge in her voice, "How much money *could* you put your hands on *right now*?"

"I'm sorry, I just can't help," Veronica said, sounding aggrieved at being asked. "I'm sure you'll think of something. I've got to go." Then she hung up on Ruth.

As it turned out, Charles had taken out a small life insurance policy on himself at his first job in his hometown, Milwaukee. It was the first policy he'd ever sold, one he had never mentioned to Ruth and had forgotten about himself. Not long after her conversation with Veronica, at the peak of her stress over losing the house, Ruth got a call from an insurance company in Wisconsin. The woman wanted to verify her address so the insurance company could mail her twenty-five thousand dollars as beneficiary of the previously unknown policy.

It was years before she'd spoken to Veronica again. Ruth still hadn't forgiven her when Veronica had called, asking for a ride to chemotherapy.

Of course I hung up on her. Look how she treated me, Ruth thought as she got ready for bed the night before the chemotherapy session, as though justifying her feelings to herself.

Ruth muttered while climbing into bed, unhappy at what she'd agreed to, about how early she'd have to leave the house, how much of her day it would probably consume. Not to mention spending that kind of time with Veronica.

She wished it was over.

She wished she'd said no when Veronica had called—and stuck to it.

And yet, in the end, Ruth had said yes.

Now what?

CHAPTER 13

Driving to Veronica's house in Minnetonka to pick her up for chemotherapy, Ruth had a moment of clarity: *so this is what they mean by an emotional roller coaster.*

How appropriate. She'd always hated roller coasters.

As children, Ruth and Veronica had begged their parents to take them to Excelsior Amusement Park, which sat along the southern shore of the Lower Lake of sprawling Lake Minnetonka, west of downtown Minneapolis. The facility's identifying structure was the Cyclone, a large wood-trestle roller coaster that dated from before the Depression but always sported a fresh coat of whitewash. Once a summer, the family would go.

To the young Ruth, Minnetonka felt like an endless drive from their house in Richfield, though it was only a little over twenty-five miles. Yet she didn't mind how long it took to get to Excelsior because the trip's terminus was a beautiful lakeside amusement park.

She loved everything about it—except the roller coaster. She hated the massive roller coaster at first sight. To Ruth, the wooden structure looked as rickety as if it were made of random Tinkertoys. Every pass of the coaster made the framework shake and rattle. The sound of the coaster's ratchety rumble—as the ancient motor powered the chain that tugged the cars up the steep incline to the first drop—gave her a chill.

Ruth rode the roller coaster only once, on the Abraham family's first visit to Excelsior. Ruth and Ronnie both came off the ride shrieking—Ronnie with delight, Ruth in sheer terror.

It became Ronnie's favorite ride, of course. On the family's subsequent annual visits to Excelsior, Ruth refused all pleas to board what looked to her like an invitation to certain death. Her mother would sit with Ruth on a park bench, and they would talk while her father took Ronnie on the ride. When she returned from the roller coaster, Ronnie would tease Ruth about being a chicken.

Ronnie got a taste of her own medicine in the fun house, the first year the two girls were allowed to go into the attraction without their parents. Among the fun house's features was a horizontal spinning barrel, large enough for an adult man to walk through. With timing and balance, you could stroll through the barrel by walking against the rotation, as though on a cylindrical treadmill.

In previous years, when their parents had accompanied them into the fun house, the barrel had been off limits to the girls. Neither parent was physically courageous, so they had forbidden their daughters from entering the attraction. They didn't want to have to follow the girls into the barrel, should a rescue be necessary.

On their own in the fun house for the first time, the sisters made a beeline for the spinning barrel. Ruth went first; she found her footing and waltzed through the whirling cylinder with an ease that Ronnie tried to emulate.

But Ronnie lost her balance and fell on her rear end. The spinning barrel quickly dumped her on her head, flipping her like a sock in a clothes dryer. Ronnie started crying as she tumbled helplessly, over and over. Finally, a blasé-looking attendant with slicked-back hair and a stained white T-shirt strolled through the barrel to rescue her.

Excelsior Amusement Park closed in the early 1970s, lingering only in the memories of baby boomers and their surviving elders. The real estate on the shores of Lake Minnetonka became too valuable to devote to a facility that produced revenue only from Memorial Day through

Labor Day. Even in Minnesota, where lakes were available by the thousands, lakefront property would always be a precious commodity. So the old amusement park was torn down. The property was subdivided into a housing development of condos, luxury homes, and mixed-use commercial. Veronica's house was on an exclusive part of Lake Minnetonka proper on its southern shore, near where the park used to be.

Ruth turned off the highway and stopped to put gas in her car at a self-service station. The clerk who took her credit card—a young man whose neck and arms were festooned with dark tattoos—wore a T-shirt that said **Sorry I'm Late. I Didn't Want to Come.** *I should be wearing that,* Ruth thought.

She made her way through a maze of streets, as dictated by the GPS on her iPad (which Jane had helped her program). The tablet now directed her to a guard shack at a gate that was bracketed by seven-foot hedges: "Your destination is on your left." The gate led to a private road that served about a dozen lakefront estates.

When she rolled down her car window, the guard said, "Can I help you?"

Ruth said, "Ruth Winters. I'm going to Veronica Mills's house."

"Mills?" the guard said. "No one on this road by that name."

"Oh, wait—that was one of her other husbands. Her name is Snelling now."

"Oh, of course, the Snellings. And you are?"

"Ruth Winters," she said again.

The guard went down the list on his clipboard. "Winters . . . Winters . . . no, sorry, I don't have a Ruth Winters here."

This is so typical of Veronica, Ruth thought.

"Oh, wait," the guard said. "I have a Ruth Abraham down here for the Snellings."

"Abraham was my maiden name," Ruth said, adding, "hers too."

"OK, put this on your dashboard," said the guard, who wore a name tag that said **Randy**. He handed her a laminated powder blue card with the word **Guest** on it. "Can you please return this on your way out? Take a right—that's Incognito Lane—and the Snellings' will be the sixth house on the left."

Had Veronica forgotten Ruth's married name was Winters? Veronica had met Charles Winters only once. It was at the funeral for one of their mother's sisters. Ruth introduced Charles to Veronica without incident.

Later, as Ruth waited for the buffet after the service, she found herself two people behind Veronica in line. Veronica, however, was clearly unaware that Ruth was within earshot when she said to a friend, "Oh my God, I think my sister married Willy Loman." Veronica and the other woman had erupted in shared giggles as Ruth's face had burned.

Driving down Incognito Lane, Ruth took a deep breath and exhaled. This was not the time to dredge up past grievances. There were too many; where would she even start? *Better to simply do this thing—however long it takes—and be done with it,* Ruth decided as she turned into the long driveway and drove toward what appeared to be a lavish lakeside home.

When Veronica answered her front door, she looked so shrunken and helpless that Ruth's anger evaporated. It was all she could do not to gasp audibly.

"Are you all right?" Ruth asked.

"Sure. I was going to run a 10K but thought I'd go to chemo instead, because it sounded like more fun. Come in for a minute—I'm almost ready," Veronica said and disappeared into a powder room.

Ruth suffered a moment of cognitive dissonance, whiplashed between the obvious seriousness of Veronica's condition and the opulence of Veronica's home.

The living room was done in soothing yellows and creams with the right splashes of bright color and tasteful eccentricity among the luxe trappings. Veronica had expensive taste, at least since her first husband, and she'd found a series of mates who'd continued to subsidize her decorating choices. The living room, a matching collection of overstuffed easy chairs and sofas, looked like something out of *House Beautiful.*

Then, through a sunlit doorway on the other side of the living room, as though in a picture frame, Ruth could see another full sitting area in a glassed-in sunporch, with a suite of furniture that could accommodate at least ten. The windows of the sunporch revealed a manicured lawn that sloped gracefully down to the lake. At the shoreline, there was a dock with a large speedboat tied to it and a canoe tipped over in the grass.

For Ruth, it was a glimpse into a life she had never imagined for herself—a room of opulent, glossy indulgence.

Veronica, by contrast, looked like she'd stepped out of an Edvard Munch painting.

Her once-creamy complexion had a grayish cast, with dark circles prominent under her eyes. Neither of the svelte sisters had ever struggled with their weight, but Veronica had always looked sleek rather than skinny, a living illustration of the adage that you can never be too rich or too thin. Now she appeared gaunt and frail. Her legs didn't look sturdy enough to support her skeletal frame.

Veronica's thick mane of honey-brown hair had varied in shade over the years as the quality of her colorists had improved. What little hair she retained now was encased in a magenta turban, which clung to her head like a skullcap and made her look like a matchstick with a brightly colored tip.

Ruth heard a toilet flush. Then Veronica emerged from the powder room. She gave Ruth a wan smile and said, "Would you believe this is the best I'm going to feel all day? Let's go get this over with."

CHAPTER 14

Veronica filled the drive to the hospital with chitchat about Chloe's pregnancy. She mentioned the rainy winter weather in the Bay Area and their plans—hers and Irwin's—to spend a month out there after Chloe's baby was born. Then she explained that her housekeeper, Marta, had a long-standing family commitment that required her to take the day off today, which was why she needed Ruth to drive. And she nattered on about Irwin and a story he'd told her when they'd FaceTimed after he had gotten to New York.

Ruth drove silently, understanding that this wasn't meant to be a conversation. Surprisingly, she didn't resent being talked at. Veronica's words filled the car in bursts meant to approximate normalcy and good cheer. What Ruth heard was Veronica's desperation not to talk about the thing they were both thinking: *this is not going to end well.*

Ruth had a feeling she couldn't put her finger on, something unfamiliar and painful. Then she recognized it. It was actual concern for her sister and fear about what her future might hold.

At almost that instant, Veronica turned to her and said, "Do you remember the time you vomited in the hall in junior high?" Then she chuckled, which made her cough.

Ruth stiffened as she drove. *Really? She brings that up to mock me now? Why do I never learn this lesson?*

Veronica continued, "I was in the gourmet-cheese aisle at Lunds & Byerlys last week, and the smell of stilton triggered my gag reflex. Like, bam! Nothing I could do. I threw up on the carpeting, right next to the brie. Even as I was doing it, I was remembering how mercilessly I razzed you when we were kids. And I thought, *OK, this is karma biting me in the ass.*"

She coughed again, hard enough to concern Ruth. She caught her breath, then said, "Funny the things you think about when you're puking your guts out in public."

"That must have been awful."

"What could I do? I apologized profusely to the clerk who helped me clean the vomit off my favorite Lululemon in the ladies' room. As I was sitting there, with my stomach rolling like a cement mixer, I felt bad for teasing you."

Ruth was alarmed at how slow and unsteady Veronica appeared as they walked the hospital corridor to the chemotherapy clinic at the University of Minnesota Medical Center. But, at the clinic door, Veronica brightened, picking up her pace as she entered the pastel-colored room full of leather-covered recliners, each surrounded by a privacy drape. A large East Asian nurse with an infectious smile greeted her.

"Mrs. Snelling, looking beautiful as usual. How are you feeling today?"

"I'm ready for calisthenics, Jamilla," Veronica said, trying to sound carefree. "How about a footrace to the elevator? If I win, I get to skip chemo."

"Look at the size of me, Mrs.—of course you'd win," Jamilla said, indicating her own girth and chuckling heartily. "Now, hop into the chair, and we'll go for a spin."

Ruth excused herself to go to the waiting room, where she flipped through an aging pile of magazines that had an average publication date of 2015. *Golf Digest*, *Popular Mechanics*, *Martha Stewart Living*—Ruth had trouble imagining the people who would read them. Well, not *Martha Stewart Living*: she could definitely see Veronica reading that.

As she'd aged, Ruth had developed a wary relationship with longevity. She enjoyed relatively good health, so she seldom dwelled upon her age. She thought of her recent trip to the dermatologist for the removal of what had turned out to be a benign growth on her shoulder blade. Compared to what her sister was going through, her own health problems were, well, skin deep.

While she feared many things, death wasn't one of them. She had gone through a brief fascination with metaphysics and spirituality in college, after taking a course with an inspiring professor. She'd read volumes about the ways different religions and cultures thought about death and what happened to the soul or spirit when the body ceased to exist. None of it had particularly bothered or frightened her. She had come to the conclusion that it was something she could neither know nor control. So why devote energy to worrying about it?

"Why borrow trouble?" as her grandmother used to say.

She'd long ago stopped worrying about her own death and what came after. But being with Veronica was shaking Ruth in ways she hadn't anticipated. Her sister, someone whose self-involved joie de vivre made Ruth envious, was fighting for her life and appeared to be losing the fight. It made Ruth uncomfortably aware of the general fragility of existence, something she didn't like to consider.

Sitting in the waiting room, Ruth thought of her phone call with Chloe the previous day.

"Auntie Ruth, what's going on with Mom? Is she OK?" Chloe had said.

"Why do you ask, dear?" Ruth said, unsure how much Veronica had told her daughter. Her deep ambivalence toward her sister made her wonder why she would bother to hide Veronica's secret from her niece. But she did.

"She sounds so tired and out of sorts when we talk. Out of sorts, I could understand—when has she ever been satisfied with anything?"

Welcome to my entire life, Ruth thought.

"But this was different," Chloe continued. "She sounded exhausted, as if she didn't have the energy to complain."

"That *is* unlike her," Ruth allowed.

"I swear, the last time I spoke to Irwin, he sounded on the verge of tears. It was as if he couldn't get me off the phone fast enough or he would start crying. Maybe I'm imagining things."

Conflicting impulses paralyzed Ruth as she considered her response to Chloe. She knew that telling Veronica's secret would make her sister angry, and the urge to sting her sister was hardwired into her DNA. But Ruth disliked the vindictive streak in her own nature, particularly under these circumstances.

She had said to Chloe, "You know your mother. She's a complicated woman," and let their history tell the rest of the story.

On the ride home after chemo, Ruth said to Veronica, "You need to tell Chloe about this. She called me yesterday. If she calls again, I'm not going to lie to keep this secret for you. In fact, promise me this minute that you'll call her, or I'll go home and call her myself right now."

Ruth had assumed her sister would put up a fight. Instead, Veronica nodded a halfhearted assent, then closed her eyes and rested her head against the car window, dozing the rest of the way home.

When they got back to Minnetonka, Ruth helped Veronica into the house, where they found Veronica's housekeeper, Marta, in the kitchen. Veronica introduced Ruth to Marta, then bolted for the powder room, a hand clamped desperately over her mouth. Marta followed her, out of concern that she might not make it, then returned when it was clear that she had.

Marta was a small, energetic woman in her fifties, with jolly eyes and a disarming personality. She seemed genuinely pleased as she shook Ruth's hand when she came back.

"Her sister? I've worked for Mrs. Snelling for five years. Why have I never met you?"

Ruth didn't know what to say except "We've never been close."

"But sisters? My grandmother used to say, 'Sisters should always be closer than brothers.'"

"Yes, well, your grandmother never met us."

Marta started the electric kettle, then took out cups and saucers from the cupboard.

Veronica returned from the bathroom, sat down at the kitchen table, and said to Marta, "Why are you here? I thought your daughter needed you today."

"So did she," Marta said with a shrug. "Then her doctor got stuck in emergency surgery, so she'll have to have her colonoscopy another day. I'm sorry I wasn't here for you this morning."

"It's all right—Ruth did just fine," Veronica said. She turned to Ruth and said, "I appreciate you doing this."

Ruth stood there holding her purse (even in this neighborhood, she wouldn't just leave it in the car), as though about to bolt for the door. "Well, of course" was all she could think to say.

"Would you like to stay for a cup of tea?" Veronica said. "If Marta doesn't mind getting another cup?"

Now I'm in for it, Ruth thought but couldn't come up with an excuse to leave. By that point, Marta had found another cup and saucer, saying to Ruth with a smile, "If she won't insist that you stay, then I will. Stay. Please."

CHAPTER 15

"Auntie Ruth? I'm so mad at you right now—but I'm so grateful to you too," Chloe said when she called the next day.

"What do you mean, dear?" Ruth asked.

"You knew Mom was sick and didn't tell me."

"Is that the part you're angry about or grateful for?"

That made Chloe laugh, laughter that turned to tears.

"I'm mad you didn't tell me—we just spoke! But I'm grateful you were there to take her to chemo."

"I'm sorry to keep it from you," Ruth said. "But it wasn't my news to share. And I'd just found out myself. Your mother must be quite sick to ask *me* for a favor. You know she'd rather die—sorry, poor choice of words—she'd rather go out in public without makeup than admit to anyone, particularly me, that she wasn't in complete control."

"Yes, I know," Chloe said, still in tears. She sniffled to a stop. "OK, I'll be there in two weeks."

"What about the baby?"

"What about it? I'm pregnant, not immobilized. I'm barely showing yet."

"I look forward to seeing you, dear," Ruth said warmly before they hung up.

About once a week, Jane Mallory stayed around when she came to pick up Samantha so she and Ruth could sit and talk over a glass of wine. The day after Ruth did driving duty, Jane asked, "How is your sister doing?"

"Not well," Ruth said. "It feels like she's shrinking before my eyes. If I was meeting her for the first time, I would say the chemotherapy was killing her."

"Yeah, I remember how brutal it was for my mom," Jane said.

"Your mother had cancer? I'm sorry."

"Thank you. Yeah, brain tumor, about two years ago. About a year after Sam—uh, Samantha—was born, so at least she got to see my baby. But the chemo—she would be so sick, in so much pain. By the end, it was hard to even recognize her. I swear, in a hundred years, scientists will look back in horror on the practice of injecting deadly poison into people in the hope it will kill the cancer but not the patient."

"But what else is there?" Ruth asked, surprised at her own note of helplessness.

"That's just it. After all these years, there still isn't anything. This works often enough that they continue to use it."

Ruth sipped her wine silently for a moment. Finally, Jane broke the silence.

"So do the two of you seem to be getting along any better, you and your sister?"

Ruth nodded. "She's been very conciliatory. I kept thinking of the various grievances I have with her—"

"Grievances? Plural?"

"Oh, honey, it's been a long life. My mental catalog runs for pages. But on the drive to chemo—and then while we had tea at her house afterward—she kept mentioning them before I could. Then she apologized. Don't get me wrong—she owes me those apologies. But while I appreciate them, at times, it feels like one of those Saul-on-the-road-to-Damascus conversions. I keep thinking, *How can she possibly mean this after all these years? What else is she supposed to say under these circumstances?*"

Ruth saw the expression on Jane's face and added, "Maybe I'm just cynical."

In fact, that first afternoon after chemotherapy, as Marta had asked Ruth questions about herself, Veronica would chime in with tales of unfortunate moments from their shared past, including several that Ruth had forgotten—only to put salve on the sting of those memories by apologizing to Ruth for them.

While her sister's contrition moved her, Ruth still harbored resentment. Whenever her sister launched into another memory/apology, Ruth would think, *That's just the cancer talking.*

At one point, Veronica said, "My friends and I used to sneak your art-history books, looking for pictures of statues with penises. I still feel badly about the time my friend Sally spilled Kool-Aid on that one book."

"Is that what happened to my catalog for the Monet exhibit? I remember pulling it out of a box when I got to college, and the pages were stuck together. I assumed something spilled on it during moving."

"I'm so sorry. I should have said something," Veronica said. "I was such a little shit."

The string of unasked for apologies disarmed Ruth as she sat having tea with Veronica and Marta. So much so that she had said yes when Veronica had asked if she could drive her to chemotherapy again the following week.

"You can tell me if I'm being too nosy," Jane said, pouring herself a little more wine, "but what was the most unforgivable thing your sister ever did?"

Without hesitating, Ruth said, "Suing me over the sale of our parents' house."

"No," Jane said with a small gasp. "She didn't—really?"

"Oh, she definitely did. She and her second husband, Peter."

"That must have been terrible."

"We didn't speak for a long time."

"Why would they sue you?"

"Greed? Sheer meanness? Those are my best guesses."

"If I'm not being too nosy, can I ask what happened?"

Ruth recalled a meeting she had with the lawyers from both sides, along with Veronica and Peter. Peter was a florid-faced man who sported a noticeable toupee, which clung to his head like a needy badger. Ruth got the impression he knew how ridiculous he appeared and thought he seemed angry at the rest of the world for looking at him anyway.

The lawsuit had been filed, and they gathered in a conference room for negotiations to avoid a trial and reach a settlement. But the attorneys spent so many billable hours on nitpicky issues about defining the terms of the dispute that Ruth finally said, "Can we stop the lawyers' clock for a minute so my sister and I can talk privately?"

Veronica, however, said nothing when Peter insisted on staying in the room after the lawyers left. Undeterred, Ruth said to the two of them, "What are you doing? You must understand that, if you force the sale of the house now, I have nowhere to live."

"Well, it's not as if we're going to sell it tomor—" Veronica started to say, until Peter interrupted her.

"Half the sale price of that house belongs to us."

"Yes," Ruth replied, "and that will be as true in the future, when I am ready to sell, as it is today."

"But we don't need that money in the future," Peter said, his voice dripping with condescension. "We need it now."

"That's not my concern," Ruth said. "My parents' will specifically states that I have the right to approve any sale. I'm not about to do that, at least not now." She turned to Veronica. "Why are you doing this? They're going to throw this case out of court."

"This isn't personal," Veronica said.

Peter stood and pulled Veronica to her feet. "We obviously can't talk to you if you're going to be this belligerent," he said, ushering Veronica out of the conference room and past the waiting attorneys. "We'll see you in court," he had called back to Ruth.

Ruth paused in recounting the episode to take a sip of wine. Jane shook her head and said, “I thought you said she’d never been involved in your father’s care. Why push so hard for her share then?”

“My sister always had an overly developed sense of entitlement. Apparently, her second husband exacerbated that quality in her, at the expense of her common sense.”

“So what happened?”

“We went to court over whether they could force me to sell the house—and I won, of course. The judge threw it out without hearing the case. Even so, Veronica and her husband tried to make me responsible for their court costs.”

“No. That is too much.”

“The judge had a good laugh at that. Unfortunately, while she made Veronica pay the court costs, the judge turned down my request to have them pay my lawyer’s fee for the nuisance lawsuit. I used money from the estate to pay my attorney, which meant Veronica got even less—but so did I. Call it a Pyrrhic victory.”

“I guess I understand now a little more why it was so hard for you to hear from her. I’m surprised you ever talked to her again.”

“It would have been longer. But then she had Chloe. I like my niece much more than I like my sister. So I was willing to try to reconcile. But she knew she could use Chloe against me. That’s probably why I rarely got to see her when she was young.”

They both sipped their wine a moment. Then Ruth said, “And now Veronica is sick and can’t apologize enough. I’m willing to forgive. But I don’t know that I can ever forget.”

CHAPTER 16

Veronica was off to a slow start after a rough night when Ruth arrived the following Monday to drive her to her next chemotherapy session.

"I already called the clinic to let them know she might be running a little late," Marta told Ruth. "Why don't you come in for a cup of tea?"

Marta led her into the kitchen, where she filled the electric kettle and clicked it on. Then she turned to Ruth and said, "It's good for her to have you here."

"Well, she *is* my sister," Ruth said. She felt like a hypocrite, playing along with Marta's assumption of her good intentions.

"She's been very sick," Marta said quietly. "So much pain before the surgery, and yet it took so long to get her to go to a doctor. I heard Mr. Snelling a few mornings, begging her to call her doctor. And she would say, 'What's a doctor going to tell me? That I've got a tummy ache? I already know that.'"

"I didn't know," Ruth said. "We haven't spoken in a while. How did she tolerate the surgery?"

"She came home very weak. She hardly ate, could barely get out of bed. I was very worried. He only got her to do her physical therapy by threatening to call her daughter. For some reason, she didn't want her to know."

"I made the same threat," Ruth said. "She finally told her herself. Chloe will be here next week."

"Oh, that should lift her spirits."

"I hope so. We'll see."

"Mrs. Snelling has been talking about you quite a bit."

"Yes, well, don't believe more than half of the horror stories she tells about me."

"Oh, no—she never says anything unkind. It's always 'Ruth is the smart one' or 'I wish I was as strong as Ruth.' She looks up to you."

Before Ruth could process this surprising bit of news, Veronica herself came in. "Hi, Ruth. I'm ready to go." Then she put up her index finger as if to say "Just a minute" and began to cough. She sagged against a kitchen counter, her coughing fit building in ferocity until she was gasping for air.

Ruth stood paralyzed, shocked at how weak and helpless she looked. But Marta sprang into action with no evidence of panic, moving quickly to get a kitchen chair under her. Veronica sat down, still coughing, though with less force. Marta disappeared into the other room, then returned with an oxygen tank on wheels. She placed the mask over Veronica's nose and mouth, then twisted a valve on the tank.

"You're breathing too fast—slow and steady, in through the nose, out through the mouth," Marta said. Veronica did as she was told, exhaling slowly. Her frightened eyes fixed on Marta's. It took some effort to calm her respiration, but in a couple of minutes, it was under control. Veronica slipped the mask off and handed it to Marta. Then she turned to Ruth with a weak smile.

"Ready to go?"

Ruth, shaken, said, "Shouldn't we take the oxygen tank with us?"

Veronica waved her off. "I'll be fine," she said, though her face was the color of chalk. "They have plenty of oxygen at the hospital, if I need it."

Behind Veronica's back, Ruth saw Marta give her a shrug and a look that said, "Do you see what I've been up against?"

Despite her obvious physical weakness, Veronica did her best to act upbeat in the car, offering the latest news from Chloe in California and

Irwin in New York. To Ruth, it seemed as if her sister was afraid to stop talking, for fear that she might cease to exist.

Finally, during a rare pause in Veronica's monologue, Ruth said, "Did Chloe tell you she was coming?"

"Yes. I told her she shouldn't, but she insisted," Veronica said. "I didn't want her to come."

"Veronica, you ninny—why on earth not?"

Veronica's head whipped around, her eyes wide. She stared at Ruth, as though she'd seen a ghost. Tears began to roll down her cheeks. "Oh my God," she said quietly.

"What is it? Are you all right? Do you need me to stop the car?" Ruth said, her concern mounting.

"No, I'm fine," Veronica said. "It's just that, for a moment, you sounded like Mommy. She used to say that: 'Veronica, you ninny.' I hadn't thought of her in ages, and suddenly, there she was, sitting next to me, driving the car."

Now Ruth was the one in tears, though she made efforts to brush them away. Memories of her mother sparked a flood of feelings: affection, warmth, but also longing and loneliness. It had been a long time since Ruth had let herself think about how much she missed her mother. At that moment, she felt her absence keenly.

They drove in silence. Then Ruth said, "I still don't understand why you wouldn't tell Chloe you were sick."

Veronica was quiet, then said, "Because, when I see her and see how she looks at me, then it will become real for me. Not that I haven't taken it seriously up until now. I feel too sick not to. But I've worked hard to stay in denial as much as possible. Irwin, you, Marta, even the doctors—I can make myself believe that you are all alarmists. But when Chloe gets here, I won't be able to deny it any longer."

"How do you deny this?" Ruth said. She'd pulled up at the university medical center's front door to let Veronica out and made a sweeping gesture with her hand, indicating the massive hospital complex.

"You mean my spa treatments?" Veronica said, offering a dark-edged chuckle. "Worst beauty spa in town. I never leave a tip. But I keep coming back. I'll see you inside."

Ruth parked the car, then hurried toward the chemotherapy clinic and caught up to the slowly shuffling Veronica. She offered her arm for support, and, to her surprise, Veronica took it. A rush of feelings made Ruth's eyes well again, but she fought the urge to cry.

"You can stay if you want," Veronica said when they got to the clinic, and, to Ruth, it sounded like a plea. Veronica gestured toward a chair next to the recliner where she lay while being infused.

But once the plastic bag full of poison was connected to drip into Veronica's arm, she appeared to fall asleep, and Ruth was struck by a vision of her sister as a corpse. She asked the nurse, Jamilla, for directions to the hospital's cafeteria, then dawdled over a cup of murky coffee clouded with creamer until she knew Veronica's treatment was completed.

As she approached the chemo clinic, Ruth could see Veronica through the glass in the door, seated in a wheelchair, talking to a woman who looked like a doctor. She and the doctor appeared to be having an animated disagreement, which ended when the doctor, who was leaning down to speak to Veronica, stood up with a sigh of resignation and nodded.

Veronica continued to talk up to the doctor, jabbing the air with her finger to make a final point before slumping back in the chair, apparently spent. Ruth saw the doctor speak to the nurse, Jamilla, then disappear down a hall.

Ruth was waiting outside the clinic door when Veronica emerged in the wheelchair, with Jamilla pushing her. When she saw Ruth, Veronica tried to stop the chair and stand up. Jamilla put a tender but firm hand on her shoulder to keep her seated.

"Mrs. Snelling, you know the rule. You need to ride all the way to the entrance," she said, then wheeled Veronica to the front door and waited with her while Ruth retrieved the car.

"Thank you, Jamilla, for everything," Veronica said, once the hefty nurse had all but lifted her into the car. They held each other's hand for a long moment, their eyes locked on each other.

"You take care now, Mrs. Snelling," Jamilla said with a warm smile. "I'm sure we'll see each other again." Ruth thought she saw tears in Jamilla's eyes.

As they drove away, Ruth glanced nervously at Veronica, who had laid her turban-clad head against the car window and closed her eyes.

"That sounded like a pretty final goodbye," Ruth ventured.

Veronica opened her eyes and looked at her sister. Then she said, quietly, "It was. I decided to stop the chemo."

Ruth struggled to focus on the traffic around her, even as she reeled from Veronica's calm announcement.

"Is that what I saw you talking to the doctor about?" Ruth finally said.

"Yes, she wasn't happy with the decision," Veronica said. "We agreed to disagree."

"Shouldn't you discuss this with your husband and daughter? Your family?"

Veronica took a couple of deep breaths, then said, "You're my family, too, Ruth. But yes, I'll tell them. Not discuss—tell. Because it's my decision. And I can feel it. The cancer is winning. I'm losing."

"Maybe what you're feeling is the chemo working."

"No, this is different. I'm dying, Ruth. Why torture myself with more chemo? Or, worse, more false hope? If the cancer is going to get me, so be it. Why do I need to fight the chemo too? It feels like it's killing me faster."

"And you'll call and tell Irwin that you're stopping?"

"I will."

"Chloe too?"

Veronica nodded, then turned her head away, and Ruth could tell she was crying. As Ruth drove, she realized tears were running down her cheeks again as well.

CHAPTER 17

"How are you feeling now?" was all Ruth could think to ask as she watched Veronica lie back on a couch on the sunporch when they got back to her house.

"Like shit," Veronica said, without opening her eyes. "But I'll be better in a minute. Sit down, and stay awhile."

As Ruth sank into a nearby chair and set her purse on the floor, Marta bustled into the room, carrying a long-legged TV tray, which she set in front of Ruth's chair. Marta sat down on the ottoman that went with Ruth's chair and pulled the tray toward her.

Marta reached into her apron pocket and pulled out a cigarette lighter, a small glass pipe, and what appeared to be a prescription bottle. She opened the bottle, dumped out a dried marijuana bud, and crumbled it between her fingers onto the tray. With casual expertise, she used an old playing card to scrape the crushed vegetation into a pile, then employed the card as a shovel to lift a small amount into the bowl of the pipe.

When she nudged Veronica's hand with the pipe, Veronica opened her eyes and took it from her. Marta lit it, and Veronica inhaled, held it, and then exhaled a small cloud of smoke and coughed, though not the racking cough from before.

Ruth watched, astonished.

"You smoke pot?" Ruth said, not quite believing her own eyes.

"Please—this is medicinal cannabis," Veronica corrected her. "It helps after the chemo."

"I know it's legal," Ruth said. "I never thought about someone I knew using it. Certainly not you." She thought a moment. "But where do you get it? From a drugstore?"

"No, and the medicinal stuff they sell in this state—none of it can touch the nausea I get," Veronica said. "But smoking helps. Marta has a son in Oregon, where recreational cannabis is legal. He was kind enough to send me some after I got sick."

Ruth shook her head in disapproval. "Smoking can't be good for you."

Veronica guffawed, snorting smoke through her nose. "Ruth—how could it possibly make anything worse?"

"But still . . . smoking?" Ruth tsked. "Don't they have those candies you can eat instead?"

"Gummies? Oh, I've got gummies up the ying-yang from friends in Colorado and California," Veronica said, "and those are great, especially for sleeping. But they take a while to kick in, and after some of the chemo sessions, I need something that works faster."

"What about the other thing?" Ruth asked. "The vaporizing?"

"Vaping? I tried it, but it makes me cough more, for some reason. Smoking works best."

Veronica toked at the pipe again, this time without coughing. When she stopped, she offered the still-smoldering vessel to Ruth and said, "Now—are you going to have some of this or not? I hate to smoke alone, and I always have to." She gave Marta a mock dirty look, and Marta rolled her eyes and smiled. It obviously had come up before.

"Not while I'm working—you know that," Marta said.

Ruth accepted the pipe, then sniffed at it with distaste before lifting it gingerly to her mouth. Marta lit it for her, and she inhaled. As she did, Veronica said, "Be careful. The weed is a lot stronger now than when you smoked it in college in the Seventies."

By her second puff, Ruth understood what Veronica meant. She felt light—not lightheaded but merely light, as though the weight of worry, anxiety, and concern had drifted away. Ruth felt as though she needed to concentrate on the concept of gravity, to remind herself not to float from the chair up to the ceiling. Then a thought bobbed to the surface of her consciousness, and she turned to Veronica.

"How did you know I smoked pot in college? It was only a few times during fall of freshman year, and I never told anyone that."

She looked at Veronica, intoxicated by the sudden notion that Ronnie might be a mind reader. Then Ruth thought, *Has she been able to read minds all this time and I never noticed?* The idea felt entirely plausible, even likely, for seconds that felt like hours. Then Veronica burst her bubble.

"How do you think? I read your diary."

Her diary? Ruth hadn't kept a diary for years or thought of the ones she'd kept in high school and college, September through August, one for each school year, before her parents' accident. The copious, detailed diaries, still piled in a box in her basement.

"You read my diary?" Ruth said, the emotional swirl causing her head to blur, thanks to the cannabis.

She felt as if she were outside herself, watching a separate Ruth react to Veronica. The interior Ruth was suffering the stabbing sense of anger and betrayal at this long-ago violation. The exterior Ruth was a spectator as those feelings engulfed her inner self. It was like watching waves crashing against a rocky shore.

How futile. How completely pointless, the exterior Ruth thought. *I haven't looked at those diaries in years. Even if I did, they're ancient history at this point, a story about a girl who no longer exists.*

And Ruth began to laugh.

Her mirth was so infectious that Veronica and Marta laughed with her. Eventually, they all stopped giggling at the same time, with a sigh of relief—and their unison sigh provoked another round of laughter. Finally, this, too, subsided.

They sat quietly for a moment, and Marta said, "I must have a contact high. I don't even know what we were laughing at."

"It was Veronica saying she'd read my diary," Ruth said. "I was furious for a moment. And then I thought, *That was fifty years ago. Why am I getting mad now? What difference could it make?* And that struck me as incredibly funny."

Veronica reached over, taking Ruth's hand. "I'm sorry. I shouldn't have done that back then."

Before she knew what she was saying, Ruth replied, "I'm sorry too. I was always mean to you. Because I was always jealous of you."

"Well, I *knew* that," Veronica said—and they both started laughing again. Between giggles, Veronica gasped, "But you were always the smart one."

She suddenly turned to Marta with stoned enthusiasm. "Do you remember that TV game show *Password*?"

"Word association—am I right?" Marta said.

"I remember that show," Ruth said, smiling happily.

"You should," Veronica said. "You always won. *Always.* We would watch every week with our parents, and Ruth would say the winning clue before the celebrity on the show said it. Every time! Then we got one of those home versions—in a box?—and she never lost. Never! It didn't matter who we played with: our friends, our parents. Ruth always won."

"I had forgotten that," Ruth said dreamily.

"You were always so much smarter than me—and I was always jealous of that."

Ruth gave her a pitying look and said, "Well, I *knew* that."

Then all three dissolved into laughter once more.

CHAPTER 18

The western horizon glowed a vivid purply pink by the time Ruth pulled into her driveway on that warm summer night. She marveled that she had spent the afternoon talking, laughing, and crying with her sister. It was something she had never done before.

She had taken only three or four puffs on Veronica's pipe, but Ruth had spent the time afterward with a sense of well-being and relaxation that was new to her. She also got to meet the adult version of the Veronica she now remembered liking when they were girls.

This version of Veronica was clever and funny, quick with a snarky (but witty) observation. Unlike the old Ronnie, this one made Ruth her ally, instead of her target, as they spoke about things they had never discussed previously.

"I keep having dreams about Mommy," Veronica said.

"What kind of dreams?" Ruth asked.

"Not nightmares or anything—just the opposite," Veronica said. "I'm a little girl, and she's brushing my hair. That kind of thing."

"I hadn't thought of her in a long time," Ruth said, "until we were in the car, when you said I reminded you of her." She paused, then said, "I miss them."

"Me too," Veronica said. After a quiet moment, she said, "Do you remember when they had the contest to see who could quit smoking cigarettes?"

It was the early 1960s, after news stories about the US surgeon general's report linking cigarette smoking to lung cancer. For a long time, both girls had complained about their parents' smoking, making a show of gasping and coughing whenever one of their parents lit a cigarette in the car or at the dinner table. Now they had ammunition—in the newspaper—with which to support their argument that their parents should stop smoking.

Their father jokingly proposed a contest, saying, "I can quit whenever I want. But I don't think your mother can."

"Wanna bet?" their mother snapped.

The game was on. For the next two months, the girls enjoyed a smoke-free environment at home for the first time in their young lives.

Their parents were competitive in a kidding way for the first couple of days of the contest. But they quickly turned cranky and edgy, remaining that way for the first two weeks of the showdown, when the effects of withdrawal from nicotine addiction were the worst. Their mother seemed to be gritting her teeth for the entire two weeks, as though privately battling some invisible malevolent force. She never lost her temper with them, but she lacked the note of cheer that suffused her personality most days.

After two weeks, she started to regain her usual sunniness, a little more each day. Yet she never lost the slight tension in her bearing, as though a piece of clothing was pinching her somewhere she couldn't reach.

Their father, on the other hand, turned a sharp corner at the two-week mark. He shed the jangled quality that disrupted his usual controlled exterior. If anything, he was calmer than before.

The contest led to the only moment the girls could remember when their mother raised her voice at their father.

It happened at the two-month no-smoking mark. Ruth was in the kitchen, doing homework after school, when her mother came in, slamming the door behind her. Ruth looked up, and her mother said, "Sorry.

No slamming doors. That's the rule." She took her coat off, then came back to begin dinner.

The way her mother rattled pans and noisily handled dishes made it obvious to Ruth she was upset. But she didn't say anything until Ruth's father walked in the back door, carrying an armload of shoeboxes.

Ruth's mother was on him immediately: "You're smoking again, aren't you?"

Their father looked like a moth whose wings had been pinned to a corkboard. But he held her fiery gaze and said, "Yes."

"Have you been smoking the whole time?"

"No."

"How long?"

"Since about two weeks in."

"Have you been buying them?"

"Not at first. I was borrowing from Rita and Carl."

"I can't believe neither of them said anything to me."

"I asked them not to."

"You forced our employees to support your filthy habit—*and* to lie to me about it?"

After a moment of silence, Ruth's father said, "I guess so."

"You son of a bitch." Ruth's eyes widened. Her mother never cursed.

Then Ruth's mother walked out of the kitchen into the dining room, where they could hear her open the china cabinet and rummage around before closing the cabinet again. She came back in with a lighter in her hand and a cigarette in her mouth, a Winston, which she lit with great flair.

She took a long, satisfying pull, then expelled an impressive cloud through her nose.

"How long have you had those?" Ruth's father asked.

"Since before we quit two months ago," she said, savoring another extended draw on the cigarette. "The difference is I haven't touched one since then. But I kept them because I knew there's no way you would really quit."

She took a defiant puff and exhaled a triumphant plume of smoke.

"I win," she said.

Neither parent quit smoking that year, though both agreed to stop smoking in the house and the car. Ruth's father eventually quit cold turkey a couple of years later. Ruth's mother never did stop, and Ruth had found a pack of Benson & Hedges 100s in the back of the china cabinet after her mother died.

Because of her parents' habit, Ruth had never even tried cigarettes. The one time early in their marriage that Charles had pulled out a cigar and lit it at the dinner table, Ruth had snatched it from his mouth and marched into the bathroom, where she'd flushed it down the toilet without ceremony, looking him in the eye as he watched helplessly. Then she'd given him the silent treatment for three days as punishment when he'd blustered, "A man should be able to smoke in his own house."

As she said to Veronica, "I haven't stood up for myself enough in my life, but I did then. I mean, honestly."

They were quiet again. Then Veronica said, "Can you remember the last time you talked to Mommy?"

Ruth tried to recall her final phone conversation with her mother, more than forty years earlier, in May 1973, at the end of senior year. It was probably one of their weekly chats while Ruth was at Northwestern: every Sunday night at 7:00, after dinner, like clockwork.

"Punctuality is the courtesy of kings," her mother used to say.

They would talk about the quotidian details of the previous week and their plans for the week ahead, and her mother would fill her in on gossip about relatives and neighbors. Neither of them had said anything special during their final phone call, because neither had known it would be the last time they'd have the chance to speak.

"Mommy and I had an argument the last time we talked before the accident," Veronica said, almost whispering.

"What were you arguing about?"

"Stupid stuff—the color of paint I wanted to buy for my apartment when she took me shopping," Veronica said, speaking softly. "She said,

'No landlord is going to give you back your damage deposit if you paint your bedroom that color. I'm not paying for you to paint it twice.' And I got mad, so we wound up exchanging harsh words. It was the last time she and Daddy came to visit me at Saint Cloud and the last time I ever saw her."

After Ruth had left Richfield for Northwestern, Veronica had been involved in a running battle with her mother about the state of her bedroom the entire time Veronica was in high school. Her dirty clothes littered the floor of her room, her shoes were rioting in the closet, and her bathroom looked as though it were carpeted in wet towels after she showered. It drove Veronica's mother wild, but Veronica simply could not see what the big deal was.

The disputes continued even after Veronica left for college. She would visit home for a weekend, then return to her college dorm room to find her phone already ringing. It was inevitably her mother, with some variation on the theme of "Would it kill you to hang up your wet towels and make your bed before you leave town?"

Ruth had inherited, or simply learned, that persnickety quality from her mother and understood where it came from. Her mother had kept a spotless household, Ruth decided, because so little else in her life was under her control.

That was particularly true of the shoe stores. Veronica told Ruth a story about the time, after Ruth had left for college, when their mother had come home from work a little later than usual.

As Veronica had pieced together later, an employee had been stealing from one of the stores, and their insurance wouldn't cover the loss. Business had been off, so this would cause a shortfall that would force their father to borrow money at the bank. This was now a source of tension between their parents.

Veronica heard her mother slamming cupboards as she started dinner, then heard a crash of breaking glass. When she ran into the kitchen, she found her mother kneeling over a broken dish, crying.

"I hate those goddamn stores," she said. "I never should have said yes to the second one."

When she had realized Veronica was standing there, staring at her open mouthed, she had apologized and made her swear she would never say a word to anyone.

"I always knew she wished she was still a teacher," Veronica said.

"You could tell," Ruth said. "When she told us stories about teaching, it was obvious."

"Yet I'd tell you they had a happy marriage."

"Was it? I believe they loved each other and cared about us. But is that the same thing as a happy marriage? If she was unhappy and stressed out by her life?"

"Look who you're asking," Veronica said. "By comparison to the marriages I was involved in, I'd call theirs nearly perfect. At least they stayed together."

After returning home from Veronica's, Ruth came in the house and sat down at the kitchen table. She wasn't sure how long she'd been sitting there; the marijuana was distorting her sense of time, she decided.

Then she noticed a cold can of diet ginger ale sitting open before her on the table. Ruth had no memory of opening it or even of retrieving it from the refrigerator.

There was also the matter of the can itself. Ruth observed strict decorum in her kitchen. Beverages were consumed from cups or glasses, not from tin cans like a hobo—that was the law in Ruth Winters's house.

She almost never drank diet soda pop without diluting it with seltzer. Yet here she sat, drinking it straight out of the can. At this moment, it tasted like ambrosia.

I'd better stop smoking pot, Ruth thought, *or who knows what's next? Drinking orange juice out of the carton? Or milk?*

Ruth smiled at her effort at self-deprecation. She tentatively put the diet ginger ale to her lips for a sip and, afterward, thought, *OK, so it's not the end of the world.*

CHAPTER 19

Dear Ruth,

Thanks for trusting me enough to share your unhappy news. There is no way to prepare yourself for something like this. When my father died suddenly of a heart attack at fifty-six, it was a surprise and a shock. When my mother died after a long illness at eighty-nine, it was not a surprise at all—and yet it was still a shock. My point is, no matter how prepared you think you are, you will still suffer a shock you can't prepare for.

My wife only had eight months between her cancer diagnosis and her passing. Never one to waste time, she hopscotched over denial on that Kubler-Ross "Five Stages of Grief" list and went directly to anger. She stayed there for a while, then leap-frogged over bargaining and depression to move directly into acceptance.

Both stages were accompanied by this ferocious burst of productivity on her part. The anger made her charge directly at the cancer, like a warrior going into battle. She was someone who went to the gym every day before this happened and she kept going as long as she could. Even when she was feeling her worst after the early treatments, she faced the chemo like a champ. She went to the gym, if not every day, then way more often than I ever could have in her condition, because she believed it helped fight the cancer.

About five months before she died, when she was told the treatments hadn't helped, she pivoted in the most amazing way. She systematically created a list of the things the rest of us were going to need after she died: the kids, the grandkids, me. Then she did everything on that list, ticking the tasks off, one after the other, until she'd completed them all, right down to arranging for the person who was cleaning our house and doing the laundry to continue doing so after my wife was gone.

For the grandkids, she created a video oral history project, where she filmed herself talking about her life and her family, for them to watch when they get older. For our children, she went through her things and found something meaningful to pass along to each of them.

And she wrote each of us a long letter: personal, loving, reminding us of the things in each of us that she loved and most treasured. She did all this while she was dying. If it had been me, I'd have been wallowing in self-pity or zoned out on pain meds. Probably both.

It was all intended to soften the blow of her departure and, even more difficult, her absence. And it was a comfort to all of us. It really was.

But when she died, it still felt like I'd been flattened by a steamroller, like a character in a comic strip. Her death wasn't a surprise, but it was still a massive shock. And that's something you need to prepare yourself for—even knowing that there is no way to be ready for it.

All of which is a long way of saying that I know what you're about to go through. And I'm sorry.

Your relationship with your sister sounds complicated. But I have a hunch you can see past that to what truly matters. Because you need to remember: There is never enough time.

I apologize—probably TMI, as the young people say. Too much information.

So let me end on what I hope will be a lighter note.

I was remembering a time you and I were eating together in the high school cafeteria, because we shared a lunch hour sophomore year after German class. It was right after Homecoming—this would have been fall of 1966?—and one of the senior cheerleaders walked past our table. She was this pretty, popular girl, Marlene something, the head cheerleader, and everyone assumed she would be voted Homecoming queen.

But apparently one of the seniors on the football team twisted a lot of arms to get out the vote for his girlfriend and she won instead of Marlene. It was someone no one expected to win, and that was big news at school. Lowly sophomores like us didn't know the gossip behind the story, but we definitely knew the headline.

When Marlene walked past our table, I remember pointing her out to you and saying, "Wouldn't that crush you? To lose Homecoming queen after everyone told you they thought you would win?" And, without missing a beat or even looking up from your lunch, you said, "Her consolation prize will be when she becomes Miss Fertilized Ovaries of 1967." So fast. Sharp as a razor.

I arrive in Minneapolis on the Wednesday before the reunion, which is on a Friday night. Perhaps you can spare a few minutes Thursday or Friday during the day to get together? Let me know what works for you. And please know that you and your sister are in my thoughts. All my best, Martin

~

Dear Martin,

I don't have time to reply at the length I would like. But I think either Thursday or Friday should work. I'll know better what my availability is as we get closer to the date.

But thanks so much for your thoughtful message. It came at just the right time. Yours sincerely, Ruth

P.S. Her name was Marlene Merzynski. As I recall, she was pregnant by graduation.

CHAPTER 20

Standing near the baggage carousel at Minneapolis–Saint Paul International Airport on an overcast morning, awaiting Irwin Snelling's return, Ruth found herself next to a line of black-suited limo drivers.

Several of them wore sunglasses indoors. This struck Ruth as an affectation that smacked of self-regard.

Then she noticed one particularly towering driver, built like a linebacker, in a black suit that strained at the shoulder seams. He held a small whiteboard with the logo of his car service stenciled in one corner (**DISCREET CARS**).

The name **SNELLING** was written in erasable marker in the center of the whiteboard, in large capital letters.

As it happened, Ruth was carrying a sign of her own: a piece of typing paper with Irwin's full name printed neatly with a Sharpie in block letters. She had thought to craft the impromptu sign before driving to the airport because she had met Irwin only briefly at Chloe's wedding and was not confident she could identify him in person.

She walked up to the row of drivers, stopping directly in front of the beefy driver with the **SNELLING** placard, who was a couple of inches taller than she was. Before Ruth could speak, she was jostled from behind and pushed into the driver in front of her.

"Watch it," growled the **SNELLING** driver, not bothering to look at Ruth.

"Excuse me," Ruth said, trying to get his attention.

The driver, however, mistook her "Excuse me" for an apology, one unworthy of acknowledgment. So Ruth cleared her throat and said, louder this time, "Excuse me? Sir?"

"Yes?" the man finally said, not bothering to look at her as he scanned a new cluster of arriving passengers.

Ruth felt provoked to point out that this was extremely rude. Rudeness, however, was not the immediate concern, and she did not want to confuse the issue. But she wouldn't forget it either.

"I notice your sign has the name Snelling on it," Ruth said.

"Yes?" he said again, his voice ripe with his lack of interest in whatever she might say next. He still did not look at her.

"Does your sign refer to Irwin Snelling? Because—perhaps you can see, if you'd be polite enough to look at me when I'm talking to you"—she held the paper up in front of his face—"I'm also here to pick up Irwin Snelling."

With obvious annoyance, the driver removed his sunglasses and slowly turned his gaze to Ruth. He glanced at her paper, then looked at her again. Then he donned his sunglasses once more and said, "I'm not at liberty to discuss my passengers."

Ruth fixed him with a stern look. "We must be talking about the same person. How many Snellings can there be on one flight?"

"I wouldn't know. What I do know is this: the first one's mine," the driver told her. "You're welcome to any stragglers."

Ruth was incensed at the man's snide self-assurance. "I beg your pardon!"

But she got no further because, at that moment, Irwin himself came walking up to the driver and said, "Hi, I'm Irwin Snelling."

"Good grief. Irwin!" Ruth said loudly, now flapping her sheet of paper in his face.

"Ruth?" Irwin said, looking genuinely puzzled. "You're Ruth, Ronnie's sister, right? What are you doing here?"

"Veronica asked me to pick you up," Ruth said, giving the driver an aggressive side-eye. "Didn't she tell you?"

"*Ronnie* sent *you*?" Irwin blurted out before catching himself. "I'm sorry. I mean, she never told me you'd be here. I booked a car service."

"Which you obviously no longer need because I'm here," Ruth said, inserting the final dagger with a look at the driver.

"Hey," the driver began to protest.

"Look, I'm sorry for the mix-up," Irwin said to the man, reaching for his wallet. "Obviously, I'll pay you for your trouble."

"Well . . . all right," the driver said.

He removed his sunglasses and put them in a pocket, then pulled a handheld device out of an inside pocket to take Irwin's credit card. He ran the charge, then moved out of the flow of traffic to message his dispatcher for another possible airport passenger.

Ruth and Irwin waited together for Irwin's bag and then walked to Ruth's car in the basement garage. The whole way, Irwin chattered about his trip to New York and the sale of his business, with a familiarity and level of detail that Ruth found confusing.

This was, by her count, the second time she'd ever spoken with this man. Yet he acted as though they discussed these things regularly and at length. Perhaps his willingness to confide his business to Ruth sprang from the fact that she was his wife's sister. It was a logical leap to make, even with the sisters' unhappy history, but still one to which Ruth needed to adjust.

As they reached her car, Irwin turned to Ruth and began to say, "Ruth, I can't tell you how much . . ." But he couldn't finish the thought, because he suddenly embraced her and began crying on her shoulder.

Ruth stiffened at being touched—hugged!—unexpectedly. But Irwin was sobbing so hard he didn't appear to notice when she flinched. Gradually, as he continued to cling to her, she relaxed. She lifted her arms from her sides and put them around him in what she hoped was a comforting embrace.

He was a large man, taller than Ruth by several inches and far broader, and had to bend slightly to lay his head on her shoulder, like a little boy, as he cried. She patted the back of his head the way she did when one of the children skinned a knee. She didn't utter the words "There, there," but she thought them.

A young couple could be heard approaching in the concrete subbasement, their argument echoing as they pulled wheeled suitcases through the garage. But they fell silent when they passed Ruth and Irwin, gawking at the sight of a man weeping so loudly and publicly.

Ruth shot them a fierce glance and hissed, "Is this any of your business?" They scurried away as though pursued by hornets.

Eventually, Ruth got Irwin calmed down and shoehorned him into the front seat of her small car, a Subaru Impreza sedan. But before she turned the key, he reached for her arm and stopped her. Sniffling, he said, "I'm so sorry I never made Ronnie introduce us properly. It took me a long time to figure out why she didn't want to see you. Once I understood, I should have insisted."

Wondering what he was referring to, Ruth patted his hand, then started the car. "But here we are now" was all she could think to say before busying herself paying for parking and navigating her way up to the exit at street level.

Once they were on the freeway, Irwin asked how Veronica was doing.

"She seemed better yesterday," Ruth said. "It felt like she was out from under a burden, after making her decision. It had been weighing on her, I think."

"Her decision? Oh yeah, the chemo," Irwin said gloomily. "Oh God, Ruth. Am I going to have to go through this again?"

"Again?"

When he'd met Veronica, Irwin explained, he had been widowed for seven years, after his first wife's routine hernia surgery led to a sudden onset of sepsis that quickly proved fatal. The large malpractice award he received hardly was sufficient to assuage the loss of a partner of almost thirty years.

Irwin had had no intention of remarrying. His kids were grown, with kids of their own. (Ruth thought, *Aha! So Veronica* has *been a grandmother all this time!*) Irwin buried himself in his work, a catalog-printing concern that survived, adapted, and even thrived after the arrival of the internet. This was the business he'd just sold.

He met Veronica when they were seated together at a charity event and hit it off. He asked her out to dinner, which led to more dinners. Irwin found she added a spark to his life that he had assumed was beyond his reach at that stage of life.

So he courted her with determination. Veronica, several years removed from her marriage to third-husband Errol, was more skittish about commitment than Irwin was, based on three previous divorces. She explained to Irwin all the ways she'd been at fault in the collapse of those marriages, while placing the blame for each divorce squarely on her ex-husbands.

Irwin had no interest in competing with Veronica or controlling her in the way she felt her exes had tried to do. She still had a shine to her, Irwin said, an inner glimmer of vitality and engagement that he realized he'd lost track of since his wife's death. He was happy living in her reflected glow.

"I'm not that interesting a guy," he told Ruth matter-of-factly as she drove. "But she makes me feel I have something to offer. Do you know what I mean? We take care of each other."

She glanced at Irwin Snelling: this large, lumpish but likable man, so forlorn at the prospect of losing Veronica. He turned to her and said, "Do you think I can talk her out of quitting chemo?"

Ruth resisted the impulse to blurt out, "Why on earth would you ask me? Until a few weeks ago, she and I hadn't spoken in more than a year."

Instead, she reformulated her response as a statement: "You probably know her better than I do at this point. I will say that Veronica has never been easy to persuade once she makes up her mind."

"I know. You're right," he said, sounding defeated.

Ruth thought a moment, then said, "I think she needs us to support her decision. It shouldn't be the thing that consumes us going forward.

The decision's been made, and now we need to make her remaining time as easy as we can. Having you and Chloe there will help."

"Oh God—I forgot about Chloe," Irwin said. "When does she get here?"

"Later this afternoon. I'll pick her up when her flight gets in."

"Ruth, I'm so grateful you were willing to drive Ronnie to chemo. You don't have to be our personal taxi service as well."

"It's a way to help," she said. "There's nothing for me to do if I'm just sitting there with Veronica. Marta has that all under control."

"Just having you there is pretty big for Ronnie," Irwin said. "She values your company."

"Yes, well, there's a first time for everything," Ruth said. "I'm trying to adjust, but it's not as easy as throwing a light switch."

CHAPTER 21

"Please!" Veronica said, putting up a hand when Ruth walked onto the sunporch. "Do *not* ask how I am. The answer hasn't changed since the last time I saw you, which I believe was yesterday."

"Someone is being awfully crabby," Ruth said in her disapproving-babysitter voice, which made Veronica and Marta smile.

Because of fog at the San Francisco International Airport, Chloe's plane would be at least two hours late. That was the news when Ruth and Irwin had returned. But, in her impatience for Chloe's arrival, Veronica had already had Marta help her get dressed and into her makeup.

Veronica had also insisted Marta style and adjust an attractive shoulder-length, salt-and-pepper wig (heavy on the pepper) over the wisps of hair Veronica retained. She may have been dying of cancer, but, for the moment, that wasn't the first thing a stranger would notice about her.

"You look like you're about to walk the runway in the Mrs. Minnesota pageant," Ruth said.

Veronica snickered. "Mrs. Cancer Victim is more like it."

"If the title comes with a tiara, I'm sure you'll be happy."

That made Veronica laugh. Then she said, "When is your fiftieth high school reunion? My friend Daffy Spencer is on the reunion planning committee, and she was talking about it on the phone today."

"Spencer?" Ruth said. "I don't remember her."

"Daffy Spencer? She used to be Daphne Aldine? But everyone called her Daffy?"

"Everyone but me, apparently," Ruth said.

"Anyway, she asked me how she could reach you."

"You didn't . . . ?"

"I told her, 'Honestly, I've never been able to reach my sister—and I've been trying for years.'"

Ruth gave a short bark of laughter, then said, "You didn't tell her anything, did you? Not my email—please, God?"

"When have *you* ever responded to email?"

"I always answer Chloe . . . eventually. Most of your emails are too mean to reply to."

"You've got me there," Veronica said flatly. "I'm sorry."

"Thank you. I ran into someone from that reunion committee at the bookstore. Teddy someone, a man I didn't remember, who practically begged me for my email address. I said no."

"Are you going to the reunion?"

"Of course not. I've never gone before. Why would I start?"

"Aren't you curious?"

"About what? People I barely knew fifty years ago? Why would I want to pretend to know them now? Or act as if I care what happened in their lives? I certainly don't want them prying into mine."

Veronica let her lower lip droop in a childish pout, then dabbed at an imaginary tear in the corner of her eye with the top knuckle of her fist. It made her look like a cartoon toddler. Then she said, in a little-girl voice, "I was hoping I could experience it vicariously through you. Since I'm obviously not going to be around for my own fiftieth."

Ruth couldn't help but laugh at such a bald act of manipulation.

"No, I'm not going to go," she said, trying to sound firm in her resolve. Then, after a pause, she said, "I *have* been emailing with a classmate who's coming to town for the reunion."

"Well, aren't you the sly one?" Veronica said in her best Noël Coward–socialite voice.

"I'm the last person anyone would call *sly*."

"I'm teasing you," Veronica said. "Is it anyone I know?"

"I wouldn't think so. His name is Martin Daly. We were in the same German class for three years."

"Martin Daly—isn't he the guy who took you out on a date your senior year?"

"How could you possibly remember that?"

"Are you kidding?" Veronica said with a laugh. "It's the only date you went on that I even remember. Were you not aware of Mommy's constant agita about the fact that you had no social life?"

"Oh, Veronica—do you think I didn't know why she insisted that I work on the stage crew or at Daddy's store? She hoped it would 'bring me out of my shell,' to use her phrase. But it was obvious that what she really hoped was that I would somehow magically turn into you. You were always the center of attention."

"Because I couldn't pass math. 'Why can't you be more like Ruth?' That's what I heard from them."

Their mother's excitement, when Martin had asked Ruth out on a date, had been seismic. It outstripped Ruth's muted response in front of her parents and added a level of pressure that Ruth had not anticipated.

But, as Veronica now told her, after she found out about Ruth's date, her mother had coffee with former teaching colleagues who taught at Ruth's high school. They gave her an earful about Martin Daly: insolent, rebellious, smart mouthed, bright but underachieving. Veronica overheard their parents talking about it.

"If he's such a delinquent, why would he be interested in our Ruthie?" their mother said. "Ruth may keep to herself, but she's got a good head on her shoulders. Why would she agree to a date if this boy was such a threat?"

Veronica smiled at the memory, then said, "So he took you out, you had one date, and then—*pffft*."

"Because his family moved away from Minnesota right afterward," Ruth said, with more insistence than she meant to. "I don't know why *other* boys didn't ask me out, but not having a second date with Martin was definitely not my fault."

"So what's his story now, this Martin Daly?"

"He's a widower and lives in Denver, he said in his email. He retired, but he used to own an advertising agency."

Irwin, who had wandered in a few minutes earlier to rummage through an attaché case, looked up. "Wait—are you saying you know Martin Daly? *The* Martin Daly?"

Ruth looked at him. "Why? Is there more than one?"

"Martin *Alexander* Daly?"

"I don't think I ever knew his middle name."

"You said he was in advertising? Did he run a firm called M/A/D?"

"Mad? Like angry? I know he mentioned advertising. How do you know him?"

"I don't know him personally, but I've definitely heard of him. That guy was huge."

He pulled out his phone, tapped it a couple of times, and then showed it to Ruth. "Look at this," he said, pointing her to a Wikipedia page devoted to Martin Daly. It featured a photo that Ruth recognized as Martin, though he looked about forty, with a mustache, glasses, and a receding hairline.

As she examined the screen, Irwin said, "He was this big advertising innovator from the Rockies. M/A/D did national campaigns but would never move to New York or LA. And they had some big offers. A few years ago, Daly finally sold his agency for eight figures. There was a story in the *Star Trib* about the sale because he was this hometown boy made good."

Ruth, who still subscribed to the daily newspaper, said, "I must have missed it."

"There was a piece on him on *60 Minutes* that said he once told Coca-Cola to—pardon my French—'go fuck themselves' when they tried to change one of his campaigns. The story on TV bleeped it out, but it was obvious he was saying 'Go fuck yourself.' Apparently, someone gave a tape of the meeting to the reporter. Daly took the campaign back from Coke, rather than let them change it. *And* he gave them back their fee. Then he turned around and went to work for Pepsi—and took them to number one with the same campaign. And you went to high school with him? Wow."

Up to that moment, Ruth had never even considered using the word *Google* as a verb, let alone thought about googling a person she knew. After Irwin showed her how, she began scrolling through page after internet page on her iPad when she got home, reading about Martin Daly.

CHAPTER 22

Chloe's arrival closed a circle that comprised her, Ruth, Veronica, and Marta. It was as though this collection of women, who had never been together before, were old friends reunited for the first time in years.

They spent the rest of the night gathered around Veronica in the den, gossiping and joking as daylight turned to dusk. Eventually, even the adrenalizing effect of Chloe's arrival wore off, and Veronica's energy faded. As Chloe and Irwin helped Veronica to her room to put her to bed, Ruth and Marta straightened up the kitchen until Chloe returned to help them.

The three women sat in the kitchen, talking quietly and sipping wine, while Irwin stayed with Veronica.

"Irwin is already so upset," Chloe said. "I wonder how he'll react when, you know . . ."

"When Veronica dies," Ruth said without emotion. "That's what's going to happen, I'm afraid. We need to be ready for that."

"Winter is coming," Chloe said tonelessly.

"What?" Ruth said.

"Sorry. A line from a TV show I used to watch. 'Winter is coming.' They were talking about inevitability and how some things can't be stopped. All you can do is be as prepared as possible."

"She seemed to be in good spirits today," Marta offered.

"I'm not sure what that even means anymore," Ruth observed wearily. "I've said it myself: 'She seemed to be in good spirits.' Compared to what? When she *wasn't* in good spirits? Or is it that she seems in good spirits for someone who's dying of cancer?"

"Were you ever a teacher?" Marta said with a rueful laugh. "Because I think you would have been *really* tough. I would have hated being in your class."

Ruth had spent her life in mortal fear of being mocked. Yet she now found herself laughing along with Marta and Chloe at her own overthinking.

Chloe hugged her. "It makes me happy to see you loosen up like this. I almost don't recognize you."

"And all it took was having my sister contract a terminal illness."

~

As it happened, most of Ruth's regular children were about to start in the local preschool system, so Ruth simply stopped babysitting. Instead, with an ease that surprised her, she changed her morning routine.

She started by driving to a Starbucks drive-through to get everyone their favorite drink before proceeding to Veronica's house. Marta arrived most days with homemade pastries.

Then, while Marta worked around them (and occasionally took a break to join the chat), Veronica, Chloe, and Ruth would drink coffee while watching and commenting on TV shows Ruth had never seen. After Veronica and Chloe brought her up to speed on the history of *Live with Kelly and Ryan* ("So then Michael Strahan just *left* . . .") and the shifting interpersonal dynamics on *The View*, Ruth found she enjoyed the kibitzing and even joined in.

Who says you can't defy inertia? Ruth thought.

Ruth and Veronica struggled to scrape the accretion of grudges and resentment from their relationship, but it seemed to get easier when they began telling Chloe tales of their childhood together. Ruth felt as if she and Ronnie were using the stories to remind each other who they used to be. They were also offering each other a narrative of what had happened to them and who they'd become while living lives in which the other barely figured.

"Do you remember our dog?" Veronica asked one afternoon.

"You had a dog?" Chloe said in disbelief, turning to Veronica. "You never let *me* have a dog."

"We didn't have it for very long," Ruth said. "And there was only ever the one." She paused, thinking. "What was its name? Tiger?"

"Tige," Veronica corrected her. "Like the name of Buster Brown's dog, from Buster Brown shoes. Like Daddy sold."

Veronica's winning sales pitch for the dog had amounted to this declaration: "I promise I will feed, walk, train, clean up after, play with, and otherwise take care of a puppy, every single day, without fail. I swear." Expressed in the less succinct, more insistent words of an eight-year-old.

Ruth stayed out of her sister's pleadings to their parents. Ruth would have preferred a cat, but her father had an allergy to them.

One Friday evening, unannounced, their father came home from work with a six-month-old Jack Russell terrier and told the girls he'd named the little brown-and-white dervish Tige. Veronica, a dramatic child, professed her immediate and undying love for the energetic, high-jumping pup.

Before she went to bed that night, Veronica put down enough newspaper to cover the floor of the kitchen. She and her mother cobbled together a makeshift bed from an old blanket and half of a cardboard box. Then she gave Tige a hug and closed the puppy in the kitchen to sleep.

In the night, Tige dropped little moist puddles of dog diarrhea all over the newspapers on the floor, the effect of the saucer of milk Veronica had given him before bedtime. But something in the night, perhaps the sound of a windblown tree branch scraping against the kitchen window, frightened Tige, who apparently ran anxious laps through the kitchen, tracking excrement everywhere, including the kitchen chairs he tried to jump up on.

The unsuspecting Veronica outpaced everyone else to be first to the kitchen the next morning to greet the Abraham family's newest member. When she opened the door, the excited Tige jumped up on her, marking the front of her pajamas with the dung caked in the fur between the pads on his tiny feet.

A girly-girl, Veronica flinched, then pouted when she saw the smear: "Eww, Tige got mud all over my nice pajamas." When she caught a whiff and realized the mud was dog feces, she vomited—all over herself and the dog.

The kitchen was cleaned up and the dog forgiven by the time breakfast normally would be served on Saturday: cleaned up by Ruth's gagging parents, forgiven by Veronica. The mess was excused as the reaction of a very young dog to unfamiliar surroundings.

It was agreed that breakfast—now brunch—would be at Perkin's Pancake House, normally a rare Sunday treat, during which time Tige would be leashed in the yard. The kitchen, while clean, was left with its windows open and vent fan on. Their trip to the restaurant was meant to provide sufficient time to rid the kitchen of the odor of Mr. Clean and bleach, both of which had been vigorously employed to clean up Tige's mess.

Still, what became known in family lore as the "Kitchen Caca Incident" wasn't the deciding factor in bringing about Tige's return to the kennel the following Monday. The little dog packed enough action into the final forty-eight hours of his sojourn with the Abrahams to warrant the quick removal.

When Tige was allowed back in the house Saturday afternoon, he immediately found and chewed up one of their mother's favorite shoes. "He's only a puppy," Veronica pleaded.

That night, as the family watched *Perry Mason* in the family room, he came trotting in with Ruth's expensive dental retainer, which he'd already chewed until it was mangled beyond recognition, dangling from his mouth. "This dog is lucky I'm not a gun owner," her furious father growled.

"He didn't know any better," Veronica begged.

Then, on Sunday afternoon, while playing tug-of-war on the floor together in the girls' bedroom, Tige suddenly dropped the knotted sock they were vying for and, with a yip, leaped at Veronica's face. With unerring accuracy, the puppy sank two tiny needle-sharp teeth into one of her nostrils. Veronica yelped in pain, pushing the dog away. Before she realized she was bleeding, the puncture squirted enough blood to ruin one of her favorite outfits.

"I guess I *am* too young for a pet," Veronica said when she asked her father to take Tige back to the pound.

Chloe and Marta laughed at the story. Then Chloe looked at her mother and said, "You never talk like this about Grandma and Grandpa. Auntie Ruth, she has literally never told me anything about your parents—ever. Seriously."

Ruth turned to Veronica and found she had closed her eyes. Her lip trembled, and tears trickled down her cheek.

"I just miss them" was all Veronica could say.

"So do I," Ruth said, putting an arm around her for a moment but feeling irritation at her sister.

"So you tell me, Auntie Ruth," Chloe said. "I don't even know what they looked like."

Ruth turned to Veronica, a note of accusation creeping into her voice.

"I remember you insisted on taking the photo albums when we sold the folks' house," Ruth said. "Do you know where they are now?"

Veronica looked even unhappier, if that was possible, and cried a little harder.

"I'm sorry, Ruth," she finally said. "I think I still have them somewhere, but I have no idea where they are. My best guess would be either the attic or the basement. I can go look, if you want."

"No, Mom, stay put—I'll find them later," Chloe said. Sensing the sudden tension between the two, she turned to Ruth. "You tell me, then: What did your parents look like?"

Ruth had a memory of being fourteen, sitting with her mother in their living room, watching an old movie on WTCN on a rainy Sunday afternoon, when Veronica and their father were off doing something together. Watching movies with her mother was a rare treat, one of the few times her mother allowed herself the luxury of sitting still for more than a few minutes.

The movie was in black and white: *Mr. Smith Goes to Washington.* The star was a young James Stewart, far younger than the one Ruth had seen in films at the movie theater, like *How the West Was Won* and *Mr. Hobbs Takes a Vacation.* That actor had looked old enough to be her grandfather.

What stayed with Ruth was something her mother said to her on that Sunday afternoon together, the first time the youthful version of the actor appeared on screen as future Senator Jefferson Smith: this thin, dreamy version of Jimmy Stewart, with his sleepy eyes, slight stammer, and slow, sly smile.

"That's what your father looked like when I met him," her mother said, with a note of wistful longing so pronounced that it resonated with Ruth all these years later.

If her father looked like Jimmy Stewart, her mother had the kind of looks that made nine-year-old boys swoon. Every year that she taught, she had told the girls, she could count on at least three or four proposals of marriage from male students.

"It was very cute," Ruth explained to Chloe. "She would gently point out that the *Mrs.* before her name meant she already had a husband. Then she'd give them a kiss on the cheek and tell them, 'But if I wasn't already married . . .'"

Chloe and Veronica laughed at Ruth's delivery.

"You sound just like her," said Veronica, whose tears had gradually stopped. "Ruth looks a lot like Mommy."

"I thought the two of you were the ones who looked alike," Ruth replied.

"Ruth got Daddy's eyes and nose—" Veronica began.

"And his height," Ruth put in.

"We both got that."

"Then why am I so short?" Chloe asked.

"Unfortunately, your grandmother was about five foot four," Ruth said.

Veronica added, "Apparently her DNA trumped whatever it was that Peter brought to the table, genetically speaking, when it came to creating you."

Ruth snorted a laugh.

"I'm just saying, genetics are funny," Veronica said. "You see these seven-foot-tall professional basketball players with their mothers around Mother's Day on *The View* or *Extra* or one of those stupid shows I watch. The mothers are these tiny little women, and their sons are these giants. How does that even happen?"

Ruth thought about her own parents, picturing them laughing, joshing, and kibitzing with each other and the girls at the dinner table or Sunday brunch. She turned to Veronica and said, "Do you remember how mad Daddy would get if we left the car radio tuned to WDGY or KDWB?"

KDWB and WDGY ("Wonderful Wee-*Gee*!") were the dominant Top 40 AM radio stations in the Twin Cities of the 1950s and '60s. They were the stations that first played Elvis Presley and Chuck Berry and, later, the Beatles, the British Invasion bands, and everything that followed.

Veronica had been more of a fan of individual bands than Ruth, but, as kids, they had both insisted on tuning to one of those radio stations when they were in the car with their mother. Their mother indulged them and joined in singing along with the radio. She liked the energetic new music and the way it captivated her daughters.

Their father, on the other hand, venerated the bands that had been popular when he was a teen: Duke Ellington, Count Basie, the Dorsey Brothers, Glenn Miller. He'd seen most of the biggest names when they played at the Prom Ballroom in Saint Paul when he was a young man.

So he resented it bitterly when artists like Elvis Presley—and, later, the Beatles and the other so-called rock bands—began to dominate the music being played on the radio and featured on TV shows.

There were no radio stations playing the music he liked. So he would play his old big-band LPs on the living room phonograph. When he did, Ruth and Veronica, both under the age of ten, would dance, spin, and skip around the room to songs like "Take the 'A' Train" or "One O'Clock Jump." Inevitably, one of them would jump too hard and make the record skip.

"You'll scratch the record doing that," their father would say with exasperation, and the listening session would be over.

Ruth recalled one particular school morning when she was fifteen. As Ruth and Veronica ate their breakfasts before catching the school bus, their father left for work at his usual time. They heard the garage door go up, his car door opening and closing, his car starting—and then his car door opening again. Ten seconds later, he was back in the house, wild eyed as he confronted his family.

"OK," he had said, "who left the radio tuned to the goddamn Rolling Stones?"

"The Rolling Stones?" Chloe said with a laugh. "Those guys are ancient."

Veronica chuckled and said to Ruth, "Did I ever tell you about my high school boyfriend who tried to convince Daddy to listen to the Grateful Dead?"

Ruth's jaw dropped a bit, and she said, "I can't imagine who would be so stupid."

The boy's name was Bobby Richards, and in the early 1970s, he was among a then small but rapidly growing group of musical aficionados known as Deadheads. As a devotee of the rock band known as the Grateful Dead, he always carried all his Dead records around with him in an army-surplus knapsack.

In any conversation in which Bobby was involved, there would always come a moment when Bobby would shift the subject to the

Grateful Dead. It didn't matter whether he was at work, or a dinner party, or a late-night gathering at someone's house, it was inevitable and, perhaps, unavoidable. No matter what the subject, there was a Grateful Dead lyric Bobby could cite to explicate it. After which he would say, "Let me play you the song. You'll see. Where's your record player?" And he would reach for his knapsack.

That's what happened the night Bobby Richards, the latest in a string of Veronica's high school boyfriends, came to dinner with Veronica's parents. Their father made an effort to be polite and listen as Bobby, a high school senior, sermonized on the unique profundity of the lyrics by Jerry Garcia and Robert Hunter.

"I mean, 'Truckin''—am I right?" Bobby said.

"About what?" Veronica's father said.

"Oh, man—where to start? I mean, it's all right there in the lyrics: you're either in the spotlight or you're in the shadows. That's, like, life, right? In a nutshell. Shadow and light: where there is shadow, there must be light. Like, it's soooo Zen. Here—let me play it for you."

"That's not necessary . . ."

But Bobby was already up from his chair, extracting a Dead album from his tattered backpack: *American Beauty*.

He turned, scanning the living room even as he said, "I really should play you the live version from the *Europe '72* album, but you need to hear that entire album side from beginning to end—and, really, you should listen to the whole concert, start to finish, without stopping. But that's, like, a triple-album set. And I mean, sorry, much as I'd like to, I really don't have time for that tonight."

The relief on Veronica's father's face was short lived, as Bobby said, "There."

Spotting the family hi-fi at the other end of the living room, Bobby sauntered over and, without hesitation, slapped the vinyl LP on the turntable. He then placed the needle at the beginning of "Truckin'," the final cut on the second side. As the song played, he stood next to the hi-fi like a sentinel, guarding against anyone who might try to interrupt the wisdom of the Dead, while silently mouthing the words along with the record.

When the song was over, Veronica's father said, "Thank you. Now you'll have to excuse me," and went down to the basement, leaving them to imagine the important business that pulled him away from this particular discussion. When he left the room, Bobby turned to Veronica and said, "I think he dug it."

After Bobby had left, Veronica's father had emerged from the basement, come to her bedroom, and said, "Why are you wasting your time on that schmuck?"

Ruth laughed and said, "Daddy never did mince words." She thought a moment, then said, "Do you remember who Daddy loved to listen to when we were teenagers? While everyone was going crazy for the Beatles? It was sooo corny."

Ruth and Veronica said it together—"Herb Alpert and the Tijuana Brass!"—then giggled like schoolgirls.

"Who?" Chloe said.

Herb Alpert and the Tijuana Brass played the only music of the 1960s that spoke to their father, Ruth explained. The swing music he loved had given way to more abstract versions of jazz: bebop, hard bop, cool jazz, free jazz—the labels were as meaningless to their father as the squeaks and squawks of everyone from Charlie Parker to Ornette Coleman. He loved a melody, a sense of swing. Herb Alpert's music wasn't really jazz, but it was instrumental, upbeat, and decidedly tune based. Plus: Herb Alpert was Jewish. That was good enough for him.

"I don't think I've ever heard them," Chloe said.

Veronica thought a moment, then said, "Don't you have one of those streaming-music services on your phone? Do a search for Herb Alpert."

Chloe pulled out her phone and fiddled with it for a second, then reached for a compact Bluetooth speaker sitting on a table next to Ruth. She pushed a button, and the speaker gave a small beep. Then Chloe said, "This?"

Herb Alpert and the Tijuana Brass issued from the speaker, with the impossibly cheerful melody of "Spanish Flea."

"Oh, I know this," Chloe said. "It was the theme song for a game show my roommates and I would watch in grad school at Ohio State. We'd finish studying, then roll a joint—"

"TMI, honey," Veronica said.

"And we'd laugh at these old reruns of *The Dating Game* that one of the Columbus stations showed at eleven p.m. each night. And that was the theme song."

"Not quite how your grandfather might have imagined enjoying Herb Alpert," Ruth observed. "But to each their own, I guess. Times change, and I guess we all have to change with them."

She noticed the astonished look on Veronica's face and said, "Yes, I said it. I'm still working on believing it."

CHAPTER 23

A couple of days later, when the sisters were alone, Veronica lit the pipe and inhaled. She held it in for a count of five, then exhaled a massive cloud of cannabis smoke. "Oh yeah, good shit," she said with a chuckle, her laugh triggering a cough.

"This is some new weed from a friend of mine in Marin County," she said when the coughing had subsided. "Supposed to be a little mellower than what we had last week."

Veronica offered the pipe to Ruth, who clucked and started to demur, then reached to take it.

"You're going to turn me into a drug addict," Ruth said through clenched teeth as she tried to hold in the smoke without coughing.

"Some days, this is the only thing that helps," Veronica said. "Percocet, Vicodin, oxycodone—they work on the pain. But this is the only thing that lets me turn off my brain." She took a hit, exhaled, and said, "And it's impossible to OD." That made Ruth laugh, then cough.

Ruth experienced the same feeling of expansiveness she had enjoyed the previous time they had smoked, the sense of all tension leaving her body and mind. She felt free enough to say to her sister, "Why did you get married so many times? I've always wanted to ask."

Veronica laughed out loud. "Hey, why not?" she said, then thought a moment. "I've never liked being alone, is the short answer. The long answer is that I used to dislike being alone so much that I'd go a long way to avoid it, even if that meant being with someone I didn't like very much. Plus, I discovered I liked having nice things."

I can't imagine that was too shocking a discovery, Ruth thought, then said, "I don't think I met any of your husbands before Irwin, except Peter. I only saw him in lawyers' offices or in court. What was it that made you decide to marry them? Was it something different with each one—or some quality they all had in common?"

"Slow down, stoner Sigmund Freud," Veronica said. "Give me a minute. It's not something I've really thought about."

"You never were the introspective type."

"Thanks, I think."

"It means you're not preoccupied with the past and can focus on moving forward."

"I'll take that."

"Can you tell me about them? Please? After Charles died, I could never imagine getting married again."

Veronica had met her first husband, Tad Mills, at a sorority rush party the fall of her freshman year. They were both in the same lecture section of an American history class. She didn't notice him there, but Tad, who fancied himself a bit of a playboy with freshman girls, immediately spotted Veronica as fresh talent. He made a point of finding out who she was, then made sure she received an invitation to a sorority rush party that his fraternity was cohosting.

Tad was scion to a distant cousin of an important Minneapolis family whose company had become a nationally successful flour-milling concern. Tad's branch of the family had made a fortune in stocks and real estate investments, acquired with inherited money and generational wealth.

Tad's parents wore the family name like a crown, one that signified wealth, if not influence, and the name certainly dazzled Veronica. Tad had the self-assurance of privilege, which appeared to be the same as genuine charm to Veronica—at first.

Still, though he was persistent, Veronica was soon dating at least two other upperclassmen. She and Tad dated off and on through her freshman year, but she never regarded him as special, to Tad's chagrin.

Veronica, who had a high school reputation as a flirt and a tease, wasn't in a rush to find a steady beau. That was true even after she returned to college in the fall for her sophomore year, after her mother's death.

Tad, however, had spent the intervening summer working at a paid internship at a Chicago bank, while obsessing about Veronica and the fact that she refused to date him exclusively. It had thrown him. Tad Mills was used to being the one who dictated the terms of romantic relationships. He was the chooser, not the chosen.

Tad had a plan for his future, one that he had typed up, which carried the heading "The Plan" (and which he showed Veronica, after they were married). It began with a given: a job as a vice president at his father's firm in Minneapolis awaited him after graduation. But now, "The Plan" said, it was senior year—time for him to secure a mate with whom to launch his postcollege career.

Tad felt as though his hand was being forced. Veronica's hard-to-get act convinced him that his only way forward was to propose marriage to her.

Veronica arrived on campus for her sophomore year to a full-court press from Tad: study dates, lunch dates, frat parties, movies, dances, lunches, dinners . . . breakfasts. She had no free time to date anyone else. By homecoming, Tad had proposed, and by Christmas, they'd set the following Labor Day as a wedding date.

Veronica remembered how adamant their mother had been about the importance of a college education. But college wasn't for her, and Veronica knew it.

Most of the other boys she'd dated during freshman year had been chosen for their ability to help her stay afloat academically, in exchange for little more than a brief make-out session.

Tad, however, came from wealth and offered her a life without want. Not only without want, but with luxury, plenty, excess—and it didn't matter if she had a college degree.

So, rather than return to college for a junior year, Veronica married Tad that fall, the beginning of what she expected would be a life of marital ease.

One night on their honeymoon cruise to Hawaii, after too many rum punches, Tad outlined "The Plan" for Veronica, explaining the way he'd decided to make her his wife. He thought he was being vulnerable and self-deprecating, but he spoke of women in general—and Veronica in particular—as though they were pawns in a game controlled by Tad, one in which they had no say. The tipsy Veronica laughed along, but she shivered when she thought about it the next day. His confession could not be unheard.

When they returned from Hawaii, Tad settled into his job at his father's firm. But, as she started married life, Veronica discovered the vast canyon between what Tad expected she would be doing with her time and what she did.

Tad came home from work on the Friday of their first week of domestic life to find her exactly where he had found her each preceding evening that week: sitting in an easy chair in the den, watching television, a highball next to her chair, a cigarette in her hand.

While there was a light on in the kitchen, there were no odors of cooking. Tad went to the bedroom to hang up his coat and tie, noting the unmade bed while he did. He went back to the living room to mix himself a drink at the bar, then walked over to the TV and clicked it off.

"I was watching that," Veronica protested.

"We need to talk," Tad said, sitting on the ottoman in front of Veronica's chair.

"What about?" she said, taking a sip of her whiskey sour.

"Dinner, for starters."

"I can see what we have in the freezer."

"I'm not eating another TV dinner."

"We have chicken potpies."

Tad looked exasperated and took a gulp of his bourbon and water.

"And you haven't cleaned the house or made the bed again today, from what I can see."

Veronica looked him in the eye. "Cleaned the house?"

"You know, dusting, vacuuming, doing the dishes. My father came home every night to a spotless house and a hot dinner waiting on the table. I don't see why I can't have the same thing," he said with an air of finality.

"If that's what you wanted," she said, "you should have married your mother. Because I'm not your maid."

As Veronica also pointed out, Tad's mother had a live-in housekeeper. If Tad wanted what his father had, he needed to give Veronica what his mother had: full-time help to cook and clean. He could afford it, she pointed out, with his salary as a vice president.

So Tad let Veronica hire help, and when he got home from work, the house was spotless, and a three-course meal was waiting on the table.

Tad, however, still wasn't happy—because, at least three out of every five weeknights, Veronica wasn't home to dine with him. He walked in the door each night, expecting the greeting due to a warrior returning from the financial wars. Instead, he found a hot dinner served by the housekeeper while Veronica played tennis or bridge at their country club or had dinner out with friends.

If the cause of her absence from the household had been a meeting of the Junior League or the women's auxiliary of some men's group to which he belonged, Tad might have found that excusable. The fact that Veronica was doing whatever she wanted, though—and enjoying herself—bothered him to no end.

But divorce was never mentioned until Tad happened upon a small brown glass bottle, which held most of a gram of cocaine, while snooping in one of her drawers.

This was the mid-1970s, when cocaine was considered the drug of choice for the well-to-do, with a false reputation for being nonaddictive. Veronica would go to lunch with a group of friends, then adjourn from the restaurant du jour to one of their homes, usually in Kenwood or another neighborhood near Lake of the Isles. They would spend the rest of the afternoon—often into the evening—drinking, gossiping, and snorting cocaine.

Veronica developed an unfortunate habit: The cocaine in the afternoon made it hard to fall asleep in the evening, so she would take barbiturates before bed. Those would leave her groggy in the morning, so she would do a line of cocaine off a makeup mirror to wake up, using more as needed to fuel the rest of her day. Wash, rinse, repeat.

Rather than confront Veronica when he found the cocaine, Tad instead tattled to his family. Later, she understood why she had felt she was being watched—or, more accurately, observed—when she attended the weekly family meals at Tad's parents' house.

Veronica's behavior wasn't noticeably different when she used drugs. She didn't dance on the table or wear a lampshade on her head. But her natural tendency toward sharp-edged kidding, which had never found an appreciative audience in Tad's stiff-backed family, was amplified after a couple of between-course lines off the marble vanity in the ornate powder room. After her mother-in-law observed at a brunch that Veronica's humor might be a little coarse for mixed company, Veronica loudly proclaimed, "Well, fuck 'em if they can't take a joke." Her testimony was entered into evidence against her.

Not long after, Tad confronted her with a verdict from the family: she needed to check into the facilities at the Hazelden treatment center, north of the Twin Cities, for a month to kick her drug habit—or the marriage was over.

During her Hazelden stay, Veronica decided that she was less a drug addict than a bored suburban housewife who was acting out by using recreational drugs. At the end of her detoxification period, she had no particular craving for cocaine or sleeping pills. She finished rehab with a clear head and came home determined to find a way to be finished with Tad.

He offered the perfect exit, carelessly leaving evidence where she could find it that he had been sleeping with his secretary while Veronica was in rehab. When Tad's family tried to lowball her on a divorce offer, Veronica threatened a scandalous—and very public—divorce trial. As she told Tad and his lawyers in an early negotiation session: "I'm an inspiring success story. I'm someone who overcame drug addiction. Then I discovered that, while I was battling my dependence on cocaine and sleeping pills, my loving spouse—a respected local businessman and scion of the Mills family—was banging his secretary in our bed at home. How do you think that will play in the press?"

The payoff was quick and generous. Veronica even got to keep the house on Lake Harriet.

Veronica's divorce from Tad was final in March 1976. She met Peter a couple of years later. He was an attorney, doing pro bono work for an arts organization on whose executive committee Veronica served.

Peter had just made partner, in fact. But while he made almost as much money as Tad, most of it was tied up in a hellish divorce from his first wife. That put him in a financial squeeze not long after he and Veronica were married, around the time her father died.

"Is that why he wanted you to sue me to sell the house?" Ruth said, interrupting Veronica's story.

Veronica looked stricken. "I'm so sorry about that."

Ruth brushed it aside. "As I recall, the judge gave him quite a scolding."

Apart from Peter's performance in the courtroom, he was an otherwise reasonable man who made a diligent and dutiful husband. He also lacked the kind of intrusive family Tad had. Veronica was ready to have children, and Peter seemed like a solid candidate for fatherhood.

They were married at the end of 1981 and had Chloe a few years later. Peter handled parenthood well—when he was home. But Peter, Veronica discovered, was a workaholic. His dogged—some would say *obsessive*—attention to detail meant he was perfectly suited to contract law, dotting every *i* and crossing every *t*. It made him late for dinner on a regular basis. It also made him a much duller person than Veronica had noticed before they were married.

One evening, she realized that she'd begun to doze off while listening to him at a neighborhood dinner party. After dessert, Peter started explaining to the table something called *riparian rights*, having to do with a client's waterfront property on the Saint Croix River. Veronica unexpectedly woke herself in the middle of his lecture with a jerk of her nodding head and a small "*Snnrk*," which she tried to cover by pretending to cough. Hoping no one else had noticed, she managed to keep herself awake for the rest of the evening.

But, later, Veronica cast back over their recent conversations and realized that, minus talk of Peter's job and her daily update on Chloe's development ("She almost stood up!"), they had nothing to talk about.

That can't be true, Veronica thought. *After all, we met through our work for an arts organization. We have the arts in common.*

When she asked him about it, however, Peter revealed that he'd volunteered time with the arts group because he knew pro bono work was expected of associates on the partner track. He'd also heard that Veronica's organization was a pet project of one of the senior partners' wives, whom he had gone out of his way to befriend and flatter.

"I couldn't care less about the arts—and I still made partner," Peter said cheerfully, as though he'd pulled a fast one and gotten away with it. For Veronica, he'd dug his own grave.

"I guess we were happy," Veronica told Ruth. "Up to a point."

"Which point was that?" Ruth asked.

"The point at which he figured out I was having an affair with Errol."

"Dear God, Veronica—why would you do that?"

Veronica had strayed after realizing she'd married two men in a row who'd exhausted their entire supply of charm by the time they walked down the aisle. Compared to a human stick of wood like Peter, Errol, a financial daredevil riding a hot streak, looked positively dashing.

Peter was furious when he discovered the affair—and angrier still that Veronica admitted it so easily. A friend had spotted Veronica in one of the skyways in downtown Minneapolis one weekday morning and mentioned it to Peter. That night, as they got ready for bed, Peter said, "What did you do today?"

"Me?" Veronica said. "Not much. Mostly stayed around the house this morning. Went to the grocery because I was out of a couple things."

"That's funny. Ernie Meyers said he saw you around lunch hour in the skyway near the Marquette Hotel."

Veronica paused while brushing her teeth, looked at him in the mirror, and said, "Oh, that." Then she looked down at the sink and resumed brushing her teeth.

Peter came up behind her. When she looked up at their reflection, his eyes found hers in the mirror, launching what felt like an aggressive staring match—until she casually looked down.

When she sneaked a glance at him, he looked as though he was working through pieces of a puzzle in his head. Then he found her eyes in the mirror again and said, "Are you having an affair?"

"Yes," she said flatly, holding his gaze, before returning to brushing her teeth.

Their exchange was heated and brief:

"You don't even do me the courtesy of denying it?"

"How is lying to you a courtesy? Isn't your pride taking enough of a beating?"

After the divorce, Peter paid generous alimony and child support, including tuition for private school for Chloe. But he punished Chloe for Veronica's sins by not seeing her for months or, sometimes, years at a time.

Errol was more interesting than Peter. They had met at a fundraiser for the capital-improvement fund of the Guthrie Theater and, after her divorce, had been together a couple of years when they decided to get married. But, after their spur-of-the-moment wedding during a business conference in Las Vegas, Veronica discovered Errol was much needier than she'd realized.

Their nuptials, in a Las Vegas chapel, were a case of mutual drunken impulsiveness: "We're going to do it eventually," he told her. "Why spend all that money on a big wedding? Let's just do it now."

"I've already had a couple of big weddings," Veronica allowed. "Why do I need another one?"

The next morning, however, Errol revealed that he was, at that moment, teetering financially. He was the principal in a deal to import wholesale furniture from China, in which his money had been tied up for several months—and the first shipment was being held up offshore in Long Beach, California, in a customs dispute. If things tipped the wrong way and a tariff was assessed for the furniture, he told her, he might need a cash infusion as a bailout. It was only then that Veronica understood that Errol had married her for her money.

As it turned out, Errol's deal tilted in his direction—that time. But he refused to learn one basic lesson: he was not a genius but, rather, a lucky guesser. Veronica, meanwhile, began sheltering the money she'd received after her divorces, even as Errol chased investments with more risk than reward.

"Near the end, I could tell he was working up the courage to ask me for money again," Veronica told Ruth. "I had no interest in being the sacrificing wife, supporting the valiant struggle of her spouse. His struggles weren't valiant, and they had nothing to do with me. So I left."

"How could you even think about getting married again after that?"

"I didn't. In fact, that's what I told Irwin when we first went out. I was a three-time loser—three strikes, and you're out. I spent the decade after I divorced Errol playing the socially prominent rich person, getting involved in arts organizations and civic groups. I had friends I saw and traveled with. I dated occasionally but never seriously, until Irwin. But Irwin was very sweet and very persistent. I finally realized that, at long last, I'd found one of the good ones. Plus, you know, the money and the big house on Lake Minnetonka."

"Ever the pragmatist," Ruth said.

"I like to think of myself as a romantic."

"Yes," Ruth countered, "a romantic pragmatist."

Their talk drifted from Veronica's marriages to the family gatherings of their youth. They giggled while remembering how, as teens, they had both mocked one of their cousins the summer she wore an unfortunate combination of bangs and braces.

Their mirth apparently triggered a partial memory for Veronica, leading her to forget the old adage "Never ask a question you don't want to know the answer to."

And so, buoyed by the high spirits of the moment and the effects of cannabis, she said, "Do you ever wish you'd gone to work at an art museum, like you wanted when you were in college?"

Ruth's anger flared spontaneously, and her vision darkened, just for a second. She spoke without thinking, a bad habit of long standing. "Wishing is for children," she said with more ire than she meant to. "I wasted too many years on that wish. I had to stop because it hurt too much."

Veronica gasped and looked stricken, before she dissolved into tears.

Ruth could not believe it: *She's the one who's crying?* Her temper rose further, but she stopped herself. Before she could say something harsh, she pulled herself to her feet and mumbled, "I forgot something in my car," then rose and walked out the front door.

She got behind the wheel of her car, closed the door, and turned the ignition. The car started, but she simply sat there, feeling the air conditioner blow tepid air that gradually cooled. After a minute, she turned the ignition off again but continued to sit there, fulminating inwardly. Her anger surprised her in its ferocity. It sprang from her sense of betrayal after actually opening up to her sister.

How could she not know what she was asking? How could she be surprised when I got upset? I knew this was more about convenience than contrition.

She reached for the key again, then stopped when she thought of Jane. Jane would point out that her sister was dying and, perhaps, Ruth should allow for that when judging her.

Then she thought of her own mother. "Be the bigger person," she could hear her mother saying, an act that never brought the level of satisfaction her mother always implied it would.

But the thought of her mother pushed Ruth over a line in her own head. After invoking her mother's memory, if she didn't go back inside now and something tragic happened—and something tragic was *going* to happen—she'd be haunted by it forever.

Ruth took a deep breath, held it for a moment, and then exhaled before getting out of the car to go back in the house. It was meant to be a cleansing breath. *So why,* Ruth thought, *did it feel so much like a sigh of resignation?*

Because, she realized, *the right thing is always the hardest thing to do.*

CHAPTER 24

When Ruth got to the front door, she found that it had locked behind her. Aggravated, she pressed the doorbell and heard its lengthy ringtone, as elaborate as the chimes of Big Ben.

After a long moment, she heard Veronica shuffling to the door, the sound of her sobbing audible as she came. When she opened it, her eyes were red from crying. But when she saw Ruth, her face blossomed into a wet-cheeked smile.

"You came back!" Veronica said, her smile immediately giving way to more tears.

"I just went out to my car for a moment," Ruth lied but got no further because Veronica enveloped her in an embrace.

Veronica felt insubstantial in Ruth's arms, as though she were constructed of balsa wood. Ruth thought of a CPR training video she'd watched, which cautioned against using too much pressure when doing chest compressions on a child. Ruth worried that she could unintentionally crush her sister if she wasn't careful. She guided the still-weeping Veronica back to her couch on the sunporch.

"I ruined your life," Veronica said, her sobbing subsiding only slightly. "Oh God, Ruth, I'm so sorry. It's all my fault."

At last. Finally.

Veronica had said out loud the thing that Ruth had thought and felt and wanted to hear—but kept inside—for most of her life.

"How can you ever forgive me?" Veronica wailed. "You put your life on hold to take care of Daddy, and I let you do it. And everything that came after. If you did any of that to me, I would never have spoken to you again. I'm so sorry."

"I did what I had to do—so did you," Ruth said. "I forgive you, if that's what you need me to say."

These events had festered for so long that Ruth had assumed herself incapable of actual forgiveness for her sister. But Veronica surprised her. She was not merely apologetic or contrite—she also confessed the corrosive sense of shame she felt at what she'd done to Ruth. Veronica blamed neither husbands nor circumstances, nor anything else but her own selfishness, with all that encompassed.

Ruth heard the remorse in her sister's voice; it moved her because she could hear the pain that Veronica carried, beyond that of her illness. As she listened to her sister, Ruth felt a weight lift from her. *Finally,* she thought. *Veronica acknowledged she's wrong and I'm right.*

So why didn't Ruth feel vindicated? Or triumphant?

Nor was she moved to use her advantage. Instead of the urge to say "Yes, but what about the time you . . . ?" she found she had no interest in pressing any of this further.

Indeed, what came to mind were the many unkind things she'd said to Veronica in their lives, the numerous uncharitable thoughts she'd harbored, some for a half century or longer.

And so, she interrupted Veronica: "It wasn't only you. I played a role in how our relationship was." But Veronica waved her off.

"I'm the one trying to apologize here," Veronica said, perhaps attempting to lighten the mood. "I'm too old to change, but that won't be a problem for much longer."

She gave a throaty laugh, and Ruth smiled with her.

"I hope it's not too late for us to still be sisters," Veronica said. "And friends too. Do you think we can?"

"Let's not get ahead of ourselves," Ruth said with a straight face. But something in her eyes gave her away, and Veronica laughed and reached for Ruth's hand.

Veronica found a tissue to wipe her eyes. She looked at Ruth and said, "Now—when is your big lunch date with the famous Martin Daly?"

Startled, Ruth said, "My God, what day is it today?"

"Thursday. Why?"

"Where's my phone?" Ruth, who had recently started carrying it in her purse, dived to unearth it and turn it on. Sure enough, there were several emails from Martin, the most recent of which was dated that morning.

> Dear Ruth,
>
> I'm assuming you are with your sister, and understand if that means you won't be able to meet. But if you get this message and can, in fact, get together on Friday for lunch, let me know. All my best, Martin

Ruth turned to Veronica and said, "Do you mind if I take a minute to answer this?"

"Who am I—your boss?" Veronica joked. "Go ahead."

> Dear Martin,
>
> I'm so sorry for not responding sooner. Friday will be fine. Send me the name and address where you'd like to meet, along with the time, and I'll meet you there. And I promise to pay closer attention to my email so I don't miss your response. Best, Ruth

Ruth turned back to Veronica. "Friday," she said. "We're having lunch Friday."

Veronica's eyes widened. "Tomorrow? Oh, I hoped I could take you shopping first."

"The clothes I have are perfectly fine," Ruth protested.

Veronica gave her a pitying look, then said, "We've always been about the same size. Let's see what we can find in my closet."

Though she'd had the run of Veronica's house since she had begun visiting her regularly, she'd never taken a moment to look in her closet, for fear of being accused of nosiness. When Veronica opened the double doors to her wardrobe, Ruth saw a chamber the size of her own bedroom.

"Let's see—it's summer, it's lunch . . ." Veronica began riffling through the top rack of dresses on one wall.

"I would never buy clothes like these," Ruth said, watching as Veronica turned to a second wall of dresses.

"Now you don't have to," Veronica said. "Take your pick. I'm obviously not going to be needing them. Find something nice to wear for your date."

"It's not a date," Ruth said. "It's just lunch."

But she couldn't keep herself from feeling a small thrill. *Yes, just lunch—but with Martin Daly.*

Veronica selected a handful of colorful dresses, in shades far brighter than anything in Ruth's wardrobe—magenta, cobalt, canary. Givenchy, Saint Laurent, Fendi—the designers had names she recognized, even if she wasn't familiar with the fashions themselves.

"Do you really think these would suit me?" she said, slightly dazzled by the brilliant hues. She felt herself about to say "I couldn't" and gave herself a mental pinch on the arm, then turned to Veronica and said, "Which ones do you think?"

They spent the next two hours playing dress-up. *Like when we were girls,* Ruth thought. Instead of trying on their mother's clothes and pretending to look grown up, it was Veronica crafting the right outfit for Ruth to go to lunch with Martin. And this wasn't pretend.

"Here—this one would be perfect," Veronica finally said, selecting a cheery frock in an abstract pattern of pastels: green, yellow, and blue. "Try it on. It'll be great with your coloring."

When Ruth looked at herself in a mirror, she had to admit that, for a moment, her gray hair looked silvery.

"Now," Veronica said, "go slay him."

CHAPTER 25

The pastel print dress turned out to be from Ann Taylor. When she put it on, Ruth felt as though she were wearing a costume.

I am in disguise: I'm dressed up as my sister, Ruth thought as she left for the café where she was meeting Martin.

Ruth had been thinking about Martin, about what she'd read about his success and apparent wealth, and what it would be like to see him again. She was surprised how readily she could access the secret attraction she'd felt for him in high school, a feeling she'd tried to keep at arm's length at the time. She had no illusion that he shared those feelings in any way, after all this time. Then she thought about his original letter and subsequent emails.

What if he does?

Don't be foolish. That was fifty years ago. He was just getting in touch with an old acquaintance out of curiosity—like finding an old photograph and thinking, *I wonder whatever happened to her?*

As she parked her car on the street near the restaurant and plugged several quarters into a meter, she thought, *But what if he does?*

Then she pinched her own arm. *Stop that. You're not some teenager.*

Ruth rarely dined out. Even when she overcame her concerns about the cost of a restaurant meal, she couldn't overcome the feeling of being an insect under a magnifying glass when she dined alone in public. She felt like the center of attention, scrutinized for what she ordered and how she ate it. She was always sure that she could feel caustic pity emanating from other diners: "That poor woman, reading a book, eating by herself—what's wrong with her?"

The same anxious feeling took hold when she walked into Eggy's, a homey café near Minneapolis's Loring Park, on the fringe of downtown. She was convinced all eyes were trained on her as she stood at the host's stand, waiting for the young hostess to finish taking a phone reservation. Ruth tried to ignore what she imagined was a packed room of lunchtime diners, all staring at her as she stood there by herself. But when Ruth sneaked a glance around the half-full dining room, no one was looking her way.

As the hostess finished her phone call, Ruth felt a hand on her elbow—and turned to look up into the smiling face of Martin Daly. He was still a gangly six feet two, with only a little more meat on his bones than when he was in high school, a pair of modern-looking glasses, and somewhat less hair. Ruth decided she liked his golf shirt's vivid shade of lilac.

"Ruth—how are you?" he said, sweeping her into an impromptu hug. He turned to the hostess and said, "Hi—table for Daly? I called for one by the window?"

As soon as they were seated at a window table with menus, Martin reached over and took Ruth's hand.

"I'm so sorry about your sister," he said, and, for the first time in a while, Ruth was able to talk about Veronica and her illness with someone who wasn't directly involved. After the waitress came for their order, Ruth said, "That's enough about sad subjects, Martin. I want to hear about your fabulously successful career."

"Oh, it wasn't *that* fabulous."

"Don't be so modest. I googled you."

"Uh-oh," Martin said with mock embarrassment. "Not that."

"Very impressive. You're even in Wikipedia. Of course, I always knew you'd be a star."

"You did?" he said, laughing in surprise.

"You were the most enthusiastic person I knew."

"C'mon, in high school, I was an aspiring hoodlum with literary pretensions and smart-aleck tendencies."

"No, I've been remembering things about you," Ruth said. "It seemed like every week, you had a new passion, whether it was an author or a new movie or some obscure rock band. You tried to get me interested as well. I should have listened to you more than I did."

They ordered lunch, and then Martin said, "Do you remember Renee Stafford?"

"Of course. She's the most famous person in our graduating class. Though I think you're probably a close second, Mr. *60 Minutes* Profile."

"So you *did* google me. Anyway, the reunion committee wanted her to emcee the reunion, so they asked me to reach out to her, because she and I worked together when my agency produced some spots for her syndicated show. Renee agreed, so she's going to be the emcee for the dinner."

"Oh, that will be nice," Ruth said, not sure what else to say.

"It's been really good reconnecting with her," Martin said. "We started out just talking on the phone. But then I was going to be on the West Coast, so we had dinner. In fact, we've seen each other a couple of times, getting ready for this reunion."

Martin continued talking about various ideas he and Renee had considered for the reunion program. Ruth didn't really hear him, because she felt as though someone had hit her in the back of the head with a shovel.

Martin is involved with Renee. Of course.

Ruth reached for her water glass and took a long swallow.

He's a widower and wealthy; she's a TV star and divorced, I think. Of course they would have a mutual attraction.

She watched him as he continued to talk about Renee, the warmth in his voice as he spoke. This wasn't just someone he happened to work with on a project. There was obviously romance involved. *How could I have been so stupid?* The disappointment cut deep, like a sharp knife she'd grabbed by the blade in a sink full of soapy water.

"Ruth?" Martin said. "Are you still with me?"

She realized she'd been staring at him, trancelike, for several seconds. "I'm sorry," she said. "Senior moment."

"I get it," he said with a laugh. "I do tend to go on."

Ruth tried not to let her smile droop as they chatted through lunch. The talk flowed naturally; whatever anxiety Ruth had felt previously vanished in the face of Martin's good humor. But disappointment hovered over her afternoon, as she felt this new distance between them.

Yet after they finished eating, Martin reached over and took Ruth's hand again. It was a natural, affectionate gesture that both comforted her and filled her with regret. She found herself really looking at Martin: A witty provocateur as a teen, he retained the spark of subversive youthful humor, under the exterior of a bespectacled senior citizen. *Of course Renee would be a match for him.*

Ruth realized that Martin had stopped talking and was smiling at her expectantly.

"I'm sorry—I *am* listening, but my mind is in a million places," Ruth said. "I've been so scattered lately, and it's not just because of my sister. Something is changing; I can feel it, but I'm not sure what it is. And it has put me in a state. I'm sorry—you were saying?"

"I said that Renee and I were discussing what she needed for the reunion. But the only thing she asked about was you."

"Me?" Ruth said.

"She wanted to be sure you would be at the reunion. She said it's the only way she would agree to come: if she knew you were going to be there."

"Me?" Ruth said again.

Renee Stafford's family had moved to Richfield from North Minneapolis midway through junior year, making them only the second Black family in the suburb at that point in the late 1960s. There was an empty locker next to Ruth's, to which Renee was assigned.

Not naturally comfortable with new people, Ruth mustered the courage to offer a shy "Hello" the first morning Renee appeared at the locker. After that, they would greet each other at the beginning and end of each day, exchanging bland pleasantries about homework ("Boy, Mr. Swenson piles on the reading!") from the American history class they shared. During senior year, they were in the same advanced-placement classes and were both chosen for a select humanities seminar, where they shared an amused disdain for their humanities teacher.

The teacher, Mr. Calman, was a former athlete with intellectual pretensions. He let his receding hair grow below his collar, which was mildly controversial: this was the autumn of 1968, when a school dress code still existed that dictated, among other things, appropriate hair length for male students and skirt length for females.

Mr. C., as the students he cultivated as his pets called him, had a well-crafted reputation as one of the school's "hip" teachers, a "cool" guy who found a way to tie the dusty classics they were assigned from the Great Books series to the headlines and popular culture in the daily newspapers. But Ruth and Renee agreed he was a pretentious show-off who made no effort to disguise his interest in the prettier girls in the class—Renee in particular.

She could remember eating lunch with Renee during senior year. Not that they shared personal confidences; instead, the topic was the latest antics of the humanities teacher, whose class was right before their lunch period.

Mr. C. was the kind of teacher who routinely played devil's advocate in discussions, as a way to engage (Ruth would have said *provoke*) his students. Both Ruth and Renee spotted the technique immediately, even as they identified him early on as a poser and a phony.

It turned out Mr. C. was easy to flummox, if they took his side in the debate. No matter how wrongheaded or contrarian his argument was, they understood they could undercut it by agreeing with it.

At lunch they'd chuckle together over the look on his face when they'd parroted something ridiculous back to him, telling the teacher, "But you just said . . ."

"You're missing my point," he would say in frustration. "You're taking me too literally."

They both were able to do it with a straight-enough face that he could never be sure if they were putting him on, a fact they'd delight in as they recapped the class discussion over lunch.

Ruth and Renee were friendly classmates, though neither existed in the other's world outside of school. As Ruth thought about it later, she remembered that Renee suggested studying together at least a couple of times. Ruth deflected, even in the face of the new girl's overture to be friends.

Renee starred in the senior musical, *Oklahoma!*, for which Ruth was the chief scenic artist on the stage crew, painting impressively detailed backdrops. While waiting for the activity bus home after the final practice before dress rehearsal and opening night, Renee told Ruth she hoped she'd see her at the cast party after the opening.

"I have to get up early Saturday to work for my father," Ruth said. "Otherwise, I would."

"My mom is letting me use the car to go to the party," Renee said. "I could give you a ride. We could leave the party early if that's what you needed to do. I think you'd have fun. You worked so hard on the show."

But Ruth couldn't imagine putting herself into a socially aggressive environment like a high school party, certainly not voluntarily. She yearned to be as confident and upbeat as Renee but knew that kind of ease was reserved for her sister, Veronica, not her.

When Ruth would stand in the wings and watch her rehearse, Renee radiated a presence that was more than personality or style. It was as though, onstage, she was able to access every emotion she'd ever felt and make you believe she was feeling it for the first time. Her singing voice was rich for a high school student: full, clear, and sweet, showing both ability and control. She could glide effortlessly from the soprano register of a choir soloist to the soulful shout of a blues singer, in a way that more experienced singers would have envied.

It was considered quite daring when the drama teacher cast Renee as Laurey in *Oklahoma!*, due mainly to the fact that she was Black and the student who played her love interest, Curly, was white (as was everyone else in the cast). Their characters shared a kiss at the end of the play, and that fact was controversial before they'd even rehearsed it.

Renee, however, ignored the brouhaha and got on with the performance, bringing such wit and spunk to her character that she stole the show. By the time she and her costar went in for the climactic smooch, the audience was cheering. They gave her a standing ovation at the curtain call.

Renee earned a scholarship to Juilliard, then left the performing arts school early for a regular role on a network soap opera, where she stayed until the mid-1980s. After that, she turned up in guest-star roles on TV series and TV movies and small roles in a few feature films. Then, starting in the mid-1990s, she hosted a syndicated TV talk show that was successful enough to air for almost a decade. Since then, she'd become a successful health-and-beauty entrepreneur and spokesperson, with her own signature cosmetics line distributed by one of the major brands.

Over the years, Ruth had seen regular (and breathless) coverage of Renee's career in the *Star Tribune*. Renee was a hometown Hollywood celebrity, even if her main visibility lately came from hosting a series of infomercials for an electric juicer.

"She was quite specific," Martin said. "She said, 'If Ruth isn't going to be there, I don't want to come.' So what I'm confessing right now is that I promised her I'd make sure you were there tonight. That's why she agreed to be emcee. I hope you won't make me into a liar."

And, before she knew it, Ruth agreed to accompany Martin to their class reunion that evening.

CHAPTER 26

Ruth tried not to sound panicked when she got home and called Chloe and Veronica.

"I have to go to my fiftieth high school reunion tonight, and I'm being picked up at seven p.m.," she said when Chloe answered. "I have no idea what to wear. Would you mind helping me get ready?"

Ruth could hear Veronica in the background, saying, "Put her on speaker." There was a click, and then Chloe spoke again, though her voice had a tinny quality.

"OK, go ahead, Auntie Ruth," Chloe said.

Before Ruth could say anything, Veronica said, "Did I hear you say you're going to your reunion?"

"Yes, and I need a little help—"

"Oh, oh, oh!" Veronica said with such excitement that it made her cough. "Chloe, get the car. Ruth—we'll be there in twenty minutes."

Ruth knew how short Veronica's energy reserves were and quickly said, "No, I'll come to you. You'll need all your strength for this kind of transformation. I'm leaving now. What should I bring?"

"Take a quick shower; put on clean underwear and a housecoat. When you get over here, we'll do the rest."

When Ruth arrived at the house thirty minutes later, Veronica practically vibrated with excitement. "Wait until you see what we've picked out."

They had selected a black cocktail number by Givenchy, which came with an emerald-green bolero jacket that added a sense of authority. "You look like a boss," Chloe enthused when Ruth came out wearing the dress.

"What do you think?" Veronica asked.

Ruth realized she was smiling admiringly at her own reflection in the full-length mirror. "I look . . . I look . . ."

"You look amazing, Auntie Ruth," Chloe said.

Veronica added, "You look better in that dress than I did," and began to mist up.

Ruth joked, "Well, if you're that jealous, I'll take it off."

Veronica laughed through her tears and said, "Thank you."

"I should be thanking you. You're the one who is working magic here on my behalf."

"Thank you for letting me help you," Veronica said. "And for going to the reunion. I know you're not going because I asked you to. But it will mean a lot to me to hear about it afterward."

"Have you given any thought to what you want to do with your hair?" Chloe said.

Ruth hadn't but admitted she was resistant to a radical makeover. "Who am I trying to fool?" she said.

"Anyone who ever underestimated you in high school—which would be just about everyone," Veronica said. "By the time we get done with you, they're going to want to crown you homecoming queen—retroactively."

Chloe's application of cosmetics erased fifteen years from Ruth's face, a feat Ruth knew she'd never be able to replicate on her own. Then, employing a few well-placed bobby pins and a handful of foamy hair mousse, Chloe pulled and shaped Ruth's short hair into a sleek, upswept pompadour.

"I look like Elvis Presley," Ruth marveled as Chloe applied final touches to the hairdo.

"Don't touch that for about ten minutes until it dries," Chloe said.

"Let's go make a cup of tea to calm my nerves before I get dressed," Ruth said.

"You're going to look great," Chloe said. "So this Martin Daly asked you out at lunch today?"

"Yes, it was a last-minute thing."

"Did you two have chemistry?"

"What? Oh no," Ruth said. "This was a classmate who looked me up after fifty years." She stopped. "Fifty years. Saying that number makes me a little dizzy."

"Was he easy to talk to after all this time?" Veronica asked.

"Yes, Martin's very funny and offhand." Ruth smiled as she fussed with the now-boiling teapot, then poured tea for the three of them. "He was very nice," she said. "Very comfortable to be with."

"When was the last time you were on a date?" Chloe asked.

"Oh, it's not like that. I'm only going with him because he promised Renee Stafford I'd be there and offered to give me a ride."

"I remember her," Veronica said. "I knew she was in your class. I didn't know you were friends."

"We weren't, really. We knew each other. For some reason, she wanted to be sure I was going to attend. I'm only going as a favor to Martin, because he promised her that he'd make sure I came."

"Call it a date, and take the win, Ruth," Veronica said. "Go and have some fun tonight. You deserve it."

"Yes, I do," Ruth said but had her doubts. Still, she didn't want to disappoint Martin—or Renee, she supposed.

"So you didn't answer," Chloe pressed. "How long since your last date?"

"Let's see: I was thirty-five when I married your uncle Charles, so I would have to guess the early 1980s."

"I'd say you're overdue," Veronica said. "OK, your dream date, Martin—"

"Please stop saying that," Ruth said.

"Will be picking you up at your house in ninety minutes. Go put your dress on, and we'll take last looks."

Ruth emerged from the bedroom, hair and makeup in place, sheathed in the elegant black dress with the green jacket, wearing shoes with a low heel and a certain strappy elegance. Veronica let out a whistle.

"You're a total badass," Chloe said.

"Now go knock them all dead," Veronica chimed in, adding, "I expect a detailed report with tomorrow morning's coffee." She paused and smiled. "Unless you get lucky."

Ruth laughed in surprise, then turned to take another long look in the mirror. She tried to imagine herself as the person Chloe and Veronica were seeing, then as the one Martin and Renee would encounter. Perhaps if she squinted . . .

CHAPTER 27

Ruth answered her doorbell to find Martin Daly, dressed in a tan summer suit with a crisp white shirt, the shirt collar open, with no necktie. He smiled as she opened the door.

"Now I know I'll definitely have the best-looking date at the reunion," he said.

Ruth blushed and said, "Fortunately for me, I've always been able to coast on my good looks."

"No, really, you look amazing," Martin said.

"I'll do, until Renee makes her entrance," Ruth said, trying to make a joke of it all.

"Boy, I don't know about that" was all Martin could say, and he laughed, then helped her into the back seat of an SUV as the driver held the door. It was another new experience for Ruth. She had ridden in limousines for funerals, but never an SUV.

Ruth harbored strong opinions about SUVs: She disapproved of them. Aside from the obvious environmental hazard they represented, she resented how large they were. When she drove her aging Subaru sedan, she felt as though these massive vehicles were trying to bully her with their size, even as she tried to fight back with her pip-squeak horn.

This vehicle was a behemoth: a Cadillac Escalade, a black luxury vehicle with a leather interior and enough space in the back seat for a prom. There were liquor decanters, an ice bucket (filled with fresh ice), and crystal glasses in a rack on the back of the front seat. The car smelled faintly of spice.

"I understand a couple of our old teachers are going to be there," Martin told her as they rode, launching into a funny account of reunion-committee machinations and squabbles. Ruth tried to keep an attentive smile on her face, but, mentally, she was already hopelessly adrift on the sea of "What if . . . ?"—which was where she inevitably marooned herself .

What if I spill on myself?

What if I trip and fall?

What if people can tell this isn't my dress? My makeup? My hair?

This, of course, was compounded by her feelings about Martin and Renee, which collided in her head like tectonic plates. Ruth was having difficulty keeping the seismograph's needle from jumping wildly.

Martin paused in his recounting of reunion politics, turned to Ruth, and said, "Is something wrong? You look worried."

Ruth hesitated, then said, "I think this may have been a mistake."

"A mistake? What do you mean?"

"I shouldn't have agreed to come. I'm afraid I'll embarrass myself or, worse, I'll embarrass you and Renee."

"Embarrass us? How?"

"Oh, Martin—you're both so accomplished. And what have I ever done with my life? I'm a babysitter who used to be a bookkeeper."

Martin smiled, then said, "Let me ask you a question."

Ruth nodded glumly.

"How many of the people who will be there tonight have you talked to since high school? I mean, really talked to?"

"Me?" Ruth said. "None. No one."

"And how many of them do you think have been keeping track of your activities?"

Ruth looked up. "No one, I assume."

"Exactly. For them, you're a tabula rasa. The way you look tonight, you could have been anything from a secret agent to a school lunch lady all these years."

"I hardly think—"

"I'm exaggerating, but you get my point. Maybe you're an entrepreneur. Or a university professor. Or a retired ballerina. Use your imagination. I know you've got one."

Ruth laughed. "Are you suggesting I pretend to be someone I'm not?"

"Isn't that what everyone does when they're out in public?" Martin said. "You don't have to go that far. Let the other person do the work for you. It's all about perception; perception was always more important than reality in my business. So when someone asks what you've been doing, tell them, 'I can't go into that.' If they're rude enough to ask why, tell them, 'The NDA.'"

"NDA?"

"Nondisclosure agreement."

"Why would anyone believe that?"

"Why wouldn't they? NDAs are all over the news."

"I don't know," Ruth said. "I'm not a very good liar."

"So leave out the part about the NDA. If you say, 'I'm afraid I can't discuss my work,' you're not lying to anyone, because you really don't want to discuss it. But saying it that way will stop people cold. They'll fill in the blanks themselves. Meanwhile, you distract them by asking one of the big-three questions: Are you retired? Do you have grandchildren? And, of course: How's your health? That will get them talking about themselves and pull focus away from you."

Ruth looked at him, smiled, and took his hand. "Thank you, Martin. I appreciate your patience with me. And your ingenuity."

"Are you kidding?" Martin said. "I've been waiting fifty years to go out with you again."

And now I'm your placeholder date, until Renee finishes her emcee duties.

CHAPTER 28

The Escalade pulled up at the entrance to a country club in a western suburb as the sun hit that golden window in the early summer evening known as the *magic hour*. Ruth had to shield her eyes against the early-evening glare as they walked up the steps. Martin took Ruth's elbow and said with quiet encouragement, "Follow my lead."

They went to the check-in desk to get their table number and their name tags and found that they were seated at different tables. Registering the look of blooming panic on Ruth's face, Martin said, "This is a mistake. Don't worry, I'll take care of it." He seemed so casual and confident that Ruth thought, *OK, no need to get upset.*

The badges featured black-and-white senior pictures of each attendee from the school yearbook. Ruth's showed a young woman with a darker, fuller version of the low-maintenance haircut Ruth still wore, in a white crewneck sweater, with a thin chain around her neck. She appeared impossibly carefree, staring earnestly off into the future.

Who was that girl? And what would she think of me tonight?

Then she and Martin plunged into a scrum of classmates. Ruth recognized some of the half-century-old photos on the badges but had a harder time connecting the pictures with the current edition of the people on whose name tags they appeared.

Ruth found herself pulled into conversation after conversation alongside Martin, who knew and remembered everyone. Each time he greeted someone new, he said, "And of course you remember Ruth

Abraham Winters." The classmates would take a long look at her name tag, then give the current Ruth an impressed once-over before saying, "Of course, Ruth—how are you?"

That, inevitably, led to a follow-up question: "So, what have you been doing?"

The first time, the question caught her by surprise, and she started to say, "Oh, not very much." But Martin nudged her, and she added, "I'm afraid I'm not at liberty to discuss it." Almost as soon as the words were out of her mouth, Martin took her arm and said, "There's Tom Abalone. Let's go say hi. Excuse us," and they moved on.

"Nice seeing you," Ruth called back as Martin led her away.

At the bar, he said, "See? When you say that, it makes them wonder about what you're not telling them."

As the cocktail hour wore on, Martin excused himself for a minute, leaving Ruth at the bar. Though she'd been drinking ginger ale all evening, she now ordered a vodka tonic and, after the first sip, thought, *This tastes good.* So she finished it and ordered another.

Ruth's head bubbled with new sensations. Martin had made it seem as if she was his date, so she had played along. She decided to spend the evening pretending to be another woman named Ruth Winters, someone who could give the impression of being important or dangerous or bored. This mythical version of herself affected a haughty silence about her personal history that spoke of sought-after answers to mysteries both ancient and contemporary. This Ruth Winters was Martin Daly's date. Yes, she knew it was only a role for the evening, but she decided to take as much pleasure from the experience as she could.

As she watched meet and greet moments happening all over the room, someone tapped her shoulder and said, "Ruth?"

Ruth turned to find Teddy Arnold in an ill-fitting sport coat over a tieless madras plaid shirt and khakis. He seized her hand to shake it as he said, "You came! That's so great. What happened to your trip to Sioux City?"

"Plans change," she said vaguely. "You know how that is."

"Sure, sure. Well, great—you're here. So tell me what you've been doing."

It was now automatic: "I can't really talk about my work," she said. She scanned the room for Martin, but there was no sign of him.

"What do you mean?" Teddy asked. "Like you were a spy or something?"

"I'm sorry, I really can't discuss it."

"Wait—didn't I hear something about you being a babysitter?"

Emboldened by her second vodka tonic, Ruth fixed him with a dark look and, after a significant pause, said in an expressionless voice, "If I told you that, I'd have to kill you."

Teddy's eyes grew wide, even as Ruth thought, *What am I saying?* and worked not to laugh as she saw the look on his face. Then Martin magically appeared at her elbow.

"Excuse me, Teddy, but I'm going to reclaim my date. Time for dinner," he said as he whisked her away from Teddy's interrogation. He offered her his arm with a familiarity that Ruth was enjoying, even as she told herself, *He's pretending he's my date too. Why not?*

As they walked toward the dining room, Martin said, "I told you there was nothing to worry about. Renee had them put you at our table. You're quite the big deal, mystery lady."

CHAPTER 29

Ruth and Martin stood talking near their table, waiting for the salad to be served as their cue to be seated. Then the crowd in front of them parted like the Red Sea—and through the opening strolled Renee Stafford.

To Ruth, Renee looked like a real celebrity. Polished to a sheen, under an elaborately braided hairdo and an alluring face of makeup, Renee was luminous in a shimmery silver gown, camera ready for a more prestigious event than a high school reunion. She made a beeline for Ruth and Martin.

"Finally—familiar faces," Renee said as she moved in to dole out air-kisses to them both. She stepped back and gave Ruth a once-over. "Honey—you look fabulous. Whatever products you're using, I need to know about them—like, right now."

Ruth could only laugh in surprise as Martin said, "Can I get anyone a drink?"

And so, after her third vodka tonic, Ruth discovered that she had opinions she was ready to express.

Not that she wasn't opinionated before. Ruth held many opinions, most of them about other people and almost all of them low. She maintained high standards and expected others to live up to them as well. When they didn't, she noted it on a mental scorecard, though she kept those thoughts to herself, unless pushed into a corner. Having opinions and expressing them were two different things for her.

But her third drink had the pleasant effect of erasing that line, freeing Ruth from the fear of being embarrassed or ridiculed.

She spent the dinner at the center of a lively trio that comprised herself, Renee, and Martin. The discussion on their side of the table began with local politics (both Martin and Renee paid close attention to their home state, it turned out), segued to Renee dishing about movie stars who seemed too nice to be real (most of them, according to her), and finally landed on an exchange about the Marvel Cinematic Universe, which, according to Ruth, was destroying the movies.

A movie buff who took herself to matinees at a local art house multiplex, Ruth had never seen Marvel films, even ones that featured actors she liked, such as Paul Rudd or Robert Redford. But she couldn't avoid seeing the blanket coverage in newspapers and magazines, the endless commercials on TV, the product tie-ins at the grocery store, and the booming trailers at the movie theater.

So there she sat, quoting Martin Scorsese (or at least referencing something she'd read that he had said), exchanging rapid-fire quips with Martin and Renee, and holding her own as they all laughed and talked over each other, like old friends who'd been doing this regularly since graduation.

Ruth was enjoying the fact that, for the first time in her life, she knew exactly what to say and had the confidence to say it. The rest of the people at their table could have been watching television, the way they gawked at the show of energy and wit.

Eventually, the discussion turned to their old teachers—at which point Ruth roasted Mr. Calman, their humanities teacher, as a *pretentious perv*. "He'd be talking about René Descartes, and, at the same time, he'd be trying to look down your blouse." Ruth paused, smiled, and then, motioning to her own slender bosom, said tartly, "Well, not *my* blouse. Nothing to look at there." That made Renee laugh.

Ruth's assessment of the otherwise popular teacher was so brutal that one of their tablemates, a reunion-committee member whose name tag identified him as Bruce Smith, felt compelled to defend the teacher.

He said, "That's kind of harsh. Mr. C. was a pretty cool guy when I took his class."

"Would you be saying that if he'd put his hand on your ass every damn day?" Renee responded, which drew an astonished gasp from the rest of the table.

"Bruce is probably jealous that he didn't," Ruth muttered, loud enough so only Renee and Martin caught it. They both burst out laughing.

"What did you say?" Bruce Smith asked, a hand cocked to one ear against the room's high-decibel ambient noise.

Swept up in a wave of vodka-lubricated confidence, Ruth fell into an exaggerated pantomime, mimicking Bruce's hand-at-the-ear pose and, eyes widening, shaking her head while silently mouthing the words "I can't hear you." She kept it up as Bruce went on struggling to be heard, pulling a series of puzzled faces as she mimed her continuing inability to make out what he was saying over the room's racket. At last she made a show of giving up with an exaggerated shrug and a goofy grin and ducked in close to Martin, cocking an ear as though he'd said something to her.

Martin and Renee had been laughing all along, but now the entire table, save befuddled Bruce, had succumbed to giggles. The cool kids at the table were laughing, and they didn't want to be left out.

And, for the first time, Ruth was one of the cool kids.

The feeling was deliciously unfamiliar. She was being smart and funny and even a little rude, in public. It wasn't that she felt in control of the situation, but, rather, she was in control of herself.

This is what it feels like to be Veronica, she realized.

Then she remembered Veronica begging Ruth to attend the reunion so she could live vicariously through her. *She'll never believe this,* Ruth thought.

"Boy, Ruth—get a couple of cocktails in you . . . ," Martin marveled. "You could do your own talk show."

"I'm afraid I can't talk about that. Because of the NDA," Ruth said saucily. Which set them both off on another laughing jag.

When dinner was over, Renee emceed the festivities, telling stories and jokes. She handed out awards to class members ("Most Remaining Hair," "Most Grandchildren") and handled mundane chores, like a pitch for contributions to the scholarship fund for students at their alma mater.

She did it all with a polished professionalism that still let her personal warmth shine through. Ruth recalled the hour-long daily TV talk show Renee had hosted for ten years. For a few seasons, her show had hovered between second and third in the syndication ratings, behind only *Maury* and, of course, *Oprah*.

That's one of the reasons her show was successful—her sincere quality, Ruth thought. *Of course Martin would be interested in her.*

Renee had many admirers in the class, who mobbed her after the program to ask for an autograph or a selfie. As the servers began to clear their table for dessert, a DJ started to play "Hold On, I'm Comin'," by Sam & Dave, and a few people drifted from the tables to the small dance floor. Martin turned to Ruth.

"May I have this dance?"

Ruth understood: Renee was otherwise occupied. Still, it was a question she'd been waiting to be asked her whole life.

Martin stood up and extended his hand. Ruth took it, trailing him to the dance floor. There was, indeed, a first time for everything, she thought.

She'd never been asked to a dance when she was a girl. Now, for an evening, Ruth got to act like the teenager she'd never had the chance to be, while pretending to be a woman she never was.

On the dance floor, Martin was enthusiastic if not precise. In a crowd of boogying senior citizens, it hardly mattered. Ruth danced and felt free, and when the DJ played "Cherish," by the Association, she let Martin sweep her into his arms for a slow dance. It had been more than two decades since a man had embraced her like that, and she was determined to enjoy it, even if they were just playing roles for a night.

She and Martin fit together comfortably, and as they danced, she held him close, her head resting on his shoulder. She drifted along, buoyed by the warmth of his body, with its slight scent of Old Spice, intoxicated by the music and the human contact and the evening's unexpected magic, trying to pretend it was all real, if only for a moment.

CHAPTER 30

Ruth stood at a sink in the country club's ladies' room, awash in positive sensations, still feeling the effects of her third drink, as she momentarily escaped the DJ's sound system. She found it difficult to recognize the woman who looked back at her from the mirror. She looked so . . . self-possessed. It was not an adjective Ruth had ever conjured for herself before.

The door of the stall behind her opened, and Renee Stafford stepped out, adjusting her gown. When she saw Ruth, she quickly washed her hands and said, "Come with me."

The two of them left the ladies' room, then found a door to a patio terrace overlooking the country club's deserted driving range. They stepped from the air-conditioning into the humid late-summer dusk, the blast of music disappearing with a whoosh of chilled air as the door clicked shut behind them.

"There—now we can talk without being interrupted," Renee said, lighting a cigarette and taking a long, relieved pull on it. "Girl, how are you?"

"I'm fine. It's good to see you, Renee."

"You look fabulous—how do you do it?"

"Well," Ruth began, "I had some help . . ."

"Hey, who doesn't? I have a whole team," Renee said. "So—what have you been up to?"

Ruth paused, then, with a straight face, said, "I'm not really allowed to say."

Renee whooped with laughter, giving her an affectionate hug.

"Martin told me about that," she said. "I love it—shuts people right down. Your top secret life. That's the best." She gave Ruth a scrutinizing look, then added, "You always were a hard onion to peel, Ruth. It's so good to see you again."

"You too. I've followed your career and was proud to think I knew someone as famous as you."

"Trust me—I'm not that famous," Renee said.

"Well, you're the only famous person that I know." She paused. "And now Martin, as it turns out. You're both pretty famous." She worked to recapture her train of thought and, happily, found it. "But I have to ask: Why did you want to see me? Martin said you insisted that I come tonight. I was surprised. We never knew each other that well."

"Ruth, you were the first and only person who was nice to me at that school that first year my family moved to Richfield. You were the one person who treated me like a friend. At least until I won an award at the state one-act contest. Then everyone wanted to know me."

"But I didn't do anything."

"You said hi. The very first day. And every day after that. No one else did. Most of them looked at me like I had some contagious disease. Now they can't take a selfie with me fast enough."

"Yes, well, I didn't have many friends," Ruth said, "and it seemed like you didn't either. Because of, you know, racial bigotry."

Renee guffawed, showing a gorgeous mouth of perfectly crafted teeth.

"You always were direct, Ruth. Always told it like it was, even if you were kind of quiet about it. Yeah, that was quite the lily-white school you had there. When we moved to Richfield, a lot of people made it clear they wanted it to stay that way. Or else it was the reverse—the white guys who wanted to get with a Black girl. But my parents told me that as long as I minded my manners and did my best, I'd be able to get by. So I never made a big deal about it."

"I liked talking to you back then. I didn't have a lot of people I could talk to."

"Ruth, that's why you stood out to me. You were a good person, with no agenda. That was rare in high school. It still is. You accepted me at a point when no one else did. And I've never forgotten that."

"Well, that's nice of you to say."

"Take a compliment, girl. I wouldn't say it if it wasn't true."

She pulled Ruth into an impromptu hug, though Ruth towered over the still-petite actress. As they separated, Ruth said, "I'm glad I could help you and Martin with, you know, tonight."

Renee smiled. "What do you mean?"

"With filling in for you tonight." Pause. "As Martin's date."

Renee still gave her a blank look. "Martin?"

"I'm assuming there's some reason the two of you didn't want people to know about you two. But I didn't think it was any of my business. I'm just happy to help."

"I have no idea what you're talking about."

"Aren't you and Martin, you know, involved? With each other?" She paused and, seeing the confusion in Renee's face, added, "Romantically?"

Renee burst out laughing, a raucous guffaw that so unnerved Ruth that she began to laugh nervously as well.

"Honey, I've got a husband back in Silicon Valley who would love to hear that," Renee said, wiping a tear from one cheek as her chortling subsided. "Wait until he finds out Marty's given him grounds for divorce. Ever since this reunion business started, my husband's been on my case to introduce him to the famous and wealthy Martin Alexander Daly, in the hopes that Marty will invest in his start-up idea. I keep telling him, 'He's not that kind of friend.' This is hilarious."

"I'm sorry—when Martin said you two had been seeing each other while you were working on the reunion, I assumed . . . I mean . . ."

"Ruth, we had lunch once when he was in my city on other business, and we did the same thing, once, when I was passing through Denver. And you know what? All he could talk about was you."

"Me?"

"Yes, you. And how to get you to come to the reunion." She grinned. "And I guess he got you here. Now let's go back inside, before someone else walks away with your date."

That made Ruth laugh.

When they went back in and she didn't spot Martin, Ruth continued talking to Renee, who immediately attracted a claque of women. Ruth found herself at the center of their conversation—or adjacent to the center. The women would say something to Renee, then turn to Ruth for affirmation, as though this was her assigned role for the evening: best friend and sidekick to the star.

When Renee excused herself for a moment, Ruth found she was still surrounded by the same crowd, women who had barely known Ruth existed when they were in high school together. Ruth was sure most of them didn't remember her at all.

These had been the most popular girls in their class. They were the cute ones, the pretty ones, the rich ones, the sexy ones—and Ruth's tall spindly frame had contrasted with their curvier figures when they were teens.

Now most of them—and their husbands, Ruth noticed—had figures that showed the effects of a midwestern diet and a half century of gravity on the human body.

Ruth's weight hadn't fluctuated by more than five pounds up or down in that time, thanks to the metabolism she'd inherited from her father. She looked like an aging supermodel by comparison to her classmates.

Did I really go to school with all these old women? Ruth thought as they gathered around her—Ruth Winters, friend to the star, famous by association—with endless questions.

"How long have you and Renee been close?"

"Have you been to her house? What's it like?"

"Is that a Norma Kamali?"

"Where do you go during the cold weather? We love Tampa."

"Ruth Abraham—you're fun! Why didn't we know each other in high school?"

CHAPTER 31

When Martin and Ruth left the country club at the end of the night, the air-conditioned Escalade was so chilled against the evening's humidity that Martin offered Ruth his coat. He put his arm around her shoulders, and they snuggled together in the frigid back seat as they were driven to Ruth's house.

Ruth found Martin's hand and held it, thinking about what Renee had told her. *What does this all mean?* she wondered.

She thought again of Veronica. She could imagine her sister's amusement at Ruth's attempt at making sense of her feelings, to plot their place in the larger order of things.

"Why does it have to mean something, other than what it is?" Veronica would say. "You're holding hands with a man you like. Why does it have to be anything else? Relax. Enjoy it while it lasts. This moment will end. All moments do."

Before Ruth could consider it further, Martin said, "Do you remember the time we went out?"

"Of course," Ruth said. "I only ever had a couple of dates when I was in high school, so that one stood out." She paused, then squeezed his hand. "You kissed me good night."

"I'm so glad you remember that," Martin said, his voice filling with emotion for a moment. "I've thought about that kiss so often that, I swear, I wondered if I imagined it. Thank you."

"You're very sweet," Ruth said, snuggling in a little closer.

"I think I said to you earlier today that I'd been waiting fifty years for this. You don't know how true that is or what it means to me to finally see you and talk to you."

"When you said that, I assumed you were exaggerating," Ruth said. "We were friends in class. But we never saw each other outside of school. We didn't even go out on that date until the end of senior year, right before you moved away. You always had the air of being above all of that dating and going-steady business. I can even remember you making a joke about it that time we went out."

Ruth looked up, but Martin was staring straight ahead, as though lost in thought. Then he said, "I never gave a shit about German or any of my classes, really. But I always got a kick out of making you laugh. And you were a tough laugh. So guarded, so quiet. You always appeared to be amused at something no one else was aware of. But you looked nervous that someone might find out."

"Honestly, there is a lot less to me than meets the eye," Ruth said. She thought a moment, then said, "Why did you wait until senior year to ask me out? As I recall, you had a reputation for being *fast*, as they used to say."

"When the legend becomes the truth, print the legend—isn't that the line?" Martin said. Ruth looked at him blankly. "It's from an old John Wayne western."

"Didn't they call you the Martinizer?"

"Oh my God, how do you remember that?" he said with a laugh. "Now *I'm* embarrassed."

"What did it mean?"

"It didn't mean anything. I saw it on a sign at a dry cleaner, and, because my name is Martin, I thought I was being clever."

"But I thought it was your nickname?"

"I came up with it, as a joke," Martin said. "Then a couple of my friends started saying it—at school, in gym class—and the Martinizer thing took on a life of its own. It was this legend that had nothing to do with me. The Martinizer was the one who had the reputation for being fast, not me. Plus, it wasn't true; having a reputation covered a multitude of shortcomings, like a lack of confidence."

"Now I know you're kidding me," Ruth said. "You never lacked for confidence."

"Oh, I was good at pretending. But it took me so long to ask you out because I couldn't convince myself that you'd say yes. I knew I'd be shattered if you said no."

"But as you may recall," Ruth said quietly, "when you did ask me, I said yes."

"Oh, great—now all I need is a time machine so I can go back and tell that to the teenage me."

"Yes, a time machine would be handy for a lot of things," Ruth said.

"Finally, it was do or die. The end of senior year. I had to ask you on a date or risk missing out forever."

"So you did—and then you never called me again," Ruth said with mock reproach. Then she smiled and said, "No, I know. Your family moved away. It wasn't your fault."

"You have no idea how much I argued with my parents to let me stay. I even convinced my friend Dave's parents to let me live in their basement until graduation so I could finish the school year here, after my parents moved. But my parents made me go with them."

He was quiet for a moment, then said, "I think I said in one of my emails that I came to the reunions every ten years, in the hope that I would run into you."

"Yes, that was very flattering."

"No, that's true. If I'm honest, every time I've come to Minneapolis over the years, on business or with family, whenever I'm walking around downtown or in one of the malls, I'm looking at people in the hope that I'll run into you. I've thought about seeing you so much over the years."

"But, Martin . . . why?"

"I've been asking myself that same question. What I decided was this: You were someone who meant a lot to me—and I never told you. I felt as if we had a connection that could have turned into something—and I never told you. And I wanted to. And I've thought about that all these years."

"But you were married and had a family."

"And I wouldn't trade those years for anything. I love my wife and still miss her. My kids and grandkids mean everything to me. Yet I will tell you that not a month has gone by since high school that I haven't thought about you."

"Oh, Martin," she said and squeezed his hand.

"And here's the strange thing," he continued. "As I got older and would think of you, I realized I was thinking of the version of you that I remembered from high school. I knew intellectually that, somewhere, you were aging, the same as I was, and having a whole life I knew nothing about. I realized I was thinking about the person I imagined you'd be. I was obsessing—well, not *obsessing*, but preoccupied—I was *focused* on an imaginary creation. I mean, you—you here now—you're a real person."

"Thanks for noticing," Ruth said with a smile.

"I can't tell you the pleasure I got imagining your life and who you were. I could live inside the version of you that I'd created in my mind. As strange as it sounds, it made me feel close to you. In my mind, you became like a character in a book that I was writing in my head."

"Most people have already judged this book by its cover and found it lacking."

"That's hard to believe, based on tonight," Martin said.

"Yes, well, is it midnight yet? That's when I turn back into a pumpkin. Believe me, tonight is a big departure from my usual Friday night. Or my life in general."

The Escalade pulled into Ruth's driveway, and Ruth and Martin sat quietly for a moment. Then, before Martin could say anything, Ruth took a deep breath and said, "Would you like to come in for a cup of tea? I can drive you back to your hotel afterward."

"You don't have to ask twice," Martin said as he helped her out of the car.

CHAPTER 32

As they stood in Ruth's kitchen waiting for water to boil in the teapot, Martin turned to Ruth.

"I probably sounded like some crazy stalker just now," he said.

Ruth took his hand, looking up into his still-boyish face.

"Martin, you ninny—an attractive man just took me out on my first date in decades," Ruth said. "Then he told me he'd been pining for me for fifty years. That kind of thing doesn't happen to me every day."

Then she elevated on her toes to reach up and kiss him.

Martin pulled her into an embrace. It was a lingering kiss that ended naturally, and Ruth laid her face against Martin's chest. They stood there, arms around each other, swaying a little, until the kettle's squeal interrupted the moment.

Ruth reluctantly disengaged from Martin and busied herself getting tea, the teapot, honey, and cups. Martin leaned against a kitchen counter, watching her.

Ruth's head felt ready to explode. Martin's kiss, Renee's laughter, the whole evening at the reunion—why was this happening now? What did it mean?

That kiss. It had felt as comfortable and enveloping as a warm bath but also exciting enough to give her wild thoughts that she worked to sort through. She definitely wanted that feeling again—and right now. But then what?

What had Martin said? That he'd been waiting fifty years for this evening? *If I'm honest,* Ruth thought, *so have I.*

She poured the tea, handed a mug to Martin, and then took his other hand and said, "Let's go sit in the living room."

They sat down on the couch, set down their tea—and then Martin turned to Ruth and kissed her again, a deep, fulfilling kiss that pulled Ruth all the way in, until she found herself swimming eagerly through the feelings of warmth, affection, and, most of all, longing, for the first time in ages.

For too many years, longing had gnawed at Ruth, even as she'd worked to bank those fires. Longing for what? For a connection, for someone to see and want her, to care for her the way characters did in books or films.

Even if the romance didn't end well—those were the best stories, weren't they? Would *Casablanca* or *The Way We Were* or *A Farewell to Arms* have lodged so deeply in her consciousness if they'd ended happily?

Yes, romantic disappointment was a possibility.

But even romantic disappointment required a partner.

All this longing now found a welcome outlet in Martin as Ruth sat kissing him. For the first time, she understood the origin of the verb *necking* when he began to nuzzle behind her ear, sending a thrill through her that aroused her so much it alarmed her.

Kissing Martin, being kissed by Martin—Ruth understood where this sort of thing was meant to lead. What did she expect? What did he? She put her head against Martin's chest, and he stroked her cheek in a way that made Ruth melt.

Was she going to sleep with this man? Tonight? Modest even in marriage, Ruth found it difficult to imagine taking her clothes off in front of Martin. Or making love with him. Did she want that? Did he? At their age?

What would Veronica do in this situation? she thought. And then Ruth thought, *Veronica always did exactly what she wanted, every single time, her entire life.*

If it feels good, do it. Right or wrong, Veronica had things her way. Veronica came first, and Veronica always had. She demanded it, something Ruth had never thought of doing, until now.

Then Martin enveloped her in his arms and said, "I can't tell you how often I've imagined having this kind of closeness with you. To know you in a way no one else did, and to have you know me the same way, and want me in the way I wanted you."

Ruth took his hand and said, "I could do this all night."

She kissed him again, lost in the sensations that washed over her. The two of them sat on the couch late into the night, relishing the sweetness and wanting to make it last.

CHAPTER 33

When Ruth woke and looked at her watch, it was eight thirty Saturday morning. She was asleep on the sofa, still in her dress, a pillow under her head and a blanket thrown over her. She was alone on the couch, and Martin was gone.

Ruth deflated.

Of course he was gone. He'd probably called a taxi or summoned an Uber back to his hotel. He'd tiptoed out to avoid having to talk to her again.

It was all pretend after all. Why would she have expected otherwise?

But before her sense of defeat could truly sink its claws into her, she smelled it: coffee. And was that bacon? When she listened, she could hear cooking noises coming from the other room. She got up and went to the kitchen.

Martin stood at the stove, barefoot, wearing an apron over his pants and undershirt, tending a frying pan full of scrambled eggs and bacon.

"You spoiled my surprise," he said with a grin, indicating the stovetop with a flourish. "I was going to serve you breakfast in bed. Oh well, get a plate and sit down. This is almost ready."

"Didn't you say last night you had an early meeting?"

"I rescheduled for after lunch," he said, dishing eggs, bacon, and toast onto her plate. "I still have to pack and check out of my hotel, but my plane isn't until six."

As they began to eat, Ruth worried they might not have the kind of ease they'd felt the previous evening. But then Martin smiled and said, "So how long are you going to keep babysitting? There must be other things that an amazing woman like you would rather be doing."

"You overestimate me," she said, returning his smile.

"Are you kidding? Ruth, you're smart and funny and perceptive. Given that, if you could do absolutely anything at all, what would it be? Try thinking a little bigger, or a little different. For example, do you still need this much house if you're alone?"

"What would I do if I sold my house? Where would I live?"

"Where would you like to live? Every day I see headlines on the internet like 'Best Undiscovered Places to Retire' and 'Best Cities for Retirees' or even 'Best Small Towns.' The point is to widen your lens. Do something for yourself that makes you feel good."

They held hands talking at the table. Finally, Ruth said, "I should get you back to your hotel so you can pack."

"I've got time. Let me clean up breakfast while you change," Martin said. As he began to wash dishes, Ruth came up behind him and put her arms around his waist, hugging him as she laid her head against his back. Then she went to get ready.

She brushed her teeth, took a quick shower, and then stood at the bathroom sink staring at her freshly scrubbed face. Once again, it looked as old as it was, with her hair brushed back to its normal unfussy configuration.

Martin was putting his jacket on over his unbuttoned shirt when Ruth emerged. "Back to the *real* me," she said with a shrug.

He took her in his arms and said, "For the record—I've had a thing for the *real you* since I was sixteen." And then he kissed her.

Ruth remembered many films and TV shows, both comedies and dramas, built around the sensitive matter of saying *I love you* to another person for the first time. There were stories about people who were afraid to say it, stories about people who were unwilling to say it, stories about people who said it too soon, and stories about people who said it too late.

Those stories struck Ruth as so much self-absorption. Charles had said *I love you* to Ruth exactly twice—once when he'd proposed, once on their honeymoon—and she had dutifully parroted the words back to him. None of it had felt like much.

Martin hadn't even said those exact words, but that was what Ruth heard—and his casual declaration hit Ruth like a punch. She realized he'd told her how he felt through his actions and his presence over the past twenty-four hours, and even in his earlier emails. Now it squeezed her heart in a way it hadn't before, because she realized she shared the feeling, that it was an extension of the feelings she'd hidden in high school.

The uncertainty? Who cared? She was experiencing sensations she'd never felt and was greedy for more.

The two of them talked about how Minneapolis had changed as she drove him downtown: "I spent a summer making pizzas at a Shakey's that used to be there," Martin said, pointing to a building that now housed an all-you-can-eat Chinese buffet. When they reached his hotel, Ruth parked in front, then turned to him and said, "Can I see your cell phone?"

He looked at her with curiosity as he dug the phone out of his pocket. She took it and began punching in numbers confidently, saying, "My niece taught me this." Momentarily, they heard a phone ring—Ruth's. She took it out of her purse, silenced it, and looked at the screen. Then she smiled and returned his phone to him.

"Now we have each other's cell numbers," she said. "And I never give my cell number to anyone."

"I'll guard it with my life," Martin said, raising three fingers on one hand as though taking the Boy Scout oath.

Ruth laughed. They both got out of the car, and she kissed him, then said, "I expect you to use that number, Martin. Just so there's no confusion: I *want* to hear from you."

They kissed once more, long and affectionate, and then Ruth got back into her car as Martin went into his hotel.

CHAPTER 34

As she drove to Veronica's after dropping off Martin, Ruth was abuzz with unfamiliar feelings, amplified by her sleep deficit. She found herself singing along with the oldies station on the radio, a song they'd played at the reunion: "Build Me Up Buttercup," by the Foundations.

Irwin and Marta were having coffee in the kitchen, and Veronica was asleep when Ruth arrived. "She's been having stomach issues since last night," Marta said. "Chloe picked up her new prescription for the pain, and it knocked her out."

"Should I go in?" Ruth said.

"Of course," Irwin said. "She wanted you to wake her when you came."

Ruth pushed the door to Veronica's room open and stepped into the darkened chamber, trying not to make noise as she crossed the spacious room to a chair near her bed. But her sister's eyes popped open, and she looked at Ruth.

"Tell me everything," she said, with a weary smile.

Ruth turned on a lamp, then narrated the evening for Veronica, who lay back and closed her eyes, taking long slow breaths as she listened. At one point, her breathing became so steady that Ruth thought she was asleep. But when Ruth paused in the telling, Veronica's eyes opened, and she said, "I'm not dead yet. Go on."

When Ruth reached the end of her account of the reunion, Veronica said, "So you thought, after all the trouble he went through to find you after all these years and the lengths he went to in order to get you to go to the reunion, that Martin Daly was actually involved with Renee Stafford and was just using you as his cover? And that he hired a car as part of the charade? Oh, Ruth, you're too much. Give yourself a little credit once in a while."

Veronica coughed for a moment, then said with an insinuating grin, "So you didn't sleep with him. But did you want to?"

That made Ruth laugh. All she could say was "Honestly? At our age?"

"That's what those blue pills are for," Veronica said.

Ruth blushed and said, "Oh, please."

Ruth's story complete, Veronica appeared to nod off again for a moment, then sat up with a start and looked at her in confusion. Her eyes flashed back and forth, then came into focus as she appeared to realize where she was. Something must have clicked in her memory, because she turned to Ruth with urgency.

"Promise me," she said.

"What?"

"Chloe's going to need help after the baby is born. Promise me you'll go out to California and help Chloe and David do the vetting when they hire a nanny."

"Veronica . . ."

"Promise! Enough babysitting for strangers. Stop hiding from the world. You have my permission to go live your life. In fact, as the dying person in the room, I command it."

"Yes, well, there's plenty of time to think about that," Ruth said, scolding herself for uttering such an obvious lie.

Veronica, however, wouldn't let it go. Her eyes moistened as she said, "I'm never going to get to meet Chloe's baby. I know that. I need you—I'm counting on you—to take my place. You have to be the grandmother *and* the fairy godmother."

"Yes, well, my magical powers aren't what they used to be."

"I mean it!" Veronica said fiercely through tears. "You have to tell her about me. And not only the bad things. You've got to tell her the good things too."

Ruth cocked an eyebrow and said, "You wouldn't want me to lie to a baby, would you?" Veronica laughed, and Ruth laughed with her.

Veronica sighed and said, "I thought about making some sort of scrapbook or memory book, but, really, I don't have time. Or strength. Or, if I'm honest, the interest in doing it. As you said, I don't really *do* introspection. That's why I'm counting on you. You must live long enough to tell my story."

"Tell your *story*? Who are you—Cleopatra?" Ruth said, eyebrow arched again.

Veronica laughed. "That did sound a little grand."

"A *little* grand? It sounded like you're passing along Norse sagas and I'm one of the tribal elders: 'I will tell your story. I will regale the children of your children with your many brave adventures, shopping on Fifth Avenue in the land of New York, and hunting the bargains of Rodeo Drive in the mystical Beverly Hills. And they will sing your praises.'"

They were both laughing now. Then Ruth said, "Yes, I will make Grandma Ronnie a legend to her grandchildren."

"As long as you don't make me a legendary bitch."

With a straight face, Ruth repeated what Martin had told her: "When the legend becomes the truth, print the legend." Then they both dissolved in giggles.

~

A few days later, Veronica was napping on the couch on the sunporch as Ruth sat reading in a recliner next to her. Everyone else was out, running errands or attending to lives that needed to go on even as Veronica's life dwindled to a close. Ruth was happy to keep Veronica company, talk when she felt like talking, fetch whatever she might need, help her to the bathroom.

When Veronica's pain had worsened, the doctor had increased her pain medication. This, in turn, made her sleepier—and loopy when she wasn't asleep. At one point, she woke from a nap and said to Ruth, "Was there a buffalo in this room just now? Were you and I talking about it?"

"You've been sound asleep for a half hour," Ruth said, adding with a chuckle, "and I have not seen any buffalo."

"It was so vivid. I was dreaming about the time Mommy and Daddy took us to the Black Hills."

"I remember that," Ruth said. "I must have been ten. So you'd have been seven."

"I was dreaming about driving through that park where we saw the buffalo. But you and I were right here, watching it all happen. And I said, 'I think that buffalo is getting a little too close to us,' because one of them was walking right up to us here in the sunporch. Was I hallucinating? Dreaming?" She chuckled quietly and said, "Same difference at this point, I guess."

Veronica had been in and out like that for a couple of days. She would describe impossible scenes as though she'd experienced them moments earlier, including conversations with their parents and her ex-husbands. But she also slept more and more. Ruth would rouse her at regular intervals to help her to the bathroom. When she no longer had the strength for that, they began using diapers.

Now, as she sat reading a book next to the couch where Veronica slept, Ruth heard the chime of her cell phone ringtone in her purse in the other room. She glanced at Veronica, who was asleep, then went into the kitchen and dug out her phone. The screen said M/A/D.

Martin Daly.

"Hello, Martin?" she said, in a half whisper.

"Hi, Ruth. Is this a good time?"

"Martin, no. Sorry, here—" She stepped around a corner into the breakfast nook, farther from the door so as not to wake Veronica, but close enough to stay in earshot.

"There—my sister is sleeping in the next room, and I don't want to wake her." Ruth paused, then said quietly, "It's nice to hear from you."

"You told me I better call. I don't take that kind of thing lightly. Plus I wanted to hear your voice."

"It's good to hear yours as well," Ruth said. "How was your trip back to Denver?"

Before he could reply, Ruth thought she heard Veronica's voice. She cocked an ear.

She heard, faintly, "Ruth?" from the other room.

"Just a second, Martin," she said as she went to the kitchen door.

She could see Veronica, who was lying on her side on the couch. But she had struggled to one elbow and was trying to say something.

"Are you OK?" Ruth said. She remembered the phone in her hand and said, "I'm sorry, Martin, I have to go," then clicked the phone off.

As she did, Veronica said, "Oh, Ruth." It sounded like a sigh, an exhalation.

And then she closed her eyes, lay back, and was gone.

Ruth stared at her in disbelief. "Veronica?" she said, then, with increasing urgency, said, "Ronnie? Ronnie?"

She leaped to where Veronica lay and touched two fingers to the artery in her neck, then to her wrist. Nothing. She put her ear to Veronica's chest and found no sound there either.

She pulled Veronica off the couch and laid her on the floor on her back, with a pillow under her head. After a couple of tentative thumps on her breastbone, Ruth began CPR compressions, counting the pumps, counting the seconds between, putting her mouth on her sister's while pinching her nostrils, trying desperately to breathe life back into the one person who had done the most to make her own life a misery.

After fifteen frantic minutes spent trying to correct an irreversible transition, Ruth stopped the compressions. Veronica lay on the floor where Ruth knelt.

Winter is coming. Wasn't that what Chloe had said?

She looked out the window of the sunporch to the backyard and the lake. On this unseasonably warm morning in early autumn, Ruth felt a chill. As she had at many key moments in her life, she thought, *What now?*

She looked at Veronica. *She doesn't look asleep,* she thought. *She looks devoid of life.* She could see that the pain that had pinched her sister's face for so long was gone too. That gave Ruth a small measure of comfort.

Despite her life of solitude, Ruth suddenly felt alone in the world in a way she never had. She was the last of her family still alive. She'd been a widow for decades, an orphan even longer. Yet she had never been as aware of how alone she was until that moment.

She fought the urge to cry, but it assailed her, with thoughts of Chloe and Irwin, and memories of herself and Veronica as girls. Then the old Ruth—the methodical, dutiful Ruth—reasserted herself. She pulled back on the emotional reins, regained control, and went into action.

Ruth smoothed a blanket on the couch, then lifted Veronica's frail form—so shockingly light—onto it, covering her body with another blanket. Then she went into the den and began making phone calls: Chloe. Irwin. Marta. Veronica's doctor. The mortuary they'd been talking to.

The doctor told her she'd be over within the hour. Ruth sat on the sunporch with Veronica's body until the doctor arrived. She briefly examined her, then covered Veronica again.

When Chloe and Irwin arrived a few minutes later, the doctor told them, "From all appearances, she had some sort of cardiac event. That's not surprising. The chemo and the cancer both put a big strain on her heart. And she had an arrhythmia for a couple of years, which also compromised her cardiac function. Her heart wasn't up to the demands her body was making."

After the body was removed, Chloe was teary but strong enough to help Ruth and Marta with the funeral planning. While the funeral service would be at the synagogue to which Irwin belonged (but seldom attended), they would avoid the full week of shiva dictated by Jewish tradition. Instead, they'd host a tastefully catered gathering at the house after the burial, per Veronica's wishes.

"A week of *shiva*?" Chloe said. "Mother would have been bored out of her mind."

"I can hear her," Marta said. "'Just get on with it already!'"

The three women took turns shoring up the devastated Irwin, who seemed inconsolable and unable to focus on anything except his immense grief. He sat in his basement workshop on a straight-backed chair, elbows on knees, head in hands, unmoving for hours, except for the sobbing. The next day, Chloe's husband, David, arrived from the West Coast to keep Irwin company while Chloe and Ruth organized the funeral.

Veronica had prepared an extremely specific spreadsheet of funereal preferences in advance. The unctuous funeral director at her mortuary of choice noticed the expensive taste in Veronica's selections for her interment and, sensing wealth, tried to upsell Ruth on pricier features and decorations, an effort Ruth squelched.

Ruth took charge of Irwin on the day of the funeral. She sat next to him in the limousine, where he clutched her hand as though it were a talisman. He gripped it, kneaded it, squeezed it—all with an intimacy that would have made her uncomfortable under other circumstances. Instead, she recognized it as his attempt to remain connected to something he knew was already gone.

As they rode to the synagogue, Ruth's cell phone suddenly began to ring. The unexpected intrusion flustered her for a moment, and she reached angrily for the device in her purse. But she softened when she saw the display, which read M/A/D.

She answered the phone and said, "Hello, Martin. I'm afraid you've caught me at a bad time. We're in the limousine on the way to my sister's funeral."

"Oh my God, I am so sorry," Martin said. "I'll let you go." He hung up.

Ruth turned to the gloomy Irwin, and Chloe, sitting on the other side of Irwin. "I should probably turn this off before we get to the synagogue," she said. "Although I don't know anyone else who has my cell number."

"We all should," Irwin said, adding, "I was at High Holidays last year when someone's phone rang in the middle of the service, and the ringtone was 'Fuck Tha Police,' by N.W.A."

Chloe laughed at that, Ruth smiled, and even Irwin let the clouds part, if only for a moment.

Ruth felt surprising tenderness for Irwin as she comforted him at the service. They now shared a bond of grief for Veronica, deeper than any feeling they would ever have for each other. She rode next to him in the limo to the cemetery, then sat with him graveside. He clutched Ruth's arm and wept as Veronica's coffin was lowered into the ground.

Ruth thought of all the unfamiliar and long-ignored feelings she'd experienced since this had begun with a phone call from Veronica—how long ago? Five weeks? Six? Feelings of connection and belonging she didn't know she had missed, a warmth for her sister of which she hadn't thought herself capable.

On the silent drive back to the house, Ruth thought again about something that nagged at her since Veronica had said it a week or so earlier.

"I ruined your life," Veronica had said, and Ruth had accepted both Veronica's guilt and her apology. Yet the more she thought about it, the more she confronted an uncomfortable fact: blaming Veronica meant she would never accept her own role as the real culprit here.

Veronica didn't do this to me. I did it to myself. And once again, Ruth thought, *What now?* Because everything had changed.

But had it?

Then they were back at the house, and Ruth clicked into gear with Marta to facilitate hospitality and supervise the caterers: food, drinks, plates, silverware, glasses. Chloe, David, and Irwin shared tears, laughter, and conversation with the people from Veronica's life who came to share their condolences and recollections and pay their respects to Veronica's memory, while Ruth and Marta helped the catering crew clean up after them.

At one point, Ruth took a moment to check on Irwin, who was bearing up a little better, though it may have been the brave face he put on for company.

"Did any of Veronica's other husbands come today?" Ruth asked.

"Well, Errol died last year," he said, swirling the ice in his glass.

"I didn't know—I'm sorry."

"Why? Ronnie wasn't," Irwin said. "I reached out to Tad, and I think Peter called Chloe."

"Are they here?" she said, scanning the crowd. "I never met Tad."

"No," he said in disgust before draining his glass. "Chloe was less upset than I expected that her father didn't show. But her relationship with Peter was never great after the divorce and certainly not since he didn't turn up for her wedding last year. Tad, as it turns out, is in a memory-care facility in Saint Paul."

"I guess that's an acceptable excuse for not coming, but he might have sent a note," Ruth said dryly, which made Irwin laugh.

"Thanks," he said, adding, "Hey, did you see the flowers from your friend Martin?"

"Where?"

"In the den," he said before returning to his station as bereaved widower.

Ruth went into the den, where a number of floral arrangements were on display. She immediately saw a tall green vase of lilies she hadn't noticed earlier. She read the card, which said, "So sorry for your loss. Sincerely, Martin Daly." Ruth smiled, then went back to work.

Later in the afternoon, as the crowd was thinning out, Chloe said, "Auntie Ruth, you should sit down. You've been on your feet since we came back from the funeral."

"It's all right, dear," Ruth said. "I need to distract myself from my own thoughts. Staying busy helps."

But not enough. No matter how many plates and napkins she cleared, how many leftovers she wrapped for the refrigerator, or how many dishes she washed, dried, and put away, no distraction was sufficient for what Ruth was feeling.

CHAPTER 35

To get to sleep that night after the funeral, Ruth took the strongest drug in her medicine cabinet: Tylenol PM. She never used it more than once a week and never more than one tablet at a time. On this night, she took three.

As she lay there restlessly, hoping to nod off, she thought, *I should look at what's in Veronica's bathroom. There must be a stray sleeping pill I could have.* She made a mental note to ask Chloe.

Then, of course, Ruth second-guessed herself. *I can't ask for that. They'll think that I'm drug seeking. What if they give it to me and I become an addict?*

The thoughts raced in a circle, arriving back at the same starting point. *But I need the pill to sleep.*

Why?

Because Veronica is gone.

What now?

So much of what Ruth had perceived as unfair over the course of her life had been embodied by her sister. Now her sister was gone, and nothing in Ruth's life felt different in any tangible way. Yet it felt as though it should. The only difference she could pinpoint was the unexpected hole Veronica's death left in her life.

Ruth had outlasted Veronica. She'd lived longer. She'd won. But won what?

The next day, thinking she might hear from Martin (or, perhaps, work up the courage to call him herself), Ruth took out her cell phone and turned it on. She checked her email in the hope that he had written but, instead, found a message from an unfamiliar sender, with the subject line Urgent. When she opened it, the email said, You've been selected to receive a valuable prize! Log in now before it's too late! and showed a link to click on.

But when the inexperienced Ruth made the mistake of opening the link, she found herself bombarded by a noisy advertisement for used automobiles, complete with loud music and flashing lights. It startled her, and she frantically began pushing buttons on the phone. Finally, the noise stopped, and the screen went dark. Both were a relief. She put the phone back in the drawer, as though it were a misbehaving child being sent to its room.

A couple of mornings later, Ruth sat in her kitchen, drinking coffee and mentally planning her day. There was a knock on her back door, and Jane popped her head in.

"Hi, hi!" she said. "Do you have a minute?"

"Come on in," Ruth said. "Would you like some coffee? I made a pot, and I'm not going to drink it all."

"No, thanks. I wanted to check in because I hadn't seen you in a while. Is everything OK?"

But the words Ruth started to say—"My sister died"—caught at the lump in her throat. She was silent for a moment, breathing in and out. Having to say it out loud brought on a wave of emotion. She took another deep breath and said, "My sister died. The funeral was Saturday."

Jane gasped, then took Ruth's hand and said, "I'm so sorry. That had to be terrible for you."

Ruth's emotional defenses finally collapsed. Ruth, who had made it a point to be the calm and calming center of the emotional storm brought on by Veronica's passing, now found herself laying her head on her arms on her kitchen table and unleashing all the tears she had kept in check while she was with her family.

As Jane put a comforting arm around her shoulder, Ruth cried. She cried for Veronica and for Chloe and for Irwin. She cried for her mother and her father.

And, finally, Ruth cried for herself and for all the things she'd put aside in the name of being the dutiful one, the one who did what was expected, the one who did what she was supposed to do, instead of the one who got what she wanted.

She cried because she felt as though she never got anything she ever wanted, at any point in her life.

And then she cried because she had no idea what it was that she did want, at this moment when the end of her life was so much closer than the beginning.

When she finally exhausted her supply of tears, she excused herself to wash her face in the powder room. As she looked at puffy red eyes set amid a landscape of gray hair and age spots, she muttered to the mirror, "I thought catharsis was supposed to make you feel better."

Later, as Jane was leaving, she gave Ruth a hug and said, "I wish there was more I could do."

"Oh, honey, you've been very kind to a sad old woman, and I appreciate it," Ruth said. "Say hello to Samantha for me. I'd love to have her over to play one day soon."

"She would love that," Jane said. "She asks about you all the time. Now that she's in preschool, her social life is more complicated than mine."

Ruth drove to Veronica's house to help Chloe sort through Veronica's voluminous belongings. As she drove, she tried to reorient her thinking to focus, for a change, on herself—someone whose interests she'd rarely put first at any point in her own life.

What if I did go to California? she thought. *What would I even do there? I don't know anyone, other than Chloe.*

Then Ruth pinched her own arm angrily and admonished herself: *Stop being so timid. What are you doing in Minneapolis that's so special? There has to be more to life than this. And with better winter weather.*

As she drove up to the security gate to Veronica's neighborhood, she lowered her car window to greet the now-familiar guard.

"Just me, Randy," she said. "How are you today?"

"Good—I took the wife to the Wisconsin Dells for a few days after Labor Day," he replied. "Say, Mrs. Winters, I was really sorry to hear Mrs. Snelling passed. She was one of the good ones."

"That's very kind of you," Ruth said. "Havc a good day."

When she got to Veronica's house, Ruth let herself in and found Marta in the kitchen. It had been a couple of days since they'd last seen each other, at the funeral. They exchanged the kind of hug shared by combat veterans who'd survived something harrowing together. They talked a little about Irwin, who'd thrown himself into a full fall cleanup, including supervising workers who were getting his boat and dock out of the lake before winter—anything to consume his time, attention, and energy and distract him from his grief.

Chloe came in, saw Ruth, and said, "Good, you're here." She enveloped her aunt in a tearful hug before they turned to the not-inconsiderable task of going through Veronica's belongings.

Irwin had already gone through and put Post-it notes on the things that were his, or at least the ones he wanted to keep, in the attic and basement. Ruth started in the attic while Chloe focused on Veronica's office and closet.

The attic offered boxes filled with old china and silver, discarded furniture, a few crates of Chloe's toys and board games that Veronica had hung on to—in essence, the final distillation of everything that Veronica couldn't bring herself to discard over the course of a single lifetime and a multiplicity of marriages.

When she turned her attention to the basement, Ruth found the family photo albums on a shelf, sealed in a large Tupperware bin, behind a pile of boxes. When Ruth dusted the bin off and opened it, she realized that the top albums were from Veronica's first two weddings.

As she paged through them, Ruth found that she didn't recognize anyone in the pictures except Veronica, a few of Ronnie's childhood friends, and a couple of cousins. Her sister looked radiant, born to play a bride, in photographs if not in real life.

Then she opened another album and found her parents' wedding photos—and another one underneath, full of baby and childhood pictures of Ruth and Veronica. *Thank God, somehow Veronica managed to hang on to these,* Ruth thought, fighting down a wave of emotion at the photos of her parents.

As she paged through the album, she recognized her grandparents, aunts, and uncles—people long since gone—at her parents' wedding. Her parents looked young and fresh, unaware of what the future held in terms of sickness and health, for better or worse. Ruth set the albums aside, lest she disappear into them for the next several hours, like Alice down the rabbit hole.

Instead, she followed her instructions from Chloe, who had said with a smile, "Auntie Ruth—be ruthless."

Her task involved sorting through boxes filled with tchotchkes and souvenirs from Veronica's travels, including sculptures, novelties, loose photographs, and guidebooks. There was evidence of numerous pastimes past: tennis rackets; golf clubs; riding gear; fins, snorkel, and mask; a virtually untouched box full of multicolored yarn, complete with a pair of knitting needles that still held the two inches of knitting Veronica had completed before setting it aside. There were several boxes filled with back issues of *Bon Appétit* magazine, next to a shelf of dust-covered kitchen appliances and gadgets.

It took Ruth and Chloe the better part of two days to sort through the attic and basement. At the end, Ruth felt exhausted but confident in their selections for the piles marked for discard or donation and the much smaller one for things Chloe and Ruth had decided to keep.

Chloe had pulled out a pile of Veronica's clothes for Ruth to take home, try on, and either keep or donate.

As they shared a glass of wine with Irwin at the end of the day, Ruth brought out her parents' wedding album. The three of them paged through it.

"It's amazing how much like your mother both you and Veronica looked," Irwin said quietly.

"Look how handsome Grandpa was," Chloe said, running a finger over a photo of Ruth's father in the morning suit he wore for the wedding. "He does look like Jimmy Stewart. What year was this?"

"It was 1950; I was born in 1951 and Veronica in 1954," Ruth said. She turned a page and looked at a photo of her father feeding wedding cake to her mother.

"They look so young," Chloe said.

"He was twenty-three; she was twenty-two," Ruth said.

"Children," Irwin muttered.

Ruth took her bifocals off and peered at a photograph, her nose practically touching the picture. "He looks nervous," she said. "And she looks excited. I'd say that was about right."

CHAPTER 36

On the morning Chloe flew back to California, Ruth came over for a farewell breakfast, prepared by Marta as her way of saying goodbye.

"Have you heard from your classmate?" Chloe asked. "The one you went to the reunion with?"

"Yes, he called the day of the funeral—remember? You were in the limo when he called, on the way to the synagogue."

"I meant since then."

"Well, no."

"Did he text you?" Chloe pressed.

"I'm not sure how I'd know if he had."

Chloe held out her hand for Ruth's phone. "Here. I'll show you."

Ruth pulled out the phone and handed it to Chloe, who opened the messaging app (*So that's what that is,* Ruth thought), then said, "Look. He sent you a text last weekend."

"What? Let me see," Ruth said, her eagerness betraying her. Chloe glanced at the phone again before handing it to her.

Ruth looked and saw the lone text message, which the phone showed as having been sent by M/A/D. But when she looked for the message itself, all she saw was a cartoonish image of a tiny red valentine heart, which was animated to look as though it was beating, emitting tiny red hearts of its own.

"I don't understand," Ruth said.

"What's not to understand?" Chloe said. "He sent you a heart emoji. You must have swept him off his feet."

"Even I know that," Irwin put in.

"That must have been some reunion," Marta said.

Ruth blushed again but also smiled. "I'll call him later," she said and put the phone away.

They finished coffee, and Chloe went off to gather the last of her belongings for her trip. Irwin turned to Ruth and said, "Do you have any plans for the rest of the morning?"

"I don't think so."

"Would you mind riding along when I take Chloe to the airport? I was hoping we might have a chance to talk on the way back."

"Yes, of course, Irwin," Ruth said.

"You're riding with us to the airport?" Chloe said as she walked back in.

"I don't have that many chances to see you, sweetie," Ruth said. "Why not make the most of the time we've got?"

On the drive, Chloe talked about David, who'd flown home shortly after the funeral, and all the baby preparations they were making, as well as the list of things they had yet to do. She bubbled with excitement, a little of the old Chloe after a long, sad few weeks. She was enthusiastic again about the future, talking about the baby shower her friends had planned for her a few months hence.

"When is the shower going to be, honey?" Ruth said, turning to look at Chloe in the back seat. "I want to come out to California, if it isn't too much bother for you. I could stay in a hotel and rent a car."

"Don't be silly. We'd love to have you stay with us. We have plenty of room. Oh, I hope you will come."

"You let me know when it is, and I'll make arrangements to be there," Ruth said.

The funeral had been a week earlier. Scar tissue was slowly forming over the wound caused by Veronica's death. But saying goodbye to each other at the airport reopened it temporarily for Ruth and Chloe as they cried and hugged.

"Thank you, Auntie Ruth. I couldn't have gotten through this without you."

Ruth smiled through her tears and said, "After all the years your mother tried to keep us apart, her illness brings us all back together. And then she dies. Oh, the irony."

Then she hugged Chloe again and said, "I love you, honey. Travel safely, and we'll see each other soon. Give my love to David and his parents."

"I love you too, Auntie," Chloe said. "I can't wait to see you on the West Coast."

One more quick squeeze for Ruth, a hug for Irwin, and then Chloe disappeared into the terminal.

On the ride back to Minnetonka, Ruth turned to Irwin and said, "You said something the day I picked you up at the airport, that you had figured out why Veronica didn't want to see me. What did you mean?"

Irwin didn't speak for a moment, then said, "Well, that's kind of what I wanted to talk to you about. Let me start here: I didn't even know Ronnie had a sister until right before we were married."

"What do you mean?"

"We were at dinner with some of her friends and their husbands, a couple of weeks before the wedding, and we started talking about it. One of them said, 'Will Ruth be there?'" Irwin recalled. "So I said, 'Who's Ruth?' And she said, 'My sister,' then very deliberately changed the subject.

"In the car on the way home, I asked about you and said, kind of as a joke, 'What is she—a serial killer?' She didn't say anything; you know how she could be. So I said, 'Were you ever planning to tell me you had a sibling?' And she said, 'Not if Susie hadn't opened her fat yap at dinner.'"

Irwin turned to Ruth as he drove and said, "Just like that, to my face. Ronnie could be very blunt."

"The Abraham family curse," Ruth said.

"Yeah," he said. "I guess I *have* noticed."

Irwin had grown up with two older sisters who doted on him like surrogate mothers, acting as his lifelong cheerleaders and support system. When his first wife had died, his sisters had been the ones who had gotten him through the funeral and what came after. He had no personal context with which to understand Veronica's relationship with Ruth.

The casual way in which Veronica dismissed her sister from her life distressed him, and so he continued to ask about Ruth, generally drawing minimal response. Finally, one night at dinner, she gave him a hard look and said, "I'm so tired of this." So the topic faded and did not resurface, until Chloe's wedding.

Irwin had met Clark and Marlene, David's parents, only one time before the wedding weekend in San Francisco. In the receiving line after the service, he stood with Marlene, introducing her to Chloe's and Veronica's various friends, most of whom he knew fairly well.

Then he and Marlene found themselves face to face with a woman who bore a striking resemblance to Veronica, who introduced herself to the mismatched couple as Chloe's aunt, Ruth Winters.

When Ruth moved down the receiving line after the encounter, Marlene turned to Irwin with a questioning frown, as though she'd been told that her son had married one of the help. Irwin heard himself say, "I think that was Veronica's sister. I've never met her before tonight."

In the car from the church to the reception dinner, Irwin said to Veronica, "Did you know your sister, Ruth, is here at the wedding?"

"Yes," Veronica said. "I saw her. I didn't talk to her."

When Irwin pointed out that Ruth had come halfway across the country for the wedding of Veronica's daughter—which took both time and expense—Veronica dismissed him, saying, "She just wants to make me look bad."

After the reception and dance, back in their hotel room, Veronica admitted she had never spoken to Ruth, and she and Irwin argued. They'd both had too much champagne, and Irwin's half of the conversation took on a harsher tone. Veronica, dressed in her slip and sitting on the edge of the hotel bed, slid to the floor and dissolved in tears.

"What?" Irwin said. "What did I say?"

But Veronica was inconsolable, sobbing loud and long before the emotional outburst began to subside.

"Don't you understand?" she said. "I ruined her life. Every time I see her, all I can think is how much she must hate me. That's why I don't want to see her. Because it reminds me what I did to her. When I went home that summer after the accident, it was like I had a crystal ball that told the future—that awful future being stuck in that house taking care of my father. I knew Ruth would stay with Daddy until the bitter end, and I wasn't going to do that. I was nineteen. I wanted out. So I left."

Veronica began to cry again, saying, "Her whole life was this big detour because of me. Ruth knew what she was giving up, and she did it anyway. And that's all I think about when I see her."

Irwin paused in retelling the story and drove quietly for a moment. Then he turned to Ruth and said, "She felt she'd ruined your life, and she couldn't handle that responsibility."

"Yes, she told me—finally," Ruth said. "If I'm honest, I spent most of my life feeling the same way: that she was to blame for everything that was wrong in my life and always had been. But when she said it, I realized it was too easy to make her the villain, the reason that I let my life happen to me, when I should have taken charge. That's been my problem for as long as I can remember."

They were at a stoplight, and Irwin looked at Ruth for a moment, then turned his eyes back to the road when the light changed to green.

"After Chloe's wedding," he said, "I started telling Ronnie that she needed to talk to you. I guess I made a pest of myself about it, because it was one of the only things we ever argued about. But she was a stubborn woman about certain things."

"She was a stubborn woman about almost everything," Ruth corrected him, which made him laugh.

Then, after ignoring several weeks of stomach distress, Veronica's pain had grown so extreme that she'd let Irwin convince her to see her internist. A series of tests were scheduled, each producing increasingly alarming results—until finally the diagnosis, liver cancer, was reached.

When he heard the word *cancer*, Irwin's heart seized for a moment. Then he said, "What can I do to help?" Surgery was scheduled; the two of them cried together, then tried to lift each other's spirits, with Irwin saying, "I know you can beat this."

But when Irwin mentioned calling Chloe to let her know what was happening—or Ruth—Veronica bridled. At dinner a few nights before the surgery, Irwin said, "You need to call your daughter. And I really think you should call your sister. What if—God forbid—something goes wrong?"

Veronica refused, forbidding him from telling anyone. "It's nobody's business until I say it is."

It took several weeks for Veronica to recover from the surgery, before she could start chemotherapy. Irwin began to press her again about calling Ruth—until the night Veronica began to cry again, saying, over and over, "Why would Ruth care? She hates me. I made her hate me. It was my fault Mommy and Daddy had that accident."

Irwin stared at her, then said, "Veronica, that doesn't make sense. You weren't even in the car."

But Veronica could not be dissuaded. "They were driving back to Minneapolis after visiting me at college. Mommy and I had an argument—and she was driving when they crashed. It was my fault."

Irwin turned to Ruth as he drove. "She always believed she was to blame for what happened to your parents."

"That's ridiculous," Ruth said.

"Which part?"

"For starters, I didn't know they'd been visiting Veronica that day. I assumed they were driving home from work, because the accident happened near one of the stores. How could I have never heard that before?"

"I can't imagine Ronnie telling you. She said, 'It's my fault they're dead. If they hadn't come to see me, my parents would have been alive, and Ruth wouldn't have given up her life for Daddy.'"

"But that wasn't her fault," Ruth said. "I do remember. My mother was excited about going up to help Veronica find an apartment for sophomore year. She wanted to do that. That wasn't Ronnie's fault."

"Apparently, when your mother got up there, they had an argument over something—I couldn't tell you what, but I guess it didn't take much with those two. Then your parents had the accident on the drive back. The two things were forever linked in her mind. She believed she'd ruined your life because she felt responsible for your parents' accident. There was no convincing her otherwise. The shame ran too deep."

Ruth's eyes brimmed, and she could see that Irwin was brushing away tears as he drove.

"She looked up to you, Ruth," Irwin said. "You intimidated her."

"I can't believe that."

"It's true. *Woman of steel*, she called you. She said you were incredibly smart, never showed emotion or fear. Veronica, on the other hand, was nothing but a rat's nest of insecurities."

"I'm sorry, Irwin—are we still talking about my sister? That Veronica? Because I never saw any evidence of what you're talking about."

"It would have killed her if you had. She looked up to you her whole life. But blend that kind of worship with guilt about feeling responsible for your misfortunes, then multiply it by Ronnie's insecurities—it doesn't breed rational behavior in someone like her."

"Oh my God—poor Veronica," Ruth said.

Ruth stopped. She looked at Irwin and smiled sheepishly. "I have never uttered those two words in that order before in my life. Ever."

Irwin laughed and said, “It’ll be our secret. Anyway, when she started the chemo, it kicked her ass. You saw. And I still couldn’t get her to call you. Or tell Chloe. I finally concocted that trip to New York.”

“I thought you went to New York to sell your business.”

“I did. I could have done the whole thing from here. But I had to do something to get her to reach out to you, even though it killed me to be away. I made Marta promise not to take her to her appointment; she told Ronnie some story about a family commitment. I knew Ronnie would never call her rich friends for a ride. And I told her she needed someone she knew to drive her, not a taxi or an Uber. I threatened *not* to make the trip to New York to sell my business—to forego this great opportunity to retire, which she’s been bugging me to do for more than a year—unless she called you.

“I can’t tell you what it meant to her when you said yes. Or what it meant to me. What it meant to have you back in her life, that you cared enough to help when she asked, driving out here each day, taking her to chemo. That gave her some peace.”

Ruth cried quietly for a minute, then turned and said, “Thank you, Irwin.” She reached over and gave his arm a squeeze. They rode in silence the rest of the way back.

CHAPTER 37

For several mornings, Ruth awoke feeling blue. She felt as if she'd been living in an emotional whirlwind for weeks, one that had upended everything in her life—and she was still getting used to the new configuration. Perhaps she'd become accustomed to having a little turmoil in her life.

Facing an empty calendar and no whirlwind, she thought, *Look at you, Ruth Winters, after all that excitement. So much has happened, and yet, here you are, still sitting in this house as life goes on around you—and without you.*

Some things never changed, but this had: change no longer frightened her. Now that she was ready for it, however, nothing seemed to be changing. Still, she did begin to notice little things.

Her bedroom was too bright when she awoke one morning a couple of days after Chloe's departure. Did daylight saving time end without her realizing it? She looked at her clock and found she'd slept until 8:00 a.m. *You're developing lazy habits,* she scolded herself.

Then Ruth thought, *I slept until eight and lived to tell the tale. How about that?*

She had just put on her robe when she heard a knock at the back door. She opened it to find Jane, dressed for work, with a robe-and-pajama-clad Samantha in tow.

"Ruth!" Jane said breathlessly. "Thank God. I'm so sorry—I got called in to work, just for the morning. But Samantha's preschool is closed today. Would you mind keeping her for me until then?" Her eyes were panicky and pleading.

"Of course, honey. Here—give me those clothes, and I'll get her dressed. You go along. My day was open. Now I have the company of this lovely young lady."

"You're a lifesaver, as always," Jane said. "Sorry I couldn't get her dressed, but they just called, and they need me right away." She handed Samantha's clothes to Ruth, along with a small toothbrush and a toothpaste tube that smelled like bubble gum.

"Don't worry," Ruth said. "We'll be fine."

"You're going to play at Mrs. Winters's this morning, sweetie," Jane told the sleepy little girl, "and I'll see you later." She kissed Samantha, then turned to Ruth. "Thanks again. When I get back, I want to hear about your reunion. I saw that Escalade that picked you up." She lifted her eyebrows lasciviously, saying, "Very suave," pronouncing it *swah-vay*.

Ruth laughed, then said, "You better get going or you'll be late."

"You're right," she said. "I'm angling for a promotion. See you."

Ruth's blues vanished as she dressed Samantha and oversaw her dental hygiene. The little girl reeled off an endless series of questions and theories about things like what happened to the people on the TV when you turned it off and where the clouds went when the sky was completely blue. As Ruth made breakfast, the little girl told tales of her new imaginary friend, whose name was Winkie and whom she described variously as looking like a teddy bear, a pony, and a monkey, while Ruth listened with amusement.

Finally, Ruth needed to shower and dress for the day. She sat Samantha in the middle of the linoleum in the kitchen and said, "I have a job for you."

She filled a plastic bowl with dried kidney beans and pulled out three large muffin tins, each with wells for twelve muffins.

"Samantha, can you count to twenty?"

"Yes!" Samantha said proudly. So Ruth set her task: she needed Samantha to count out twenty beans and put them into each muffin indentation.

"Bean muffins!" Samantha said.

"Exactly." She watched Samantha start the project, which confirmed the soundness of her concept: While Samantha could count to twenty, her fine motor skills were such that handling individual beans was an iffy proposition. Samantha would be consumed with this activity long enough for Ruth to take a shower and get dressed.

When Ruth returned, Samantha was on her knees on the kitchen floor, carefully placing individual bean after individual bean into the third of the three muffin pans. The other two pans stood full on the floor next to her. The tip of her tongue protruded from the corner of her mouth when she concentrated. She would occasionally drop a bean on the floor, or lose count and have to start over on an individual indentation, but she was making admirable progress.

When she saw Ruth, she said, "How's this, Miss Winters?"

"Very good, honey. Looks like you're almost done."

Ruth was finishing the breakfast dishes when her landline rang.

"Hello?" she said warily.

"Ruth? Oh good, it is you. Do you know how many *Winters* there are in the Minneapolis phone book? Or how hard it is to *find* a phone book?"

"Renee?"

"I did finally track one down, but there are about forty listings under *Winters*. Luckily, your husband's first name started with a *C* instead of a *W*, or I'd still be looking for you. There was an *R. Winters*, but a man answered and said he didn't know you. I just knew you were someone who would still have a landline—but I assumed you'd have a phone in your own name."

"It seemed easier to leave it in Charles's name after he died."

"And now I found you."

"Here I am" was all Ruth could think to say.

"You got away the night of the reunion before I could get your information."

"My information? What else do you need to know about me?"

"No, I mean your cell number, your email—that information. I wanted to be able to reach out the next time I get back to town. I got caught up with people at the end of the reunion, and by the time I got free, you and Martin were gone."

"Well, you found me," Ruth said, still mystified. After an expectant pause from Renee, Ruth said, "Oh, you mean right now?" and shared her cell number for the second time that month.

"We are going to stay in touch," Renee declared. "It's hard to make new friends at our age. But it's great to reconnect with old ones."

"Yes, I'd like that."

"Do you ever get to the West Coast? I'd love to see you the next time you're out here."

"Where are you? Los Angeles?"

"San Francisco. You should think about coming for a visit."

"Actually, my niece is having a baby shower in a few months. She lives in San Rafael. I hope to attend."

"There you go," Renee said. "Let me know the dates. We can have lunch and go shopping while you're here."

"I'd like that very much," Ruth said.

"Perfect. OK, I've got to run," Renee said, adding, "I'm glad I got to see you, Ruth."

"Me too, Renee," Ruth said.

When she hung up, Ruth was distracted enough by the call that she accidentally stepped on the lip of one of Samantha's completed muffin tins. The tin upended, catapulting 240 carefully counted beans across the kitchen floor.

Samantha stood up, put her hands on her hips, and, with exaggerated vexation, did a perfect imitation of Ruth.

"Miss Winters, I swear, you're going to make me old before my time!" the little girl said. Ruth laughed out loud.

Samantha was eating her lunch—chicken noodle soup and a grilled cheese sandwich, her favorite—when that day's mail plopped through the slot in the front door. Ruth retrieved it and brought it back to the kitchen table, to keep Samantha company while she ate.

Among the ads and bills, Ruth found a colorful catalog that caught her attention. The University of Minnesota's Continuing Education Division was offering courses for senior citizens at the Saint Louis Park Jewish Community Center, a few miles from her house.

A college class? she wondered.

She opened the catalog and began paging through it until she found a blurb for a class with the title Warhol, Pop Art, and Their Influence on the Twentieth Century.

Ruth read the description with growing interest. It was a lecture class, taught by an art professor from the U, one night a week for six weeks. Ruth looked at the dates the class met, then reached for her calendar before stopping herself and thinking, *When was the last time you were busy in the evening?*

She folded the corner of the catalog page to mark the class and set it aside. Just then, Samantha accidentally bumped her soup bowl (fortunately both empty and unbreakable), which clattered to the floor.

Exasperated, Samantha looked at Ruth and said, "I think I need a nap."

Samantha was still asleep when Jane came to fetch her in the early afternoon. Ruth invited her in for a glass of wine.

As she sat down at Ruth's kitchen table, Jane said, "I never got to ask about your reunion."

Ruth said, "I had a very nice time," and recounted the evening's events, explaining about Martin's plan that allowed her to go the entire evening without having to reveal her personal history.

"*I can't discuss it*—I've got to remember that," Jane said admiringly. "That's good."

"It was surprisingly effective."

"I'll bet it drove people crazy, especially the way you were dressed that night," Jane said. "I took a peek out the window when I saw the Escalade. You looked amaze-o!"

Ruth had never had girlfriends, or anyone, to whom she could unveil the actual anxious but eager Ruth. Though Jane was almost forty years younger, she was comfortably filling that role for Ruth, and Ruth was enjoying it.

"And then Renee Stafford came in—"

"Renee Stafford—the TV star? I knew she was from Minneapolis. What was she doing there?"

"She was in my class. She was emcee for the program."

"I love her beauty products. And you know her?"

"We had a few classes together senior year. It's not like we were close—though she made it seem that way when we saw each other."

"Still waters run deep. Ruth, look at you—connected to both the big celebrities in your class."

"I wouldn't call us *connected*." *Although she did just call me and ask me to come visit her,* Ruth thought.

"And what about afterwards? Did anything, um, happen with that Martin?"

Ruth thought for a moment, then took out her cell phone and showed her Martin's text. Jane's eyes widened.

"A heart emoji? Wow."

"Why does everyone know about these emoji things except me?"

Jane laughed and showed Ruth how to access the emoji gallery on her keyboard. Ruth found the colorful little illustrations imaginative, if childish.

"Have we regressed this far?" she mused to Jane. "We spent centuries developing and refining the written word. And now we're reduced to communicating with cartoons?"

Jane looked at Ruth's phone again, then said, "Didn't you answer his text? It's almost a week and a half old. He might think you ghosted him."

"Ghosted?"

"Blew him off. Ignored him."

"I thought it was odd that I never heard from him. Not an email or a phone call. I meant to call him, but you know how that is."

"Wait a minute," Jane said. "Let me see your phone again."

Ruth handed it to her, and Jane began flicking through screens. Finally, a look of recognition lit her face. She poked at the screen a few more times, then handed the phone back to Ruth.

"Somehow, you had put it in airplane mode, so he couldn't have phoned if he wanted to. You also had it in Do Not Disturb mode, so emails and texts weren't getting through either, I guess. What did you do? Do you remember?"

Ruth thought about the invasive spam email she'd received, the one that had startled her into frantically pushing every button she could find, as she said, "I have no idea." She looked at the phone again and said, "What should I do now?"

"Why not call him? You certainly have an excuse. Although it doesn't feel like you need one."

Without pause, Ruth summoned Martin's phone number from her "Recent Calls" list and dialed him.

She felt slightly giddy listening to it ring, then sobered when the call went to voicemail: "Hey, it's Marty Daly, and I can't take your call right now."

Ruth listened to the rest of the message, then took a breath and, after the beep, said, "Hello, Martin Daly. This is Ruth Winters. I hope I'm not bothering you. I discovered that I've been having technical difficulties with my phone, in case you've been trying to call me and couldn't get through. I hope we can speak soon. I think you know how to reach me. Goodbye." Pause. "From Ruth." Click.

When she'd finished, Jane beckoned for Ruth's phone back, and Ruth gave it to her. Jane fiddled with it a moment, then handed it back.

"There—now you'll hear a louder *ding* to alert you when you get a text."

As if to demonstrate, Ruth's phone dinged. It was a return text from Martin; the message consisted entirely of a thumbs-up emoji.

"That's why they call them instant messages," Jane said.

Later that evening, as Ruth dozed in front of the TV, her cell phone rang in the pocket of her cardigan. *What now?* she thought.

She looked at the phone's display: M/A/D and a phone number with a 720 area code.

"Hello?" she said drowsily, looking at her watch: 9:30 p.m.

"Ruth? It's Martin—did I wake you? I'm sorry."

"No, no, I fell asleep in front of the TV." She yawned and said, "Excuse me," yawned again, and then said, "How are you?"

"I've been thinking about you a lot."

His directness surprised her but excited her as well.

"Yes, me too." *Well, it's true,* she thought, fighting past her initial reluctance to admit this.

"First of all, I am so, so sorry about your sister. How are you doing?"

"I'm better," Ruth said. "But I think it might take a while to truly get past it."

"Of course. I know what you're going through."

"Thank you so much for the flower arrangement. That was so thoughtful. But how did you know where to have them sent?"

"You'd be surprised what you can track down online, if you have a couple of clues to start with," Martin said. "The internet can be an amazing tool."

"I can't even imagine."

After a moment, Martin said, "I was afraid I wouldn't hear from you. Then I wondered if you might not have seen my text."

"I'm sorry, I meant to call you back—"

"I'm so sorry to have called you on the day of your sister's funeral," Martin interjected.

"Oh, no, please, don't worry about that. Apparently, I pushed the wrong button—or several buttons—on my phone and accidentally locked you out, and everyone else, I guess. I'm sorry. I wasn't trying to spook you."

"Spook me?"

"Is that the word? I meant that I didn't intend to ignore your message."

"Ghosting. Is that what you mean?"

"Yes, that's it."

"Well, thankfully, we're talking now."

There was a pause, and then Martin said, "I was really glad to hear from you."

"How have you been?" she asked.

They spent the rest of the evening talking in a way Ruth had never been able to talk to a man before.

Something had changed. Now it was changing again.

Later that week, Ruth enrolled in the class on Warhol and pop art, getting in under the registration deadline. When the class began, she was thrilled to discover how much more there was to know about Warhol and what followed.

Her phone calls with Martin became a nightly thing. They started at 8:00 p.m. sharp in Minneapolis, 7:00 p.m. in Denver. They began an hour later on the nights Ruth had school.

"Are you enjoying your class?" Martin asked.

"Yes, very much," Ruth told him. "More than I expected. But then I never expect much."

At the end of October, Martin paused in the middle of one of their phone calls and said, "I was wondering if you had any plans for Thanksgiving."

Ruth began, "I'm usually by myself—" but Martin didn't wait for her to finish her thought.

"I'd love to have you join my family and me in Denver for the holiday, if you're interested."

Ruth surprised herself and said, without the slightest hesitation, "That sounds lovely. I'd enjoy that."

That night, as she brushed her hair before bed, she looked at herself in the mirror and smiled.

Look at you, Ruth Winters.

THE END

ACKNOWLEDGMENTS

A number of people took the time to read early sections and versions of this novel, or otherwise advise me, and their input has been invaluable. For that, I want to thank: Ellen Joseph, Melissa Hield, Rebecca Baron, Mary Johnson, Martha Moran, Mike Shatzkin, Larry Sutin, Mab Nulty, Bob Ashenmacher, Virginia Padden, Diane Lovich, Rachel Gubman, Erin Kleinertz, my sons, Jacob and Caleb Fine, and my wife, Kimberlie Jacobs. Thanks to the entire team at Amazon and Lake Union for their incredible support. Thanks also to Murray Weiss, Larry Becsey, and Devra Wasserman and to Clay and Heather Bushong. And to my editors—Erin Adair-Hodges, Selena James, and David Downing—whose suggestions helped Ruth reach her full potential.

ABOUT THE AUTHOR

Photo © 2020 Marshall Fine

Minneapolis native Marshall Fine's career as an award-winning journalist, critic, and filmmaker has spanned fifty years. He has written biographies of filmmakers John Cassavetes and Sam Peckinpah, directed documentaries about film critic Rex Reed and comedian Robert Klein, conducted the *Playboy* interview with Howard Stern, and chaired the New York Film Critics Circle four times. The author currently lives in Ossining, New York. This is his first published novel.